I IS ANOTHER:
SEPTOLOGY III-V

I IS ANOTHER: SEPTOLOGY III-V

Jon Fosse

Translated from the Norwegian by
Damion Searls

**TRANSIT
BOOKS**

Published by Transit Books
2301 Telegraph Avenue, Oakland, California 94612
www.transitbooks.org

© Jon Fosse, 2019
Translation copyright © Damion Searls, 2020
All rights reserved by and controlled through Gina Winje Agency
Originally published in English translation by Fitzcarraldo Editions in the UK in 2020

ISBN: 978-1-945492-45-7 (paperback)

LIBRARY OF CONGRESS CONTROL NUMBER
2021930154

DESIGN & TYPESETTING
Justin Carder

DISTRIBUTED BY
Consortium Book Sales & Distribution
(800) 283-3572 | cbsd.com

Printed in the United States of America

9 8 7 6 5 4 3 2 1

The translation has been published with the financial support of NORLA.

This project is supported in part by a grant from the National Endowment for the Arts.

'Je est un autre.'
—Arthur Rimbaud

III

AND I SEE MYSELF STANDING and looking at the picture with the two lines, a purple line and a brown line, that cross in the middle and I think that it's cold in the main room, and that it's too early to get up, it doesn't matter what time it is, so why did I get up then? I think and I turn off the light in the main room and I go back to the little bedroom and I turn off the light there and I lie back down in bed and I tuck the duvet tight around me and Bragi lies down against me and I think well I got a little sleep last night, even if not that much, and today is Wednesday and it's still early in the morning, or maybe it's still nighttime? I think and it was so cold in the main room that I didn't want to get up, I think and I pet Bragi, rub his back, and then I look into the darkness and I see Asle sitting on the swing outside his front door and he's not swinging, he's just sitting there, and he's thinking he can't figure out anything to do and he swings carefully, slowly back and forth a little and then Mother comes out onto the porch and she's angry and Asle doesn't know why she's so angry

Come here! she says

What's the matter, he says

Get over here, Mother says

Okay, Asle says

and he gets off the swing and goes over to Mother who's standing on the porch and she's looking right at him and he walks up the stairs

Yes, he says

There you are, she says

and he doesn't understand why Mother's voice is so angry, what's wrong with her? what has he done now to make her so mad at him? he thinks

Look at this, Mother says

and she opens her hand and Asle sees three one-krone coins lying in the palm of Mother's hand and she stands there holding out her hand with the three krone coins in it and she doesn't say anything and Asle thinks how did Mother find the three kroner? and he'd meant to hide them somewhere clever, yes, he'd meant to put them under one of the flagstones outside the front door but then he forgot, it just disappeared from his mind and now Mother is standing here holding the three coins out to him, and how did she find them anyway? Asle thinks, and then he thinks of course she found them in his pocket because he forgot to take them out of his trousers and hide them

Where did you get these? Mother says

and Asle thinks that he can't say he got them from The Bald Man, that he got them after sitting with him in his car, and he definitely can't say why he got them, no

Answer me, Mother says

and Asle thinks that he definitely can't tell her the truth, that he got them from The Bald Man, and that's because he mustn't tell anyone that he went for a car ride with The Bald Man, and that The Bald Man put his hand on his leg and then took his hand away, at least twice, that The Bald Man did that, he thinks

Where did you get these coins? Mother says

Well, answer me, she says

Don't just stand there with your mouth hanging open, she says

and then she grabs his shoulder and she shakes him and she says he needs to answer her when she asks him something and she's almost shouting

Answer me, Mother says

and he has to say something, anything, Asle thinks

I found them, he says

You found them? Mother says

Where did you find them? she says

Answer me, tell me where you found them, she says

and Asle just stands there and Mother lets go of his shoulder

On the road, he says

On the road you say, Mother says

Yes, on the road, Asle says

Where exactly, she says

Outside The Bakery, he says

You found them outside The Bakery? Mother says

and she says does he expect her to believe that, that he found them, outside The Bakery

You stole them, Mother says

I didn't steal anything, Asle says

Yes you did, you stole them, she says

I did not, he says

You did, she says

and Mother says she checked her own purse because she had a few krone coins in there, yes, she doesn't have that much money but she did have a few krone coins in there, and she didn't remember how many, but it was several, and for all she knows he stole the krone coins from her, she says, but she's not sure, because she has five one-krone coins in her purse now but she can't remember anymore if she'd had more in there, she might well have had more, yes, she could have had eight not just five

Did you steal this money from me? Mother says

and Asle says that he didn't steal the money, he found it, like he said, yes, outside The Bakery

You're lying, Mother says

I'm not lying, Asle says

and then they stand there and neither of them says anything and then Mother says that she was about to do the laundry and she checked in his pockets like usual, what hasn't she found in there, she always finds something, a stone, pine cones, nails, marbles, rope ends, she doesn't even know what all she's found, but never, ever before has she found three shiny new krone coins, and she doesn't know how Asle could have gotten them but it can't have been honestly

I found them, he says

Yes you said that, Mother says

and then they just stand there and then they see Father coming around the corner of The Old House where Grandma and Grandpa live and Mother calls Father and tells him he needs to come here and Father comes up to them just walking slowly

What's going on? he says

and he looks at Mother

Yes, she says

You don't look like everything's all right, Father says

No, Mother says

and it's silent for a moment

So what's wrong? Father says

Look, Mother says

and she holds out her hand with the three krone coins

Three kroner, yes, Father says

Yes, exactly, Mother says

And I need to drop everything for that? he says

But, Mother says

and she breaks off

But? Father says

But I found them in his pocket, Mother says

and she looks at Asle and then Father doesn't say anything and they just stand there

Where did you get them? Father says

and Asle says that he found the coins

He says he found them outside The Bakery, Mother says

Yes well that could happen, Father says

You believe that? Mother says

and Father doesn't say anything

Look in your wallet, see if anything's missing, Mother says

and Father takes out his wallet and he looks inside it and he says he can't remember exactly how many coins he had in there, so there's no way for him to know if someone took any coins out of his wallet, but why would Asle have done that? he doesn't steal, does he? Father says and he looks at Asle

I don't steal, Asle says

I've never stolen anything, he says

No, Father says

and then Father says that he might have found the coins outside The Bakery, but in that case there's someone who lost them, and maybe they've noticed they're gone, Father says, and maybe they'll think that they might have lost the money outside The Bakery, after they'd bought their bread, or maybe they'll think they forgot to get their change at the counter once they'd paid with a five and they were going to get three back, yes, and so maybe they're going to go back to The Baker or The Baker's Wife and ask if maybe they forgot their three kroner or dropped them outside The Bakery and The Baker or The Baker's Wife found them, Father says, and he says that the best thing to do would be for Asle to go to The Baker or The Baker's Wife and give them the coins, in case anyone lost them and dropped by to ask about it, Father says and Mother says she was sure that Asle had stolen the coins and Father says we can't know that for sure can we? he says

I'm glad to hear you say that, Mother says

It's a good thing, that you think like that, she says

and she looks at Asle and she says that if he really found the coins then she owes him an apology, for thinking he must have stolen them, but he might have found them, she hadn't thought of that, she says

You might have found the coins, sure, Mother says

Anyway I owe you an apology, she says

I shouldn't have suspected you of stealing, of being a thief, she says

and Father says they don't need to say anything more about it and Asle you'll go to The Bakery and give the krone coins to whoever comes out when you ring the bell, either The Baker or The Baker's Wife, and you'll say you found them outside The Bakery and then, if no one's come to ask The Baker or The Baker's Wife about some money, well then you can keep them, right? Father says

And that would mean you sure were lucky, finding three krone coins, he says

Yes I should think so, Mother says

I'll run over there right now, Asle says

and then he runs down the driveway and up the country road to The Bakery and he walks in the front door and goes to the counter and picks up the bell sitting there and he shakes it and it rings and The Baker comes out and stands behind the counter and Asle says that he found these three krone coins outside The Bakery, and now, now he really is lying, it's bad and he's ashamed, Asle thinks and he's really stammering and The Baker looks at him and he says yes, yes, he says

Yes, yes, The Baker says

and he looks at Asle

If you found some kroner then you found some kroner, you were lucky, Asle, yes, The Baker says

But maybe someone lost them, maybe they came to buy bread and then lost them? Asle says

I didn't give three kroner in change to anyone recently, at least not that I can remember, The Baker says

So they're yours Asle, he says

You found three kroner and now it's your money, he says

and Asle looks at The Baker

That's what I think, he says

and even if there's a smell of drink coming from The Baker and he's holding onto the counter as he stands there, still he's right when he says that, Asle thinks

and The Baker says that he has a custard roll around, one last one from the ones he baked, and since it'll be time to close up the shop soon, yes, he should have closed up already, Asle should just take the custard roll, since he's such a nice honest boy, The Baker says and he picks up a custard roll, the only one left, and wraps it in grey paper and hands it to Asle and he thinks that this is really really wrong, he is standing here lying and now he's getting a custard roll on top of everything, and it's a good thing he never liked custard rolls with vanilla custard and confectioners' sugar and coconut on top, it's a disgusting combination, that disgusting confectioners' sugar or whatever you call it, and the coconut, that's what that's called, but Sister likes custard rolls, so she can have it, she'll be really happy to get a custard roll, Asle thinks

Thank you, thank you, he says

and The Baker hands Asle the custard roll and he stays there for a moment watching The Baker raise a cup of coffee to his mouth and take a sip and he says today was really your lucky day Asle, finding three krone coins, no, not bad, he says

And then getting a custard roll too, Asle says

Yes well that's nothing, The Baker says

and he goes back through the door behind him, and Asle knows that the door leads to The Baker's and The Baker's Wife's main room, and Asle runs home and he tells them what The Baker said, that he'd found the money so now it was his, and he, The Baker, didn't remember giving anyone three krone coins in change to anyone recently, and definitely not today, Asle says, and The Baker said that Asle found the coins so they were his, that he'd really been very lucky, The Baker said, Asle says and Mother says well then maybe that's how it was and Father says yes The Baker's right about that, now that he thinks about it the coins are his all right, Father says and Mother asks him if he bought a custard roll now that he's come into all this money, she says, and Asle says The Baker gave him the custard roll, it was the last one left and since he'd been honest enough to try to give back the money and since The Baker was about to close up for the day anyway he should just take the one custard roll that was left, that's what The Baker said, Asle says and Mother says that was really nice of The Baker, but Asle never liked custard rolls did he, or rolls at all, not cake either, nothing like that, she says

No he never did, Father says

No, Mother says

and Mother laughs and Father says well he doesn't take after her, she likes custard rolls, if anyone does then she does, he says

And Sister, Asle says

Yes custard rolls are really good, Sister says

and suddenly Asle sees that Sister is standing next to Mother, he hadn't even noticed her, he thinks

But I don't really care too much for them, Father says

and then Mother says that they should eat that custard roll while it's fresh, shouldn't they? she says and Father nods and says he doesn't feel like a custard roll and Asle says he doesn't feel like a custard roll either and then Mother goes to the kitchen and she comes back in with two little plates with half a custard roll on each plate and she gives one plate to Sister who's sitting on the sofa and then Mother sits down next to Sister and then they sit there on the sofa eating the custard roll and Asle stands there and looks at them and he thinks what's the matter with The Bald Man? why did he touch his leg like that? and he tried to move his hand so far up on his leg, and Asle pushed it away, he thinks and Mother called him a thief, and he isn't that, but he did lie, he thinks, today he lied to Mother and to Father and to The Baker and then he got a custard roll from The Baker for being so honest, Asle thinks and he thinks he wants to go outside

I'm going to go out for a bit, Asle says

Don't go away from the house, Mother says

I thought I could maybe go to Per Olav's, Asle says

Yes, you're building a truck together aren't you, Father says

That's what you told us, he says

Yes, Asle says

But don't be late, Mother says

and then Asle goes outside and he thinks that it was nasty of The Bald Man to touch his leg, and eventually he pushed his hand away, several times too, or at least two, he thinks, and he can't tell anyone, because it's embarrassing, it's shameful, and if anyone finds out it'll be even worse so he can't tell anyone, not any grown-ups anyway, because that would be totally wrong, he thinks, now it's just a little wrong and also yes also a little exciting in a way, yes, that too, even if he hadn't liked when The Bald Man touched his leg, Asle thinks and he's never going to take another car ride with The Bald Man again, that's for sure, and he'll never go into his house, that's for sure too, Asle thinks and he goes out to the road and then he sees a tractor coming towards him from far away and it's an old tractor and it's driving slowly and the engine is making an unbelievable noise and Asle keeps walking, and the tractor is far away but coming closer to him, slowly, and now he's about to cross the country road and then soon he'll go up the other driveway and the hill to where Per Olav and his family live and he'll ask if Per Olav is home and then, if Per Olav is home and he feels like it, maybe they can start working on the truck they were building, or something, Asle thinks and he crosses the road and wow that noise from the tractor driving towards him from far away, it's a horrible screeching noise, Asle thinks and he walks up the driveway to where Per Olav and his family live and he knocks and Per Olav opens the door and Asle says hi and asks him if he wants to do something together and Per Olav says yes yes, sure, he has something he wants to show him, he says in a quiet voice and then Per Olav puts on his shoes and a jacket

We need to go somewhere where no one can see us, he says

and Asle nods

And then we can do something we've never done, he says

Maybe we should go down to The Boathouse? Asle says

Your family's Boathouse? Per Olav says

Yes, Asle says

and Per Olav says that's a good idea and then they go down to The Shore, below the country road, and they walk along The Shore and they get to The Boathouse and then they go behind The Boathouse because the back door there, or really it's more like a kind of hatch, is kept shut with just a rusty hook and Asle opens the door and Per Olav goes in and then Asle goes in after him and it's almost totally dark in The Boathouse itself and Asle keeps the hatch half open and Per Olav takes out a matchbox and strikes a match

You've got a match? Asle says

Yeah, Per Olav says

And more than that, he says

and then Per Olav takes out a pack of cigarettes

Where did you get those? Asle asks

I took them from Grandpa, Per Olav says

He left some on a shelf in his room, he says

and Per Olav lights another match

Have you ever smoked? he says

No, Asle says

You? he says

No, Per Olav says

and then the matches burn out and Per Olav says now he'll open the pack of cigarettes and they'll each have a smoke, but it's strong and Asle needs to not inhale the smoke into his belly because then he'll throw up, he says, yes, someone told him that, that he'd had a cigarette and when he sucked the smoke down into his belly he threw up right away, but it was probably also because he'd sucked all the smoke into his belly, Per Olav says and now their eyes are used to the darkness in The Boathouse so they can see fine and Asle sees Per Olav open the pack of cigarettes and he hands a cigarette to Asle and then Per Olav puts a cigarette in his own mouth and then he says that Asle has to breathe in just when he puts the match to the cigarette and Per Olav lights a match and he puts it to the white cigarette and Asle breathes in and the cigarette lights and Asle holds it away from his mouth between his index finger and middle finger and he sees the glow and he sees smoke rising from the glow and it's beautiful to watch and then he puts the cigarette back between his lips and he sucks in a breath and a little smoke comes into his mouth and he breathes the smoke out and it smells good

The smoke smells good, Asle says

and he takes another drag, and slowly breathes the smoke out, and he sees the smoke vanish into the darkness, and then he takes another drag and he holds the smoke in his mouth a little longer before he breathes it out and Asle realizes that he likes smoking, so he's going to be a smoker, Asle thinks, and he takes another drag and he sucks the smoke a little way down into his throat and he hears Per Olav start coughing

Ugh that was horrible, he says

and Per Olav throws the cigarette down on the floor of The Boathouse and steps on it

I felt sick right away, he says

and Asle sucks smoke even farther into his throat and he feels something like a nice tingling in his whole body, yes, it's like he feels calmer and somehow better, he thinks

You like it, you like smoking? Per Olav says

Yeah, Asle says

Really? Per Olav says

Yeah, Asle says

and he says that when he gets older he's definitely for sure going to start smoking and Per Olav says well not him, and then he says Asle can keep the cigarette pack and the matchbox and Asle asks doesn't he want them himself and Per Olav says no way and then Asle says thanks and he puts the cigarette pack and the matchbox in his pocket and then he thinks that the best place to hide the cigarette pack and matches is probably in The Boathouse, there are some beams running crosswise near the roof with various nets hanging on them and some of the nets are so rotted through that they fall apart as soon as you touch them and Asle thinks he can put the pack of cigarettes and matchbox up on one of those beams, one with a junky old net on it, he thinks and then he climbs up on a couple of fish crates and puts the pack of cigarettes and matchbox up on a beam

I think I'll go home, I feel kind of sick, Per Olav says

and Asle nods and then Per Olav leaves and Asle leaves and he puts the hook back in place and then they go up the path and when they get up to the road they say see you and then Per Olav goes farther up the way and Asle crosses the road and then walks up his driveway and he goes inside and hangs up his jacket in the hall and takes off his shoes and then Mother comes over to him and she says you smell like smoke

Have you been smoking? she says

Are you big enough to smoke now? she says

Breathe on me, she says

and he breathes on her and she asks how Asle got cigarettes? and who did he get them from? and he just says he got them from someone, and she asks who he got them from? and Asle says that he'll never tell her, never in his whole life, not even if she kills him, he says and then he sees Mother go up the stairs and I lie there in bed and isn't that the sound from an engine I hear, and a grinding noise? a screeching noise? yes it is, I can hear a tractor engine far away making a loud noise and I hear a plough scraping and it's cold where I am in bed under the duvet, so I probably need to just get up, I have to get up now, I think and I stand up and I turn on the light in the bedroom and I see my clothes lying there on the chair and I get dressed fast and the clothes are cold and I go into the main room and I turn on the light there and it's cold in the main room and I think that I should have started a fire in the stove and not just stood there peering into the nothingness, but I'd rather go back into the bedroom and lie down in bed again for a bit, yes, the way Bragi's smart enough to be doing, I think, because it's still early in the morning, I think, but I don't want to know what time it is, I think and wow is that tractor making a racket, I think and I look at the picture where the two lines cross, there on the easel in front of me, and I see that I've signed the picture with a big A in the lower righthand corner which means that I think the picture is done whether it is or not, I think and I look at those two lines crossing, one purple and one brown and I see Asle running downstairs into his basement at home, they were having potato dumplings for dinner and Mother asked him to go get a bottle of juice and Asle pitter-pattered on his little feet down to the basement and went into the pantry where the glass jars of preserved plums and apples and pears were, and lots of bottles of juice, because in the autumn Mother makes juice from all the gooseberries and redcurrants they have, and there's a bin full of potatoes, and Asle takes a juice bottle and runs outside, and no, no, I can't think about that, I think and suddenly Ales is right next to me and she puts a hand on my back and she just stands there next to me and it's so good to feel her hand on my back, I think and I see Asle sitting in a car and a man is holding a towel around his wrist and they're driving to see The Doctor and Asle is somewhere outside himself and he looks back at where he lives, at The New House and The Old House, and he thinks that this is the last time he's ever going to see the house and everything is shimmering slightly, in a mysterious light that he's part of and that's much bigger than him, yes, it's everything that exists, and from this light, yes, that's like it's put together out of tiny dots of flickering yellow, yes it's like a cloud of yellow dust and from that cloud of shimmering yellow he sees himself sitting there in the car with his bleeding hand because Asle slipped on the ice and smashed the juice bottle and a piece of glass cut the artery in his wrist, and Asle feels very weak, and he is in the shimmering cloud of glinting shining transparent yellow dust and he's not scared, he feels something like happiness, like a great peace, no, there's no word for what and how he feels, how he's seeing, Asle thinks and I look at the picture there in front of me and Ales is stroking my back, up and down, and I see Asle sitting there in the car with his bleeding hand and Ales rubs and rubs my back and it's so soothing and good to feel her hands, I think and I see Asle sitting there with a bleeding hand and I don't want to think about that any more, it's better to put it in my pictures as best I can, I think, and it's in the painting with the two crossing lines too, I think and then I realize that Ales has taken her hand off me and she's gone and I just stand there and look at the picture even though it's cold in the room and I should light a fire in the stove and I see Asle standing outside the front door at home and looking at Father who is looking almost without believing it at a brand new car, it's grey, and it looks like Father can hardly dare to touch the car, much less sit in it, and Mother is standing there and she says it's amazing, now they have their own car too, she says, yes it's hard to believe, but it's true, she says and Father says that it's not exactly their car yet, it's the bank that owns the car, he says and Mother says well still it's their car, and Father says yes yes and then he says look, look down at the bus stop, there's The Bald Man, he doesn't take buses very often, just when he needs to go to Bjørgvin, Father says and Asle looks down at The Bald Man and it's so cold in the room, I need to light a fire in the stove, I think, but what I really want most to do is go lie down and tuck myself nice and tight under the covers with Bragi, I think, and it would be fine for me to go lie back down in bed, warm up a little, why not, I think, and I go back into the bedroom and lie down on the bed fully clothed and Bragi is lying there and he lies down right next to me and I spread the covers around us well and I feel Ales lying down right next to me, there's Bragi on one side and Ales on the other side, and she's warm and comforting, and I think it was good to come back to bed and warm up under the covers instead of standing there in the cold main room, I think and Ales asks me if I'm doing all right and I say everything's fine, everything's the same as usual with me, yes, as she already knows, I say and Ales doesn't say anything and then I just lie there and I think that I should have turned off the lights, in the main room and in the bedroom, but that's all right, I think and I hear Ales say that we are always together, the two of us, and I stare straight ahead and I see Asle and some other kids sitting under an overhanging rock, in a kind of shallow mountain cave, there's alpine blue sow-thistle there, it's still raining out, and there are three boys and three girls and they've climbed a little way up from the country road, it's not so far up to the overhanging rock, and then they went under it and there are tallow candles they've left there and a box of matches and they light the candles and it's pretty cold so they sit close together and Asle puts his arms around the waist of the girl sitting next to him and she leans against him and she puts a hand on his leg and then Asle feels her mouth on his cheek and then she finds his mouth and they kiss and she opens her mouth and he opens his and then they touch the tips of their tongues together and their mouths kind of suck together and Asle feels his dick getting hard and he puts a hand on one of her breasts and it's small, but it is a breast, and her breathing starts to get faster and he strokes her breast, over her pullover, and then she takes his hand and puts it under her pullover and brings it up to her breast and then Asle holds her breast in his hand and it fits into his grip and then he feels that her nipple is hard and he takes the nipple between his thumb and finger and she's breathing even faster and then she moves her hand from his leg and puts it on his trousers where his stiff dick is and she keeps her hand there and then she gently moves the palm of her hand back and forth and the whole time their mouths are stuck fast to each other and then Per Olav says no look at those two and they let go of each other and Per Olav says he didn't know they were a couple but he knows it now, Per Olav says and I look straight ahead and I realize that Ales is gone now and I think is it still early in the morning? or maybe it's still night even? but I don't want to look what time it is, I think, and I should have slept more, I feel sleepy, I think, and I retuck the covers around me and Bragi but it is morning already because I hear the racket from the engine in the old tractor, and a scraping noise, like from a plough, or is that just something I'm imagining? no I hear it, a screeching noise, I think and I think that it was a good thing I drove back to Bjørgvin and that I found Asle there in the snow, because it's so cold now he really could have frozen to death, I think, but how is he doing? they took him straight from The Clinic to The Hospital and I need to drive to The Hospital to see him today, I think, and I need to drive the paintings down to Bjørgvin today and bring them to The Beyer Gallery, I haven't made any plans with Beyer about that but even if he isn't there I can take the pictures in and put them in the room Beyer calls The Bank, because the gallery is open and there's always some girl or another there, if Beyer isn't there himself, and it's always a new girl, a student, Beyer says, it's a student who wants to make a little money, he says, but they never stay long, there's always a new face to see there, so he probably pays them badly, he must, and so he always has to get a new girl, I think, because Beyer, well, he doesn't throw money around, and that's why he's become the well-off man that he is, I think and then I hear the racket from the old tractor disappear and I think that in that case Åsleik must be here already, he's parked the tractor out in front on the stoop, because he was supposed to come over today, but I didn't think he'd come so early, I think, and then I hear a knock at the door and I think that if I don't open the door Åsleik will just come inside and I get to my feet and it's so cold in the bedroom that I wish I could just stay lying in bed all day, I think and I'm so cold I start to shake my arms to warm up and Bragi is lying there in the bed, under the covers, and he looks at me with surprised eyes

You just stay right there, I say

Just stay where it's nice and warm, I say

and I hear footsteps and I hear a door open and I go into the main room and there's Åsleik standing and looking at the painting of the two lines crossing, in warm clothes and a fur hat and boots, he's standing and looking at the picture and he says boy I certainly get up late, it's been light out for a long time, he says

You didn't get up? he says

Yes I did, I say

And then you just lay back down, he says

Yeah, I say

Anyway it's ten o'clock, he says

Yeah, I say

and I think that I never would have guessed it was so late

You're usually up at five or six, he says

Is something wrong? he says

No, I say

You must have just been especially tired, he says

Yes, that's to be expected, he says

and he says that driving down to Bjørgvin and back the same day and then driving there again the same day, and in such conditions, snow and blizzards and slick roads, the way I did the day before yesterday, and then driving from Bjørgvin back to Dylgja again yesterday, yes, that would take a lot out of anyone, he himself would barely come out alive, Åsleik says and then he says that it's so cold in my living room that it's warmer outside and he'll just light another fire in the stove then, like he had to do yesterday, and the day before too, it really seems to have turned into his job now hasn't it, pretty much, he says, but maybe I could at least make some coffee? Åsleik says and I say yes

No, I shouldn't have stayed in bed all morning, I say

I don't think I've done that for years, I say

No well I can't remember the last time I did anyway, Åsleik says and then he goes over to the stove and he puts the wood chips and kindling and a log in and he lights the kindling and then Åsleik stands there and looks in at the wood and says that's good dry kindling so it'll catch in a second, he says, and who do I have to thank for that kindling? and wood? yes, for being about to have a nice warm room? it's him, yes, sure is, Åsleik says and I don't say anything because I've heard this so many times before, so many, I think and Åsleik says he's here to get something in return for the wood chips, kindling, and logs, the driest birchwood, he says, and that, that, as I know he wants a painting to give to Sister for Christmas, and every year before he's always chosen one of the small paintings but yesterday we agreed that this year he should pick one of the big paintings, or bigger ones, none of the pictures I paint are really all that big, Åsleik says and he says now he wants to choose one before I drive to Bjørgvin and deliver the pictures to The Beyer Gallery, and that's why he dropped by so early, or earlyish, because if he didn't misunderstand me I was planing to drive back to Bjørgvin again today with the paintings and take them to Beyer, who I had such trust in, such faith in, even though he, like a lot of other Bjørgvinners, was just out for money, to make money, money money money, buying low and selling high, that was the only thing people in Bjørgvin cared about, whether they bought and sold fish or paintings, yes, that's how they'd always been and that's how they still were, Åsleik says and I've heard him say this so many times before, obviously, because neither Åsleik nor I ever have that much new to say to each other and that's why we always talk about the same things, because you have to say something

Yes it's burning well in the stove now, Åsleik says

and he stands there and looks at the logs

I'll let it burn a little with the hatch open, then I'll put another log in, he says

Because damn it was cold in your room, he says

But it won't be long now before it's nice and warm, he says

At least warm enough to be in the room without a coat and hat and boots on, he says

and I go over to the stove and stand there and stretch my arms
out above the stove and it's nice to feel the warmth coming up
to my hands, my arms, my whole body, I think and Åsleik stands
next to me

Now it's warming up the room, he says

Yes, I say

But what did you do with the dog? Åsleik says

He's sleeping, I say

In the bed in your bedroom? he says

Yes, I say

and then we stand there silent

Bragi, that was his name, right? Åsleik says

Yes, I say

and again it's quiet

You've talked about getting a dog so many times, now you've
finally done it, he says

and I don't answer and then Åsleik goes over to the easel
where the picture with the two intersecting lines is and he says St
Andrew's Cross, yes, of course he says that, I think, St Andrew's
Cross he says again and he emphasizes the term, like the words
are so important, it's like he's saying he can do more than just fish
and clear roads you know, like that, wait don't go over there, I
think and then Åsleik says that that's the picture he wants even if
it's isn't finished, he says and I freeze for a second, because I want
to keep that picture myself, I don't want to sell it, so I don't want
to give it to Åsleik either no

But it's not done, I say

Doesn't matter, he says

It's good the way it is, he says

But don't you want to look at the other pictures first, the ones
in the stack there, the big ones? I say

and I point at the stack leaning solidly against the wall next
to the kitchen door

I've found the one I want, Åsleik says

But I'm not done with that picture, I say

Doesn't matter, he says

But I want to finish it, I say

Yes yes, but it's finished in a way the way it is, he says

And you signed it, he says

And it wasn't signed the last time I saw it, he says

Doesn't that mean you've decided you're done with it? he says

and I don't say anything and I think you can't pull a fast one on him so easily can you, on Åsleik, he always picks the best picture to give to Sister, often, yes, well, usually, it's been a painting I've wondered if I wanted to keep for myself, in the collection I have upstairs in the crates, but that would be just the painting that Åsleik would say and think and feel the same way about, the one I wanted to keep

But at least take a look at the other finished paintings, I say

Yes, at the big ones, I say

and I stand there and point at the stack of big paintings leaning against the wall next to the kitchen door and Åsleik says he will, yes, he'll do that if I come and bring him a steaming hot cup of coffee soon, yes, if I put the pot of coffee on while he looks through the pictures, he says and then Åsleik goes over to the stack of pictures and I go out to the kitchen and I turn on the light and I put the coffeepot on and then I look outside and wow it snowed a lot last night, my car is totally snowed in, so it certainly is good that Åsleik cleared the road, I think, and do I really need to drive the pictures into Bjørgvin today? after it's snowed so much, and with the roads so slippery? and why in the world didn't I just take them with me the day before yesterday? I can't understand why I didn't think of it the day before yesterday, I think, but the first time I drove to Bjørgvin was to go shopping, and the second time was because I wanted to check in on Asle, and actually that's really why I want to drive to Bjørgvin today too, because I want to go see Asle in The Hospital, and maybe buy him something or bring him whatever he needs from home, that's mostly why, I think and I look out at the white snow and I see Asle lying there in bed and there are all kinds of tubes and things attached to his body that are hanging down from a metal stand and he's lying there asleep and his body is shaking up and down, his body is constantly quivering and Asle wakes up and he opens his eyes and he looks to the side and he sees that three other people are lying in three other beds in the room he's in

So, you're awake, one of them says

and Asle doesn't answer

You're awake now, you've been asleep a long time, I don't know how you could sleep through that noise from the street, a tractor or something, he says

and Asle doesn't answer, he just closes his eyes again, and then he's shaking even harder and then a doctor and a male nurse come in and The Doctor says someone needs to be watching him at all times, so he needs to be transferred, and Asle just lies there and he doesn't know quite where he is or isn't and everything's confusing and he's shaking and then two men come and take the bed and the metal stand and they wheel Asle out into the hall and he closes his eyes and his whole body's shaking, jolting up and down, and then they wheel him into a lift and I stand there in the kitchen and look out at the snow and I see them wheel Asle down a corridor and then they open a door to a room and there's a bed in there and a man is lying in the bed and his hair is all grey and his face is all grey and a man is sitting next to the bed half asleep and he's watching over the people lying there because they're so sick, I think and I watch them wheel Asle's bed in and put it against the wall across from the other bed and the man sitting in the chair stands up and looks at something hanging on Asle's bed and then he sits back down and after a moment he gets up and goes over to the bed and prods Asle on the shoulder

Asle, he says

Yes, Asle says

and then I see the man who prodded Asle's shoulder, who's

keeping watch in a way, sit back down on his chair and I look and look at the snow and I think I have to drive the paintings into Bjørgvin today and then go see Asle in The Hospital, because he's really sick, I think and I turn around and see that the coffee is ready and I pour out two mugs of coffee and then go back into the main room and I see that Åsleik has set up four or five of the big paintings along the wall where the kitchen door is and now he's standing there looking at each one and I go over and hand him a mug and he says thanks

You've been painting a lot of good paintings recently, haven't you, he says

Thank you, I say

and then we both stand there, sipping our coffee, and then I go and stand and look at the picture with the two lines crossing and Åsleik says that that's the picture he wants, the one I'm look-ing at, but if I really want to keep it then there are several other very good paintings too, Åsleik says, and he's already picked out one, he says and he asks me if I can guess which one it is and I say I can try and I walk over to a picture of something that might be a kind of boat gliding on the sky, and the picture is brown and purple, a little like heather, the same as a lot of my paintings, but what really makes the picture shine is the thin layer of white paint I painted in a few places after I looked at the picture in the dark, it's these clear movements, it's this white and a couple of black movements that make the picture shine, yes, or give off a stronger light at least, yes, in its own way, and now that I look at this painting again I think that this is another one I'd like to keep for myself actually, but if I had to choose I'd rather keep the one of the two lines crossing and Åsleik asks if I remember what I called that picture

Because you're good at titling your pictures, he says

A picture needs a good name, I say

Yes I can see that, Åsleik says

and then we stand there silent and I think that I've always

given my pictures names, and not every painter does that but I always do, because after I've decided I'm done with a picture the last thing I paint is a big A in thick black oil paint in the lower right corner of the picture itself, so that it's easy to see that there's an A there, and on the top edge of the stretcher I paint the picture's title, also in thick black oil paint, and now Åsleik asks me what the painting he wants is called and I think I remember, I'm not totally sure but I think it's called Silent Boat, that's something you might call a picture, I think, actually it's an awful title, I don't know what I could have been thinking calling it that, I think, and I say that I think the picture is called Silent Boat but he can just look for himself, I say and Åsleik says that he's already done that of course and then he goes and picks up the painting and turns it around and on the top edge of the stretcher, in the middle, it says Silent Boat in thick black oil paint

You always remember, Åsleik says

I'll take this picture, he says

Sure, I say

and then Åsleik puts the picture back down on the floor but leaning against the easel now and then he steps back a little to look at it and I go with him and I too can see that it's a good picture, maybe one of the best ones I've painted in a long time, but if Åsleik wants it to give to Sister then he can have it, that's perfectly fine, I think, but the picture on the easel itself that's been given the title St Andrew's Cross I absolutely won't let him have, I want to keep it myself, and Åsleik must have realized that, that he couldn't have it, I think and then I go over to the picture and I see that I've already signed it with an A in the lower right corner and then I turn the picture around and I see that I've painted St Andrew's Cross on the top part of the stretcher and I think that I must have done that yesterday, no, my memory is just terrible, I can't remember things from midnight till noon, as they say, I think

St Andrew's Cross, I say

Yes that was really the only thing you could call that picture, Åsleik says

and then luckily he doesn't say St Andrew's Cross several times

You've finished that picture? Åsleik says

So you were trying to trick me? he says

Yes, I probably was, actually, to tell you the truth, I say

and Åsleik says that he can tell that that painting is finished, even if it looks unfinished it's still finished, of course it is, he says and then we drink our coffee and Åsleik says now do I really want to drive down to Bjørgvin again today, with all the snow we've had? and he says that he doesn't understand me, two days ago I drove to and from Bjørgvin, and then I even drove back again the same day, all without bringing my pictures to The Beyer Gallery, and now I want to drive back to Bjørgvin again today, it's almost too much, he says and I think I need to go and see Asle in The Hospital but I don't want to say anything to Åsleik about that

I'll take the paintings in today, get it out of the way, I say

It's not only because of the pictures that you want to drive to Bjørgvin, is it? Åsleik says

No maybe not, I say

You probably want to go to mass, he says

and I can hear scoffing in his voice, because it's true that I drive to Bjørgvin every now and then, and in the summertime usually every Sunday, to go to mass at St Paul's Church

You Papist, Åsleik says

and I think that he'll never stop with this word, never stop saying that, it's probably another word that he taught himself and that he's proud of knowing, Papist, St Andrew's Cross, he kind of shows off and puffs himself up with words like that

Papist, yes, he says

and I think that it would be a good idea to go to mass, but I hadn't thought of that, really I was only thinking I should go and

see Asle in The Hospital and at the same time take these paintings in as soon as I can, the paintings I kind of have to deliver
to Beyer

Or is it because of a woman? Åsleik says

and he says how dumb he was not to think of that right off,
he says and I think that I don't really like Åsleik, he can be so
annoying, but I don't let it show and I let all the foolishness just
vanish into thin air in a way, I think

No, I say

No no, he says

and we stand there without saying anything

But you probably were thinking of going to mass again soon?
he says

and I say yes maybe and Åsleik says didn't I go to mass yesterday when I was in Bjørgvin shopping? and I say I didn't go to
mass yesterday and Åsleik says well that's strange, I usually always
go to mass, every time I'm in Bjørgvin, he says and I have to say
something and then I say I'll just start getting the paintings ready
then and put them in the back of the car

You wrap them in blankets, Åsleik says

Yes, always, I say

Those blankets have seen a lot of use, he says

Yes, I've had them for many years, I say

and then I stand there and hope that Åsleik doesn't ask me
where I got the blankets, and that I don't have to tell him yet
again that I got them at The Second-Hand Shop in Sailor's Cove,
I didn't get them all at once, but one this time, one another time,
whenever I was in The Second-Hand Shop I would look for
blankets and if I didn't see any I'd ask if they had any blankets
and then they'd always ask what I meant and I'd say wool blankets and sometimes they'd have one or two blankets in the back,
sometimes not, but after a while I'd bought quite a collection and
now there was a big pile of blankets on the floor in a corner of the
attic room where I keep everything I need for painting, tubes of

oil paint, canvas, and of course the boards for making stretchers from, getting nice and dry, I think and Åsleik says he can help me pack up the pictures and carry them out to the car and I say thanks and then he hands me his mug and he says thanks for the coffee and I see that I've only drunk a little of my coffee, and that's how it is every morning, I fill up a mug of coffee and then only drink a little, I think and then I go to the kitchen and put the mugs in the sink and then I go up to the attic and I put my arms in a kind of hug around the whole heap of blankets lying tossed in a corner and I go downstairs and dump the pile on the floor in front of the paintings and I see that Åsleik is standing and looking at the picture he chose as a Christmas present for Sister that's now standing on the floor leaning against the easel and then he looks at me

Yes so that's the picture I want, he says

It's a deal, I say

and then I take a blanket and one picture from the stack of finished big pictures and I wrap it up well in the blanket and I put in on the floor and then Åsleik takes a blanket and a picture and wraps it up and puts it on top of the one I put on the floor and we keep going like that wrapping up painting after painting and it's Åsleik who takes the last painting and then all the big paintings are on the floor in a neat stack and then I take a blanket and wrap up one of the small paintings and Åsleik does the same thing and there are only four small paintings in all

There were thirteen paintings in all, Åsleik says

Yes, I say

That's an unlucky number, he says

It can be either lucky or unlucky, at least for me, I say

and Åsleik says he's never heard that before and I say that that's how it is for me anyway

Yes I guess it might be, he says

and then Åsleik says he can't understand why I want to drive back to Bjørgvin again today, and I say I've already told him, I'm going to take the pictures to The Beyer Gallery, get it over with, I say and Åsleik says there must be some other reason and I say there might be and Åsleik says that I should dress warm, yes, I should put on my coat, and then we'll need to carry the pictures out to my car, he says and I nod and then it's silent

You've always gone and done whatever you wanted to do, Asle, Åsleik says

and he wraps the picture he chose up in a blanket and puts it back down leaning against the easel

You'll get the blanket back after I've given the picture to Sister, same as always, he says

and I say yes it'll be the same as usual and I say I want to go start the car and turn on the heat and brush off all the snow of course and Åsleik says he can help me with that and then I put on my black velvet jacket and I go out into the hall and put on my black coat and a scarf and then I slip into my shoes and then I go out and start the car, and it starts at the first try like always, and then I open the back and find the snow brush and then I brush off the car and then we start carrying the pictures I'm going to drive down to The Beyer Gallery out to the car and we put them down carefully in the back and after we've done that Åsleik says well then he'll get the picture he's planning to give Sister for Christmas and I see Åsleik go into the house and I shut the back of the car and I see Åsleik come out onto the stoop and he stands there with the picture under his arm and I go back inside my good old house and go into the main room and I see my brown leather bag hanging on its hook, between the pile of small paintings and the pile of big paintings, the pictures I'm not done with yet, and I put the shoulder bag on and then I stop and I look at the picture with the two lines crossing, yes, St Andrew's Cross as it's called, and there's a lot in that picture, I think and I think that now I need to go, because Åsleik is waiting, and I go into the little side room and I turn out the light and I go into the main room and I turn off the light there and I go out to the kitchen and I see that

there's still a little water in Bragi's bowl so I fill it and then I cut
a slice of bread and break it into chunks and put them down in
the other bowl even though there's still a lot of bread there from
before and I think that Bragi is still lying asleep in my bed so I
guess he can stay here at home, I think and I turn off the light in
the kitchen and I go out to the hall and I turn off the light there
and then I open the front door and go outside and I see Åsleik
still standing where he was before on the stoop with the picture
wrapped in a blanket under his arm

That took a while, he says

Yes, I say

What were you doing in there? he says

and I don't answer

I almost got tired of waiting, he says

I guess you had to go to the bathroom and had trouble getting it out? he says

Yes that's right, I say

But here you are at last, Åsleik says

No, I know you, I know what you were doing, he says

All right, what? I say

You were looking at the picture with the two lines, St Andrew's Cross, he says

and I nod and Åsleik says that he's always been able to take
the picture he wanted to give as a present to Sister, every time
before, but then again he's never asked for a big painting before,
Åsleik says and then he says that this isn't exactly weather to
stand around outside in, so he'll go sit in the tractor, he says, and
we'll get driving, him first, so that at least the driveway will be
all clear, and the country road until the turn-off to his farm, and
I'll drive after him and he hopes I have a good drive to Bjørgvin
and drive carefully since the roads might still be slippery in some
places, because there might be ice under the new snow, he says
and I say that I always do drive carefully and Åsleik says he knows
that, of course I drive carefully, he says and we'll see each other

soon, he says and I say it's just a day trip, I'll drive home after I've dropped off the paintings, I say

You always have a show not long before Christmas, he says

Yes, I say

Because it's easier to sell paintings then, of course, yes, during Advent, he says

and I say that's true, at least Beyer says so, and my pictures especially are easiest to sell then, maybe Beyer means that they're good to give as Christmas presents but he also thinks that it's best to open an exhibition not too long before Christmas, I say and Åsleik says that that's what he thought and then he climbs up into the cabin of the tractor and starts the engine and it makes a horrible noise, that screeching, it's hard to believe an engine can make a sound that bad, I think and I go sit in my car and I put the brown leather bag on the passenger seat and the car has warmed up nicely and I turn the heat down a little and then Åsleik looks back at me and then forward again and then the tractor goes around the corner of the house and I drive after him and Åsleik drives the tractor out onto the country road and I follow him and it certainly has snowed a lot, there must be four inches on the ground, but it's not snowing now, I think and I drive ten or twenty feet behind Åsleik, he's driving slowly and steadily towards his farm, and it always takes a while to get there, and the road twists and turns a lot too, I think and I drive a good distance behind him and then Åsleik turns off and he stops the tractor and gets out and I stop the car and roll down the window

You drive carefully, now, he says

Yes, I will, slow and safe, I say

and I add that once I get to Instefjord there'll be good roads all the way to Bjørgvin, because they always clear those roads, I say and Åsleik says that I have good tires on now, newish studded tires, plus I had enough money to buy a car with four-wheel drive and so that's what I did, and with good studded tires and four-wheel drive my car or van is practically a tractor, he says and

I answer that I've had enough problems driving in winter conditions in my life, experience eventually taught me something, I say and Åsleik says that's all right then and then we each raise a hand to say goodbye and then I drive slowly on, and now it's my car that's leaving tracks in the snow, in front of me I see nothing but white snow, and then luckily there are all these snow poles with reflectors on them set up to mark where the edge of the road is, without them it would be easy to end up off the road, yes, it would be impossible not to, I think and I drive slowly, the way I always do, first I'll be on the small roads along Sygne Fjord to Instefjord, and they're not cleared, but then, after I get to Instefjord and get on the main road to Bjørgvin, it'll be easier, because those roads will have been cleared, I think and I look at the white road and I see Asle standing in front of Mother and he's thinking that he can't stand going to that damn school anymore, the teachers are unbearable, why on earth should he keep going? and luckily he's almost done with school, he thinks, and if he didn't have so little mandatory schooling left he'd have just quit today, Asle thinks, but as it is he has to just try to stick it out, and he thinks that he still wants to drop out, even if he'll be done soon, he thinks and he tells Mother he wants to stop going to school

Are you out of your mind? she says

Drop out of school? she says

Children have to stay in school, she says

If you drop out they'll come and take you away to a school for delinquent boys, and it's strict there, and the school's on an island so no one can run away, she says

And anyway you're almost done, she says

and Asle thinks can that really be true, that he might get sent to an island just because he doesn't like going to school? no, he didn't know that, Asle thinks, but he doesn't really believe it, no more than he believes the other things Mother says, neither the stuff about Jesus and God nor that you can get sent to an island for dropping out of school, but he doesn't give a damn, if he wants to stop going to school he'll stop going, Asle thinks, but there's one thing, he's heard that to get into The Art School in Bjørgvin, and he's gradually started thinking that maybe he could go there, if he gets in, anyway to get into The Art School in Bjørgvin you need to have gone to The Academic High School, and if it wasn't for that he'd have stopped going to school already, then and there, no doubt about it, Asle thinks, but he's not going to do that, he's not going to drop out of school, it was just something he said because Mother gets so angry when he says it, no, it's not that he has any desire to go to The Academic High School but it's something he has to do, and he's so clumsy that there's hardly anything he can do, so what's going to become of him? as Father always says, Asle thinks and I look at the white road in front of me and I drive slowly out along Sygne Fjord and I see Father standing in front of Asle and he says you're a good kid Asle but what's going to become of you? he says

I don't know, Asle says

But you need to get an education, you have to be something when you grow up, Father says

and Asle says that the only thing he's good at is drawing and painting and then Mother says well then he's probably going to become an artist, even if there are hardly any jobs for artists, still there must be some work for people who know how to draw, at the newspapers for instance, newspapers have a lot of drawings, and there are a lot of drawings in advertisements, someone has to draw them, so it must be possible to make a living by drawing and painting, Mother says, but you can't get into The Art School unless you go to The Academic High School, she says and Father says that true, to get into The Art School you need to have graduated from The Academic High School and Asle thinks that he doesn't understand why someone has to learn not just adding and multiplying but also what they call mathematics to be a painter

Drawing and painting aren't the same thing as doing maths, Asle says

No, no, Father says

and Mother says she doesn't understand why it's like that either, but the people in charge have decided that you have to go to The Academic High School and then you can go to The Art School, if you get admitted, she says and Asle says that he's no good at anything but drawing and painting, okay well he can read, obviously, and he likes to read sometimes, and he even thinks he can write pretty well too, well enough, but the Norwegian teachers at his school don't think so, so he has bad marks in writing, yes, same as in all the other subjects, he says

You never do your homework, Mother says

That's true, Asle says

And now you're sorry, she says

Yes, yes, Father says

and Mother says that he'll need to do something in the future, he can't just sit at home and paint, she says and Asle doesn't say anything

And if you start at The Academic High School you'll need to move into an apartment, Mother says

and Asle thinks that it sounds like Mother's glad he'll be moving out, and that makes sense, he thinks, he is sure looking forward to getting out, leaving home, getting away from Mother and her constant nagging and whining about how he needs to cut his hair or needs to paint pictures that people can understand, where you can see what it's a picture of, or about how he needs to do his homework, she nags him about absolutely everything

I want to go to The Art School, Asle says

But then you need to paint like you used to, so that it looks like something, Mother says

Yes, Father says

Not those pictures that don't look like anything at all, she says

If you keep painting those you'll never get into The Art School, no matter how much high school you've had, she says

Yes, Father says

and I look at the white road and I think that I still haven't driven that far along Sygne Fjord so it's still a long way to Instefjord, I think and I see Father standing there and he says he can call The Academic High School right now and find out what Asle's chances are for getting in and Father goes out to the hall and Asle can hear him talking on the phone and then Father comes back in

It'll be fine, he says

There's a spot for you at The Academic High School, he says

On what they call the Modern Languages track, he says

and Asle hears what Father's saying and he thinks that's good isn't it? because what else could he have tried to do when he grows up? he thinks

And so you'll need to get a room in Aga, Mother says

Yes, Father says

But there are lots of people from Barmen who've gone to The Academic High School in Aga and rented a room there, so I'm sure it'll work out, he says

I'll put an ad seeking a room in *The Hardanger Times*, Father says

and Asle says he'd be grateful if Father did that and I look at the white road and I drive toward Instefjord, and it'll be good to get there, because then I'll be on the main road that's been cleared already and then I can start driving south to Bjørgvin, I think, and I don't think that I've ever, in all the years I've lived in Dylgja, driven to Bjørgvin so many times so close together, I think, and I look at the white road and I see Father standing there and he's saying that an older woman has called and said that she has a room I can rent, it sounds like it's a hayloft that used to be a shoemaker's workshop, a room up in the attic, and the shower and toilet are downstairs, on the ground floor, she said, Father says and he says that it sounded good, all things considered, and the rent wasn't so bad, he says, so he agreed on the spot, he says and they arranged for Asle to move in when The Academic High

School starts, Father says and Asle says that's great, all things considered, and he thinks it's good he'll be living in a house by himself, not in a room in a house where other people live, Asle thinks and he sees Mother stand there looking at him

But you've painted pictures of so many people's houses and you've never painted your own, she says

Don't you think you should do that before you move out? she says

That's true you haven't, Father says

and Asle thinks that now he'll have to paint The New House and The Old House too, and The Barn and The Shed and all the fruit trees and The Boathouse and The Dock and The Rowboat and The Shore and The Fjord and everything, can he really bring himself to do all that? he thinks

No you haven't, she says

You've painted pictures of almost every single house in the whole town, and some in Stranda too, but never your own, she says

Yes well then I guess I should paint the farm then, Asle says

With everything, he says

Yes, The Old House, The New House, The Barn and The Shed and The Boathouse and The Dock and The Rowboat, The Fjord too, not leave anything out, he says

I'm really looking forward to seeing that picture, Mother says

and she says that she's been thinking about it for a long time but she hasn't brought herself to ask him about it, because he'd been having a hard time since, Mother says and she breaks off and then there's a long silence and Asle thinks why did Mother have to remind him about Sister again, about how she was gone so suddenly, how she just died, was just lying there dead in her bed one morning, yes, the thought of his sister Alida just lying there and dead he can't take it

Anyway, Mother says

and Asle notices that Mother is about to start crying

I have a good photo of the farm you can paint from, she says and Asle thinks that it's too much, that Sister was gone so suddenly, and then Mother goes and gets a photo and hands it to Asle and it's a good photo, it looks very nice, Asle thinks and Father says that he's thought the same thing, that it's really too bad that almost every home in Barmen, practically all of Stranda too before long, has a painting that Asle's painted of their house hanging in the main room, while they, his parents, don't, he says, because Asle still hasn't painted a picture of his own childhood home, he says

Yes yes, Asle says

You really haven't, Mother says

So before you move out you need to paint one, she says

and then they stand there silently and then Mother says yet again that his hair has grown so long now that it's high time he gets it cut, it's shameful, for him and for her and for Father, that he's going around with that long hair, hanging straight down his back, it's too awful, she says

I don't know how many times I've told you you need a hair-cut, she says

And you don't do it, she says

But now that you're starting at The Academic High School you'll have to cut your hair, she says

and she looks at Father and she says can't he say something too

Yes you need to cut your hair, Father says

I've never seen a man or boy with such long hair, he says

Me neither, Mother says

and after that it's silent and then Mother says that he doesn't want to get confirmed and he doesn't do his homework and he gets such bad marks that she's sure he'll end up on the waiting list to get into The Academic High School and on top of all that to run around with long hair hanging down his back, she says, yes, that shaggy brown mess, she says and again she says that Father should say something

Yes you need to cut your hair, Father says

and Asle thinks that he's had enough of all this nagging, ever since he started growing his hair out and refusing to cut it Mother has been harping on at him, you have to cut it, you can't go around looking like that, they'll talk about you in town, no man in Barmen has ever had hair as long as yours, she said and Asle answered that he'll wear his hair however he wants to, it's his hair, and those curls Mother does her hair in look totally awful, that's what he thinks, if you want to know the truth, but still he doesn't go around saying over and over again that she has to get a new haircut, what if almost every single time he talked to Mother he said that she should go get a new haircut, he said, Asle thinks, but still he had to listen to her constant, never-ending nagging, she hardly ever talked to him without telling him he had to get a haircut, didn't she ever think about anything else? was there not one single other thought in her head besides his needing to cut his hair? he thinks

I don't want to paint that picture, he says

You don't want to paint your very own childhood home, Mother says

and then Asle just leaves the room and he thinks about the time when he was in primary school and Mother took him with her to a hair salon and when he went he had nice hair, a little long, and then The Hairdresser Lady cut almost all his hair off, she practically shaved him bald it was so short, and it was like both Mother and The Hairdresser Lady were glad they'd done it, yes, it was like cutting off all his hair gave them both a kind of evil pleasure, Asle thinks and the next day he didn't want to go to school, he looked so horrible and humiliated that he was ashamed to go to school, it was totally awful how he looked, Asle thinks and he said he was sick and that he didn't want to go to school but he went anyway, but he wore a hat pulled down over his ears, he thinks and no he doesn't want to think about that anymore, Asle thinks, and no one was going to give him such a short haircut ever, ever again, that's for sure, fucking never again, he thinks, and it was so horrible going to school the next day, Asle thinks

and I look at the white road and then I see some snowflakes hit
the windshield, one by one, snowflakes, then it starts snowing
more and more and it gets even harder to see where the road is,
and I have to drive even slower, but it'll be much better after I
get to Instefjord, or Øygna, where the woman Åsleik calls Sister
but who's actually named Guro lives, I think, because then I'll
be on the cleared main road that runs south to Bjørgvin, I think
and I look at the falling snowflakes, and now they're falling so
thickly that you can't tell one flake from the others, and I look
at the white road and I see Asle sitting there on the floor of the
main room in his house and he's looking at a white canvas and
he's thinking that today they found Sister dead in bed and just
now they've left and taken her away in an ambulance to get an
autopsy, they say, because they need to cut Sister up to try to
find out why she died so unexpectedly and suddenly and since it
isn't every day that someone dies all of a sudden so young they
have to try to find the cause of death, they said and Asle sits and
looks at the white canvas and he thinks that now, no, it can't go
on, he can't anymore, he thinks, now it's just, he thinks, now he
doesn't want to paint from photos anymore, he doesn't want to
paint any more rooms and barns in the sun with a flagpole flying
the Norwegian flag, and birch trees in blossom, and a still blue
Fjord, now he doesn't want to paint house and home anymore,
now he wants to paint just his own pictures, because his head is
full of pictures, it's a real torment, yes, pictures get lodged in his
head all the time, not as things that have happened but like a kind
of photograph, taken right there, right then, and he can kind of
flip from one of the pictures in his head to another, it's like he
has a photo album in his head and the strangest things are there
as pictures, like Grandpa's black boots in the rain one time, one
day, or Father stroking him on the head, just there, just then, or
the light coming down from the sky over the Fjord, just there,
just then, and now a whole bunch of pictures of Sister dead have
lodged in there and it's like they follow one another like a series
of magic lantern slides in Asle's head, one after the other, and he

raises his hands to his eyes and pushes on his eyes but the pictures don't go away, they just get stronger, and he takes his hands away from his eyes and now, he thinks, instead of painting pictures from photographs of house and home, yes, now he'll paint away the pictures he has in his head, but he doesn't want to paint them exactly how he sees them in his head before his eyes, because there's something like a sorrow, a pain, tied to every one of those pictures, he thinks, but also a kind of peace, yes, that too, yes he'll paint away all the pictures he has collected in his head, if he can, so that only the peace stays behind, Asle thinks and he looks and sees his sister Alida's white face just there, just then, and he sees the stretcher halfway inside the ambulance, with Sister's face covered, just there, just then and he looks at the white canvas and he thinks he'll start painting the pictures he has in his head soon, he'll paint them away, but he can't manage to paint the worst of them, it's too painful, it's like they're tearing him apart, everything he is, that's how bad it is, but even the pictures that aren't so hard have something about them, something sad, yes, a kind of grief, he thinks, but also a kind of peace, yes, that too, in addition to the pain, anyway there's a kind of peace in the pictures he has lodged in his head of his sister Alida, Asle thinks and then he suddenly thinks that now, no, now he doesn't want to see pictures anymore, he simply can't deal with all these pictures, not the ones in his head and not the ones there on canvas, now he wants to be done with pictures, so now he doesn't want to paint any more pictures, he wants to listen instead of seeing, yes, now he wants to listen to music, Asle thinks and he gets up and now it's decided, he wants to play music, and he wants to play guitar, a guitar makes a lot of noise, he wants to play electric guitar, loud, with distortion, he wants to play loud loud loud, Asle thinks and I look at the white road there in front of me and now it's stopped snowing, so it's much easier to see where the road is, I think and I feel white and empty, and now I've driven all the way down

along Sygne Fjord and I'm about halfway from Dylgja to Instefjord, I think, and I'm driving slow and steady, I think and I look
at the white road and I see Asle there on his knees and the white
canvas is on the floor in front of him and he's thinking that he
doesn't want to see anymore, see all these pictures, he wants to
hear now, he wants to hear the pictures away now, and for that
to happen he has to make a lot of sound so he wants to buy an
electric guitar, Asle thinks and I look at the white road and then
I see a herd of deer standing in the middle of the road and I start
driving even slower and the deer look at me and then they hop
off, away from the road, but one is still standing there looking at
me, and I think that I've seen a lot of deer, they've leaped right
across the road many times, so it's pure luck that I've never hit
a deer in my car, I think, but I usually see deer after it's dark or
around sunrise or sunset, never during the day, but then again at
this time of year it's never really light out, not even during the
day, I think and then I drive carefully closer to the deer that's
still there and then he too bounds away and I drive on and I look
at the white road and I see Asle standing there on stage in the
Youth Centre, his brown hair is hanging down in front of his
face and hiding him, he is standing there bent over a black guitar
that's hanging on him and he's playing all kinds of chords and
Terje is on the drums playing everything he can play without
any rhythm at all, it's just noise, and Geir is thumping the bass
strings totally at random and Olve's standing there screaming and
then he starts playing something kind of like a solo on his guitar
and they all stop for a bit and then Olve calls out now they need
to pull themselves together and play a real song, because what
we just stopped playing was nothing but noise, he shouts, it's no
good just making noise like that, you need to be able to play one
decent song, Olve says and then Geir says that we can't play even
one decent song but we'll be a band anyway, he says and Terje
says that we all play terribly, not one of us knows how to play, or

actually Olve can play a little but no one else can, he says, so we might as well give up on the whole band, he says and Asle just stands there with his guitar on and says nothing

And there's Asle not saying anything, same as always, Terje says

No, his hair's too long for him to talk, Olve says

And his name's not Asle anymore, it's Ales, he says

Nope, quiet as usual, Geir says

He doesn't know how to talk, Olve says

That must be why he never says anything, because he doesn't know how, he says

and Asle just stands there and he thinks it's no good, he has tried as hard as he can to learn how to play the guitar but no matter how much he practises, no matter how much he tries, he's never any good, and Olve had been nice to him, it was he who'd taught him the little he can play on the guitar, he drew little pictures of the chords and then Asle learned them, one by one, that was easy enough, but even just tuning the guitar was hard for him, and figuring out on his own which chord should come next in a song, no, he never managed to do that, so Olve always wrote it down for him, and when he tried to play a solo it was just a mess, he never managed to learn to play the guitar, Asle thinks, and actually Asle couldn't stand Olve but to tell the truth Olve was the only reason they could do anything at all, without Olve they couldn't play a single song, Asle thinks, and ever since he started playing guitar and joined this band he hadn't painted a single painting, or drawn a single drawing, and the pictures in his head that he wanted to drive out with the loud noise hadn't gone away, they just got stronger, so it's not working, Asle thinks, because even if he's just fourteen and, sure, has a lot of time ahead of him he'll never be a good guitarist and it doesn't make sense to keep trying something you can't do, something you'll never be able to do even sort of well, it's not like with pictures, those he makes easily, like there's nothing hard about it, but as for guitar playing, well, he's just never going be able to do it, and if the pictures in his head are sort of stuck there and loud noise doesn't make them go away then, yes, well, he'll just have to try to paint them away, Asle thinks, because drawing and painting are things he can do, but he can't play guitar, Asle thinks and then he takes off his guitar and puts it down leaning against the amp and Olve looks at him and asks him what he's doing

Why are you taking your guitar off in the middle of practice, Olve says

I'll never be able to play it, Asle says

You've only just started, Olve says

Yes, Asle says

and then they just stand there and Terje and Geir don't say anything

You'll get better, Olve says

You've already gotten a lot better since we started our band, he says

Maybe, Asle says

Come on, try again, Olve says

Pick up your guitar, he says

and Asle just stands there and then Olve says that maybe they'll take a break, if that's all right with every- body, he says and both Terje and Geir say it's fine with them and Olve says he has four bottles of beer with him, so now they can take a break and have a little beer, everyone always plays better after a little drink, he says and Geir asks where he got the beer from and Olve says his dad bought it for him

You've got a nice dad, Terje says

Yeah, Geir says

Yes, he is nice, Olve says

and then he says that his father is usually nice, after he's been drinking too, but sometimes he gets so confused, yes, angry too in a way, he says and then he always talks about how he never should've started a family, that's the kind of thing he says, you know, because he misses playing, travelling around and playing at dances, yeah, he really misses it, mostly the music, the playing itself, yes, but also the travelling, he says and then his mother always falls totally silent and she leaves the room, Olve says, and then he always tends to say that father can just start playing again, Olve says, and then his father says that he's too old, he can't bring himself to do it, there were several times he just couldn't pick up his guitar even though he wanted to play, he says, and that's why he gave Olve his guitar, and all the other equipment he has, and he taught Olve most of what Olve can do, and now Olve is already better than he ever was, both at singing and at playing guitar, his father says, Olve says, and then his father drinks more, first beer, and then he switches over to spirits and then his mother comes back in and says he mustn't drink so much, and his father says he'll have had enough soon and then he drinks even more and then he starts singing, and he sings beautifully, his father, and then his mother says he needs to come with her now, they need to go lie down, he has to go to work in the morning, she says and then his father usually goes with his mother, it's only on Sundays and holidays that he keeps on drinking but then he can drink all day, yes, he starts in the morning and drinks till he goes to bed, and he drives to Stranda to buy beer even if he's had a lot to drink, and if they're out of spirits he drives to Bjørgvin to buy some, he buys as many bottles as he has money for, almost, Olve says, and today, yes, today he'd asked his father if he would buy a few bottles of beer for him to bring to practice and his father had said that both Olve and the other band members were too young, they were still going to middle school, so he couldn't buy beer for them, no, it wasn't allowed, Olve says his father said, but then, after a while, he said he was going to drive to Stranda and buy a few bottles for himself and he could buy four bottles that Olve could bring to practice, one for each of us, no more than that, because playing music without having had a drink was never the same, that's what he said, so it was kind of good for them to learn that right away, but it was important not to drink too much, because then you played terribly, and that's why it was dangerous, there've been a lot of musicians both in the past and today who drank themselves to death, so you had to be careful, his father said, Olve says and then before he had to leave for the bus to practice his father gave him a shopping bag with four bottles of beer, he says, and now, yes, now they'll sit backstage and drink one bottle each and then everything'll feel better, for you too, he says to Asle

Maybe, Asle says

and he sees Terje get up and stand next to his drum set and Geir has put the bass down against his amp and Olve is already walking to the back of the stage

Come on, Geir says

and Asle goes over to Geir and then they and Terje go sit down on some chairs backstage, and then Olve comes and hands them each a bottle and then he opens his own and passes the opener and they all open their bottles in turn and then Olve raises his bottle and says cheers and Terje and Geir and Asle raise theirs and say cheers and Olve says that now, yes, now they're real musicians, now they should drink and then they'll try to play through the songs they know, there are five songs they sort of know anyway, and three songs they know really well, Olve says, but up till today it's all been a total mess, he says and they drink and Asle has had beer before but not too many times, and he doesn't think it tastes bad but it's not exactly good either, he thinks, and then they just sit there and don't say anything, just sip their beer, sip by sip, and then Olve says that beer really doesn't taste so good but it works, he says and then he takes out a tobacco pouch and he rolls himself a cigarette and he passes the tobacco pouch around to everyone else and they each roll a cigarette and Asle thinks that he's already smoked lots of times, and he likes that, yes, from the very first time he smoked a cigarette in The Boathouse at home with Per Olav he liked smoking, and he smoked the whole pack of cigarettes Per Olav had given him and he'd hidden in The Boathouse, he'd gone down there to smoke, Asle thinks and he thinks that someday he'll be old enough to go buy a packet of tobacco and cigarette papers and matches for himself at The Co-op Store, and then he'll hide them on a beam in The Boathouse, and he thinks that he's looking forward to being old enough to buy cigarettes, he thinks and he knows that some people get sick and throw up and stuff like that the first time they smoke but it wasn't like that with him, it just tingled a little in his body, in a good way, and he felt calmer, so he's going to be a smoker, as soon as he's old enough to buy tobacco for himself that's what he's going to do, Asle thinks and Olve passes around a cigarette lighter and Asle lights his cigarette and he sucks the smoke into his mouth and then he takes a real pull and he feels a sense of wellbeing spread through his body and then he sits there and smokes and there's a mug that they use as an ashtray sitting on the floor between them and Asle smokes and takes a sip of beer now and then and Olve says it'll be fine, they can't give up now, Asle is turning into a good rhythm guitarist, or good enough anyway, he just needs to practise more, Olve says and the others say they all think so too, and Terje says that he plays the drums even worse than Asle plays guitar and Geir says that his bass playing isn't anything to write home about either, no, he says and Olve says that it'll be fine, and actually he's already talked to the guy in charge of the Barmen Youth Group and he'd said that they might be interested in having them play at the dance, so once they learn enough songs they should just tell him, the guy in charge said, Olve says, and then, once they get some gigs, they'll start to make a little money too, but pretty much the first money they make they'll have to use to pay his father for the mikes and speakers, because his father hadn't given them the equipment for good, he'd only said they could borrow it and then pay for it after they'd brought in a few kroner playing, his father had said, Olve says, and Terje says of course, obviously they need to pay for the sound system as soon as they can, but then, after a while, they can split the money they make playing at dances among themselves, it'll be a few kroner each, he says, and then they'll be getting girls too, Olve says, because girls are always crazy about musicians, that's how it's always been, he says, they used to go crazy for Hardanger fiddle players and then it was accordion players and now it's for guys in a band, Olve says and in fact that's how his father and mother met, yes, his father was playing at a dance once, and they're still in love with each other even after all these years, Olve says

Everything'll be fine, he says

and Asle thinks that maybe it won't be so bad, and maybe he isn't such a terrible player, not much worse than the others anyway, and of course he can get better, even if he never gets really good, but he doesn't really need to, he just needs to get good enough that his playing is passable, he thinks, and it is good when he smokes, he likes smoking, and it's good with beer too, yes, he thinks, beer doesn't taste great but it does good things to you, he thinks and Olve says it'll be fine and they each smoke their rolled cigarette to the end and finish their bottle of beer and then Olve says that now they'll try to get through the songs they know, more or less, he says, and it won't be long before they'll be playing their first dance, he says and then they get up and go over to their instruments and Asle drapes the guitar over his shoulder and then Olve says one two three and then they start and it doesn't sound so bad and then they play through the other two songs they've more or less learned how to play, and those don't sound so bad either, and Olve says that a little beer sure helped and then Terje starts pounding away like wild on the drums and cymbals and Geir thumps like wild on the bass and Asle thinks no, this isn't right, he doesn't want to play guitar anymore, it's the wrong thing, the noise won't get rid of the pictures he has in his head, it only makes them worse, he thinks, so he wants to stop, he can't do it anymore, he should paint now, he should be where it's quiet now, in the silence, where he'll paint away the pictures he has lodged in his head and he'll neither make noise playing the guitar nor paint from photographs of houses and barns, people's homes, he'll paint his own pictures, Asle thinks and then he takes his guitar off and puts it down leaning it against the amp and he turns off the amp and then he gets down off the stage in the Youth Centre in Barmen, and it was he who'd gone to the guy in charge of the Barmen Youth Group and asked if they could practise in the Youth Centre, and they'd been given permission to, Asle thinks and then he stops in the middle of the room and stands there and looks at the other three still standing on stage and behind them someone has painted a set, a scene of a farming village with a high cliff and a blue fjord and blossoming birch trees, it's still there from a play that was put on in the Youth Centre in Barmen sometime or another, a long time ago, Asle thinks, and then he hears Olve yell into the microphone and ask where he's going? and Asle just stands there in the middle of the room and looks at the stage set

Are you leaving? Terje says

and Asle doesn't answer

What are you doing? Geir says

and Asle doesn't answer

Answer goddammit, Olve yells

and he yells it into the microphone so that it booms through-out the whole auditorium and Asle turns around and starts walking towards the door to the hall and Terje shouts after him and says he can't leave, they've just started practice, where's he going? what's wrong with him? Terje calls and then Asle turns around and he sees Terje walking up to him and Asle stops and he stands there waiting for Terje

You're not leaving, are you? Terje says

I am, Asle says

and then Geir takes his bass off and he too comes down off the stage and over to Asle

You're just leaving, Geir says

Yes, I can't play, Asle says

I'm not going to play guitar anymore, he says

and Olve yells into the mike you can't fucking quit, I won't fucking let you, he yells

You're at least as good as the rest of us, Geir says

No I'm not, Asle says

We need you, Terje says

We need two guitars, he says

and then Olve yells into the mike that it's just fucking wrong to act like that, now that they've started a band, found band-mates, and they talked during every single breaktime at school about how they should start a band as soon as they got instruments and the other equipment they needed and found a place to practise, and now they have everything all set up and Asle is going to bail just like that, and it's extra shitty since he was the one who started talking about starting a band in the first place, yes, extra shitty, Olve yells into the microphone and it booms and echoes through the auditorium and then Olve bangs the pick as hard as he can across the open strings of his guitar and screams no fuck no into the mike so that it booms and resounds through the auditorium, yes, it echoes through the whole Barmen Youth Centre, and then Olve takes his guitar off and then he gets down off the stage and comes walking over and he stops right in front of Asle

You can't fucking do this, he says

You got us to start this band and now you're just leaving? he says

and he grabs Asle's shoulder and shakes it hard

It was you who wanted us to start a band, he says

and he holds Asle's shoulder tight as Asle just stands there and doesn't know what to say, he just knows that he doesn't want to play guitar anymore, he thinks

We can't play without a rhythm guitarist, Olve says

and Asle doesn't say anything

Say something for fuck's sake, Olve says

and Asle still doesn't say anything

You're not serious? Geir says

You'll ruin the whole band, he says

and Asle says that he doesn't want to play guitar anymore and again Olve shakes him back and forth

You can't just ruin the whole band like that, Geir says

and then they stand there, all four of them, and they don't say anything and then Terje asks what he's going to do instead of playing guitar and Asle says he's going to start painting pictures again, because that's something he can do, he says

Yeah just fucking go home and paint more of those goddamn barns, Terje says

Just keep on doing your paintings, he says

Pictures of goddamn houses, pictures of goddamn barns, he says

Or maybe you're going to go suck The Bald Man's dick? Olve says

and then it's suddenly quiet for a moment and then Geir says Asle can't just leave, they've been talking about starting a band for so long, every single breaktime for a long time they'd talk about it, and it was Asle who came up with the idea, and then the others went along with it, and now they'd gotten all the equipment, everything they needed, and gotten permission to practise in the Barmen Youth Centre, yes, everything had worked out and now he was just going to leave? Terje says

And it was me who did almost everything else, Olve says

Sound system, mikes, microphone stands, yeah, who was the one who got all of that together? he says, it was him wasn't it, Olve, and that was because it was all sitting up in the attic at home since his father had played in a band once upon a time, he'd been a guitarist and singer in a band before he got married and since then his father always said that girls had broken up a lot of bands, and he'd thought about that a lot, Olve says, but for a band, a whole band, to be destroyed just because one person didn't feel like being in it anymore and just left, no, no way, he says

So get back up here on this stage, he says

and Asle just stands there and again Olve shakes him by the shoulder

Someone else can borrow my guitar and equipment for now and then pay for it whenever he has the money, Asle says

and Olve shakes Asle's shoulders and then he lets go of the shoulder in his right hand and he raises that hand and he stands there with his fist in Asle's face

You hear what I'm saying, now are you going to do it or not? Olve says

You hear me, huh? he says

Do you get what I'm saying? Olve says

and Asle just stands there and then Geir says can't he just come back up onto the stage? and they can practise a little more? it's going so well with their three songs, he says

You can't just leave, you can't just quit, Geir says

I quit, Asle says

You quit? Geir says

Yes, Asle says

and it's silent for a moment

I can't play, he says

and no one says anything

And I'll never be able to play, he says

The only one here who can sort of play is you, Olve, Asle says

Shut up, Olve says

and his fist is still in Asle's face

And Asle, you lent me the money for the drums, Terje says

The whole band is thanks to you, he says

It's because you didn't have anything yourself, Olve says

And your parents didn't want to help you out either, he says

They couldn't, Terje says

Because your father doesn't have a job, Olve says

The bum, he says

He's barely worked a day in his whole life, Olve says

Apart from getting women knocked up, he says

Other men's wives, he says

Fuck that fucker, he says

All right, shut up now, Terje says

and then they all just stand there and Asle says that there are lots of bands with just three people, drum and bass and guitar and Geir says that those bands are good too but the best bands have two guitarists, a lead guitarist and a rhythm guitarist, he says

Someone plays rhythm and someone else plays lead, he says

And sometimes they both play rhythm, Terje says

And I'm the lead guitarist in this band because I'm the only one who can play a solo, or can learn how to play a solo, Olve says

and he says that he's the singer because he's the only one who can learn songs, both the words and the tune, so without him there'd be no band at all, Olve says and then no one says anything

I'm trying my best to play the drums, Terje says

Yes, yes, Olve says

and he just stands and holds his fist pointing right at Asle's face

Me too on the bass, Geir says

Yes, yes, Olve says

and he says that we haven't been at it very long, we've barely started, he says

I don't want to anymore, Asle says

and Olve's hand making the fist comes closer to Asle's face and then Terje grabs Olve's arm and pulls it back and Olve yells what the fuck are you doing and he jumps at Terje to shove him away and then beats at Terje with his fists but Terje is much bigger and stronger and he grips Olve's hand and then Terje hits Olve hard in the face and knocks Olve down and it's quiet and Asle sees blood coming out of Olve's mouth and Olve wipes his mouth off and then raises a hand and feels around his mouth and he says you fucker you've fucking knocked two of my teeth out, he says and Olve gets up and he opens his bloody mouth wide and both of his top front teeth in the middle are half-gone and then Olve puts a hand inside his mouth and takes out the two bits of broken teeth and Terje says he didn't mean to, he's really sorry, he shouldn't have done that, he was just so mad because Olve was talking shit about his father, Terje says and I look at the white road, and now it's probably as light out as it ever gets this time of year, and I drive slowly and carefully on the narrow winding road to Instefjord and I look at the white road and I see Asle standing in the auditorium of the Barmen Youth Centre and on stage there's Olve and Terje and Geir and also Amund, who bought Asle's guitar and joined the band, Asle thinks, and this is the first time they're playing at a dance, he thinks, and Olve has gotten new front teeth and Amund bought the guitar and the mike and amp from Asle and started playing rhythm guitar instead of him, and with a little of the money he got from Amund he bought himself a brown leather shoulder bag to keep his sketchpad and pencil in, Asle thinks as he stands there and Sigve is standing next to him and Asle thinks that Sigve is the only person he knows of who lives in a boathouse, he is a few years older than Asle and he lives with his parents upstairs in a boathouse, a little ways before The Co-op Store, and then Sigve asks if maybe they should go outside and have some beer, he's put his bag behind a rock outside a little ways off from the Youth Centre and it's full of beer, he says and Asle says a little beer would be good and Sigve and Asle go outside and Asle rolls a cigarette and lights it and he and Sigve go over to the rocks where there's a black bag of beer bottles and Sigve opens a bottle and passes it to Asle and he takes it and drinks some and then Sigve opens another bottle for himself and then he raises the bottle and he says cheers and Sigve and Asle drink and Asle notices that Sigve has already drunk a lot and then he says that Asle needs to be careful with alcohol, that's something he needed to learn himself, yes, Asle's probably heard that he's spent some time in prison, yes, The Prison in Bjørgvin, by The Fishmarket, Sigve says and Asle doesn't respond and he thinks that the night he went home after the last time he played with the band it was darkest autumn, and he'd run into Sigve on the road and Sigve was carrying a black bag in one hand and had a bottle in the other and it was the same bag he has with him tonight, Asle thinks and Sigve was on the cups of being drunk and he'd said you have to go see your parents sometime and then he'd handed Asle a bottle and Asle had taken a little sip from it and it had burned in his mouth and then Sigve had slapped himself on the cheek and said again that you have to go see your parents sometime and then Asle gave him back the bottle and then Sigve walked on carrying the black bag and the bottle, Asle thinks and now he and Sigve are sitting and drinking beer by a rock above the Youth Centre and Sigve says that Asle probably remembers the night when he was going home after being in prison, he took the bus home from Bjørgvin, because he was in The Prison by The Fishmarket, and that night he got out the bus a long way before he needed to, and then he'd walked so slowly that Asle had caught up to him, and everything he owned was in that bag, Sigve says and he points at the black bag, and to tell you the truth it was three half-bottles of spirits and a chessboard with pieces, because he'd learned to play chess in prison and the first thing he did when he got out was buy a bag, yes, the one he had the beer in now, and then three half-bottles of spirits and then a chessboard with pieces, Sigve says and he says that he was so dreading going back home to his parents but he didn't have anywhere else to go, he says and then Asle and Sigve sit there by the rock a bit above The Youth Centre and Asle smokes and takes a sip of beer and he notices how much he likes beer and cigarettes together

You've probably heard? Sigve says

Heard what? Asle says

Who my real father is? Sigve says

and Asle says he heard it was a German soldier, he says

There's nothing more shameful, Sigve says

and he says that it brought shame on both his mother and him, and he didn't understand his stepfather who married his mother, it was probably because no one else wanted to marry him, the stepfather, Sigve says and then he says that he, the step-father, was always nice to both him and his mother, it's not that, but why did they have to live like that, there was no one except him and his parents who lived in a boathouse, in a loft in a boat-house, and there was a steep flight of steps, practically a ladder, leading up to the loft, and there they had a room with a kind of kitchen, and two small bedrooms, that was it, Sigve says, and he understood perfectly well that neither his teachers nor anyone else had liked him, the German kid, he says and he drinks his beer and then he says that Asle doesn't like him either, but that doesn't matter, he's good to drink with anyway, and that was why he'd ended up in prison, because of his drinking, but now he had no money again, like so often, and so he couldn't drink either, he says, but he'd made a few kroner during the fruit har-vest and that's how he could buy a few bottles of beer, he says, and now The Labour Office had found him work at The Fur-niture Factory in Aga, he was due to start in a week, and they'd also found him a little old house right in the centre of Aga where he could live, and the rent was low, Sigve says and Asle looks at the three blue dots Sigve has tattooed between the thumb and index finger of his right hand and he has a heart, a cross, and an anchor tattooed in the same place on his left hand and Sigve says that Asle despises him as much as everyone else does and Asle says he doesn't despise him, how can anyone choose who their father is? and as for living in a boathouse, in a loft in a boathouse, what's wrong with that? Asle says and Sigve says that there's no one else in the village who lives in such a hovel and then Asle says cheers and raises his bottle and Sigve raises his bottle and they drink and I look at the white road and I think it'll be good to drop off my paintings for the next show, because almost every

time it feels in a way like I can start painting again only after
I've delivered my pictures, I think and now I've reached Øygna
and up on the hill I can see the house where Åsleik's sister lives,
Sister, as he calls her, whose name is actually Guro, and where
Åsleik always celebrates Christmas, it's a little grey house, and
you can see all the way from the road that the paint is flaking
off, and it looks like the house is on the verge of collapsing, and
then there's a barn next to the house, it's about to fall down too,
a lot of tiles have already fallen off the roof, I see, but inside
that house, that dilapidated grey house, is a whole collection of
pictures I've painted, of small pictures, yes, almost all of the best
small pictures I've ever painted, I think, and I think now I've
never even met this Sister Åsleik talks so much about and whose
name is Guro and who, every single year since the man she used
to live with left her, The Fiddler, Åsleik invites me to go visit
with him for Christmas, I think, and every year I've said no, but
maybe this year I will go with Åsleik to spend Christmas at Sister's house? I think, and I told Åsleik I would, or maybe would,
and why shouldn't I, really? I think, or maybe not, because ever
since Ales died and went away I don't really want to do anything
for Christmas and maybe it's because I like driving to Bjørgvin
on Christmas Eve to go to Christmas Mass at St Paul's Church
and I couldn't do that if I was in The Boat with Åsleik sailing to
see Sister, this Guro, no I don't know, but maybe this year I'll go
with him anyway, spend Christmas at Sister's? that way at least
I'd be able to see all the pictures again that Åsleik has bought and
given to Sister as Christmas presents, and since they're some of
the best small pictures I've ever painted it would be nice to see
them again, I think, so I can just think about that, because Åsleik
keeps asking and asking me to go with him and maybe I should
go and I think Åsleik was really surprised, I think, yes, almost
shocked that I would go with him to spend Christmas with Sister, with Guro, as her name is, and that was what the woman
I ran into the day before yesterday was called too, the woman

sitting in Food and Drink, who I saw later that night, when I was managing to get lost in the snowstorm in Bjørgvin when I was just supposed to go the short way from The Beyer Gallery to The Country Inn, it's hard to believe but whether I believe it or not it's just as bad, I think, and I must not have been entirely myself, I think, not since earlier that evening when I'd found Asle lying covered in snow in The Lane, and I really thought at first that he was dead, but I got him up and then there was everything else that happened at The Alehouse, at The Last Boat, as it's called, and then at The Clinic and everything, I think, and so I ended up getting lost in the snowstorm and luckily I ran into the woman who's also named Guro and she brought me to The Country Inn, I think, and she said that I'd been to her apartment many times, yes, that I'd spent the night there sometimes, but that I'd been so drunk that I couldn't remember it, she said and I think that I've driven past the house where Guro, Åsleik's sister, lives and I'd never noticed before how much the paint was flaking off that grey house of hers, I think and then I think about my sister Alida, who died so suddenly, no, I can't think about that, not now, it's still, even now, still, still, I think and I'm at Instefjord and I turn onto the bigger country road that runs north and runs south down to Bjørgvin, and the road is well cleared and there are lots of tracks of cars that have driven on it after it snowed and I drive south and I look at the white road and I see Asle standing outside his house looking at Father who is standing there looking at a brand new car, it's grey, and it looks like Father can barely bring himself to touch the car and Mother is standing there and she says no it's unbelievable, now they have a car too, and it's about time, everyone their age she knows has a car already, she says and both Mother and Father stand there like they're almost too scared to touch the car, much less get in it, much less drive it, and The Car Salesman, a guy from Stranda, is standing there, it was he who drove the car up to the farm and a friend is now waiting for him in another car to drive him back to Stranda and The Car Salesman holds out his hand to Father and says pleasure doing business with you and Father says thanks you too and then Father and The Car Salesman just stay standing there in silence and then The Car Salesman says, because someone has to say something, that well Father's a car owner now and Father says well it's the bank who owns it, not him, and The Car Salesman says there aren't many people these days who have enough cash to buy a brand new car outright without taking out a loan, he says, and Father says he's probably right and then The Car Salesman says that they should get into the car and he'll explain the car to Father, he says, and he wouldn't believe how many people wanted to buy a new car these days, so many, he says, yes, he can't get enough cars to sell them, he says, so Father too had to wait a little while before it was his turn, The Car Salesman says and Father nods and Mother says it certainly took a while and The Car Salesman says that people are so impatient nowadays, they can't wait to get their own car so they can drive for themselves, drive around wherever they want, he says, every day he gets calls from people waiting to get their new car, isn't it ready yet? soon? they ask, The Car Salesman says and Mother says anyway they got their car eventually, she says

This is a great day for us, she says

Yes, it truly is, The Car Salesman says

and then he tells Father that he should get into the car, in the front seat, and he'll show him how the car works, he says and Father goes hesitantly over to the car door and opens it and then Asle sees him get in and sit stiffly upright in the driver's seat and he grips the steering wheel and twists and turns in the seat and Mother says that it won't be many years now until he too can get a driver's licence and she says well it'll be a couple of years anyway and Asle says that he doesn't want a car and Mother says she knew he'd say that and then The Car Salesman sits down in the other front seat

Just think, you'll be fifteen so soon, she says

Yes, yes, Asle says

and then she says that anything she says is wrong, that he always blurts out an answer as soon as she opens her mouth, she says and Asle doesn't answer and then he hears the car start and he sees Father sitting behind the wheel doing this and that and The Car Salesman is gesturing and a nice sound is coming from the engine and then the car jerks suddenly forward, yes, almost makes a hop, and both Mother and Asle are startled and then luckily the car stops and Father is sitting looking straight ahead and he looks totally scared out of his wits, Asle sees

No, what was that all about? Mother says

I don't know, Asle says

and then the engine starts again and The Car Salesman says something and his arms and hands aren't moving and then the car just barely starts moving slowly across the gravel in front of the house, and then it stops, and then it sits there and the engine is running smoothly and then The Car Salesman waves an arm and then Father looks back and the car starts barely moving backwards and then it stops again and then the indicators come on and turn off and the headlights come on and turn off, and then Father drives slowly forwards again and he turns off towards The Barn and then the car reverses again, slowly, and then it stops for a good little while before Father turns the wheel and the car creeps forward and then the car stops and Father turns the engine off and then The Car Salesman opens the door and gets out and he tells Mother that wasn't so bad now and Father gets out and he looks pale and Asle sees that his hands are shaking and The Car Salesman says again that wasn't bad at all no, and then he says that practice makes perfect and that Father just has to take it easy and drive slowly and carefully especially the first time and that he has to get going now, on to the next buyer, because he's supposed to deliver no less than two more cars today, The Car Salesman says and then he shakes Mother's hand and says congratulations and then he shakes Father's hand and says good luck and both Mother and Father say thank you thank you and then The Car Salesman

goes over to the man sitting in the other car waiting for him
and then Mother and Father stand there and look at the car and
neither of them says a word, it's as if they don't dare say a word
and Father seems nervous and then Mother says that this summer
they'll be driving their own car and they'll go visit her parents
and brothers and sisters on Hisøy, and then, while they're there,
they can drive to Haugaland to go shopping, she says and Asle
sees Father stand there writhing not really knowing what to say

Isn't it beautiful? Mother says

Yeah, Father says

and he nods and he sort of can't stop nodding, he nods and
nods, and then he stops his nodding

Well it was sure expensive enough, Father says

Let's not talk about that now, Mother says

and then they stand there and neither one says anything

Should we go on our first drive? Mother says

Guess we have to, Father says

Yes, we really do have to, Mother says

and she asks if Asle wants to come along and he shakes his
head and says that the two of them can go for a drive on their
own and then Father goes and gets behind the wheel and Mother
goes around the other side and gets in and then Father starts the
car and then they just sit there and then the car gives a sudden jolt
forwards and then stops and Mother looks at Asle and she shakes
her head and Father looks utterly desperate and then he starts
the car again and it doesn't move and then it slowly slowly starts
to move forwards and then Father turns the wheel and Asle sees
the car slowly disappear around the corner of The Old House
and Asle walks after the car and he sees Grandma standing in
the window and Asle sees the car drive slowly slowly down the
driveway and Grandma opens the window and she shakes her
head

Foolishness, she says

Spending all that good money to buy a car, she says

and Asle says he doesn't understand it either and he sees the car barely creeping down the driveway and he runs after the car and then walks behind the car and it pulls out onto the country road and drives slowly slowly down the road and then Father drives a little faster and Asle starts to jog slowly behind the car and then he runs past the car and he turns around and he waves at Father sitting and staring stiffly straight ahead and he waves at Mother and she waves back with a stiff smile and Asle runs some more and then he stops and the car gets closer to him again and then he starts walking next to the car and Mother is tensely looking straight ahead and then a couple of boys come biking up behind them and they swerve aside and bike past the car without stopping and Asle feels embarrassed and looks away and he turns around and walks home and he turns back and he sees the car creeping slowly, slowly down the road along The Shore and it's embarrassing, never in his life has Asle seen anyone drive a car that slowly, he thinks and I drive south on the country road that runs north and south down to Bjørgvin, and it's much easier driving now because the roads are cleared, and besides it's almost as light out now as it ever gets this time of year, and I'm driving slowly south and soon I'll be at The Playground where I saw a young man with medium-length brown hair and a young woman with long black hair playing the day before yesterday, I think, and when I drive past The Playground I won't look down at it, I think and I won't stop at the turn-off either, by the path down to The Playground, I think and I drive past The Playground and I drive past the turn-off, and I don't want to stop, because I don't feel tired, I think and I get to the old brown house where Ales and I used to live once, and the paint is flaking off that house too and I look at the house and I see a young man with medium-length brown hair standing and looking out the window of the brown house and he thinks that despite everything they were lucky to find this house to rent, even if it's old and run-down, the old kitchen is good enough, and everything they needed was already there when they moved in, an old stove and a fridge that was almost as old, and all the frying pans and table linens and knives and forks they needed, yes, everything you need in a kitchen, and there was furniture in the main room and a double bed in the bedroom, yes, it was like moving into a fully furnished house, and in fact that's what it was, because the man they'd rented it from had taken only his mother's most personal belongings with him, his mother had lived in that house until she died, and she died in her bed, in the double bed where he and Ales were now sleeping, Asle thinks, so all of the furniture was already there in the house, and a good thing too because he and Ales had practically nothing, just a couple of pans and some mugs, and some sheets and blankets, that was it, so it was great for them that the house they were moving into was like a newly furnished home, it was as if the woman who'd lived there had stepped out and not come back, and then her son, the one who'd rented them the house, came by and took her clothes and gave them to The Second-Hand Store in Sailor's Cove, and threw out her toiletries and everything like that, and then he took two or three things he wanted for himself, and then he rented out the house, and Ales's mother Judit knew him, they worked together at The Hospital, and so Ales heard through her mother Judit that the house was for rent and she'd mentioned that they should rent it and so they did, because they wanted to get out of Bjørgvin and have a little more space than they had in the flat they were renting there on The Hillside in Bjørgvin, and so they rented the house and moved in, but of course they didn't want to keep the house exactly the way the woman who used to live there had had it, living there her whole life with her husband and child, and then later alone, so they'd packed up a lot of the stuff there and put it down in the cellar or in a room up in the attic, and there were bracket lamps everywhere when they moved in and they unscrewed every last one, that was the first thing they did, and then they got rid of a couple of armchairs and then they moved all their painting supplies into the main room and they put up a bookshelf that Asle had made himself, yes, they'd really been lucky, Asle thinks standing there at the window, being able to rent this old house, and the brown paint on the outside of the house was still in good shape, actually, he thinks, and when he and Ales first lived together, he thinks, they'd lived in a two-room basement flat, but they wanted to live in a house, and they wanted to live outside of Bjørgvin, and then they got this house and now they've lived here for a while and things are good, before they left Bjørgvin they bought a car and before that he got a driver's licence, something he never thought he'd do, he didn't want a driver's licence but he realized that if they were going to live on their own so far from other people they needed a car and so one of them needed to get a driver's licence and since Ales didn't want to any more than he did, well, he was the one who did it, and then they bought an old used car, mother Judit simply gave them the money to buy the car as a wedding present, because she still worked at The Hospital and made money, she was from Austria, and Ales's father was from Dylgja, and his unmarried sister, old Alise, still lived there, in their childhood home, hers and Ales's father's, she lived in a pretty white house with two main rooms and an adjoining bedroom, and with two rooms and two crawlspaces up in the attic, Asle thinks, yes, mother Judit was from Austria but it was hard to tell that she wasn't Norwegian, she had learned to speak Norwegian so well, to the point where it was hard to say where in the country she came from, there was something universal about the way she spoke Norwegian, yes, it was actually kind of strange, her language, Asle thinks, but he met Ales and they moved in together and they got married, it was like it was already settled that they'd do that, it kind of happened by itself, they were together ever since the first time they met and they got married in St Paul's Church and only they and the best man and maid of honour were there, mother Judit and Beyer, and then, before they got married, Ales got Asle to convert to The Catholic Church, he'd been confirmed, with two witnesses there, not that long before the wedding, and one of the witnesses was Catholic, Ales's mother Judit, and the other witness was Beyer, and it was also in St Paul's Church that he'd been confirmed, only the priest was there plus the two witnesses, and Ales too of course, because her mother Judit was Catholic, and that was why Ales had been baptized Catholic and went to her first communion and was confirmed in St Paul's Church, whereas he had been baptized in The National Church and confirmed there in a Protestant way, and the baptism was valid but the confirmation wasn't, which was why Asle didn't have to be baptized, and the Catholic confirmation felt good, and he can still feel the priest drawing a cross on his forehead with the consecrated oil, and afterwards he and Ales got married, also in St Paul's Church, and then they lived for a while in the little apartment on The Hillside and then they moved into this old house, Asle thinks, standing there looking out the window and he thinks he just saw someone drive by on the road, and he's seen that vehicle several times already, a large car like a small van, he thinks, so whoever owns it must live in somewhere north of here, he thinks, but now, yes, now there were rumours that the man who'd rented them the house needed it back, Asle thinks, probably one of the man's children needed a place to live, and so, yes, he didn't come right out and say it but he was talking as if they couldn't keep renting the house where they lived for much longer, he said they should move out as soon as they could, that was what he'd said without saying it outright, Asle thinks, and Ales had thought they could move in with her aunt in Dylgja, old Alise, she lived there alone and could certainly use a little help around the house, but Asle didn't want to do that, yes well Dylgja was fine and the house, yes, he couldn't imagine a nicer house to live in, but he didn't want to live with anyone else in the house, he wanted to live there with just Ales, and Ales had said she was sure they could live upstairs in the old house in Dylgja, and just keep their food

downstairs, and then they could go shopping for her aunt and help
her, she was old now, old Alise, and she could use some help with
the shopping, with keeping the house clean, with everything really, Ales had said, and maybe they should move there, because Ales
had already spoken to her old aunt Alise about it and Alise had felt
it was a good solution, yes, if Ales and Asle wanted to she would be
glad and grateful to have them move into her house, she'd said, but
Asle hadn't wanted to, he couldn't stand living so close to other
people, anyone, the only person he could stand having nearby was
Ales, he'd said, Asle thinks, and Ales had said she understood and
then they'd just acted like nothing was happening and stayed living in the house they were renting, Asle thinks, standing there in
the window looking out and then he hears Ales coming and he
turns around to face her and he holds out his hand and she takes his
hand and then they give each other a hug and Asle says that he's
seen a little delivery van drive by several times and Ales says the
owner is probably someone who lives nearby and I look at the
white road and I'm driving south and now I'm getting close to
Bjørgvin, and what a relief it'll be to drop off these pictures, I
think and I look at the white road and I see Asle standing outside
the house in Barmen in his black velvet jacket and with the brown
leather shoulder bag hanging over his shoulder and he takes out a
packet of tobacco and rolls a cigarette that he puts between his lips,
and then he takes out a matchbox and takes a match out, he lights
it, and Asle thinks that the day Father got his new car The Bald
Man was standing down at the bus stop waiting for the bus to
Bjørgvin, and that was the last time he ever saw The Bald Man, he
thinks, because The Bald Man never came back from Bjørgvin
alive, he came home in a coffin, Asle thinks and then he stands
there and sees that the boot of the car is open and there's a hot plate
in the boot, a hot plate for a studio apartment, with one burner,
and a box of clothes, underwear, socks, a warm pullover, shirts,
trousers, shoes, and a box with kitchen utensils, a bread knife and
plates and knives and forks and spoons, and he's put all his painting

supplies in the boot, and they're in a single box, and everything he owns is here, and some canvas and wood for stretchers, Asle thinks and he stands there and takes a good long pull of his cigarette and he thinks that now he's been smoking for more than a year already, almost, and he sees Mother come up with a duvet and a pillow and a burlap sack

Here's your duvet and pillow, she says

and Mother puts the rolled-up duvet and the pillow into the bag and puts the bag into the boot of the car and she says that, as he saw, the duvet cover and pillowcase were on the duvet and pillow, Mother says

Thank you, Asle says

Yes so we've probably got just about everything, Father says

Not the raincoat and boots, Mother says

and then she goes back inside and she comes out with a raincoat and boots and she puts them in the boot

So that's about it now? Father says

And something to eat for the road, we need that, Mother says

And a little food for the new place too, she says

and Mother goes back inside and Father says it wouldn't hurt if Asle brought a little food with him, but now that he was going to start at The Academic High School in Aga and live by himself he was going to have to learn how to go shopping for himself, and the old studio stove with the one burner he had had the year he went to Agriculture School and lived in a rented room was already in the boot of the car, Father said, and the pots and pans are packed, so now Asle can try to cook for himself now and then, Father says, because it can get expensive to buy dinner every day, even if there is a café in Aga and a cafeteria at The Academic High School, and even if it doesn't exactly cost an arm and a leg to buy dinner either at the café or the cafeteria, he says

And every month I'll send you the money you need, he says

And plus you'll get a little stipend since you have to live in an apartment and can't live at home, he says

Yes, Asle says

You won't have much to spare but it'll definitely be enough to live on, he says

and Father says well he also has the kroner he made selling paintings over the summer, yes, it was a good idea to have an exhibition in the Barmen Youth Centre, because sure enough he sold all the pictures, he says and he says that the agreement is that Asle will pay rent for the room once a month, the first day of the month, unless it's a holiday and he's home of course, he says

Okay, Asle says

and then they stay standing there in front of the house and they don't say anything

You were lucky to get a room for such a good price, Father says

In its own building, too, he says

Yes, Asle says

We just needed to put an ad in *The Hardanger Times* and it all worked out, Father says

and he says that the woman who called them said she was a widow and that her husband had been a shoe- maker and The Shoemaker's Workshop belonging to the deceased husband was next to the house where she lived and there was a room in the attic there with a bed and a table and a little pantry too with a window, where you could prepare your food if you wanted to, and downstairs, on the ground floor, well that's where there was a toilet and shower, it was laid out like that because her husband had always had an apprentice who lived in the attic in The Shoe- maker's Workshop, yes, that's why there was a toilet and shower on the ground floor, she'd said, Father says

It sounds great, Asle says

Let's take a look, Father says

Okay, Asle says

and he rolls another cigarette and lights it and then they stand there silently in front of the house and Father says it's a strange day, because Asle, their only son, yes, their only living child, is leaving home, moving out and moving away and going to live by himself, yes, it's a memorable day, Asle is leaving his childhood home while he's still so young, so that's the end of his adolescence, the end of childhood, but that's how it is out in the country, if you want to go to school you need to move away, Father says and Asle doesn't say anything and he thinks finally, finally, he's leaving home, he can't wait, he's going to live by himself, alone, and not have to listen to Mother constantly nagging about him needing a haircut, about how it's just not acceptable to go around looking like he does, about how he needs to paint proper paintings, like he did before, when he was younger, not these messes that don't look like anything, and nagging him about how he needs to be like other people his age, he's really no better and no worse than anybody else, he's just pretends like he's so different, she's said that and again she says that he needs to cut his hair, a boy just can't go around with such long hair, she's said and she nags him like that day in and day out, Asle thinks and then Father says again that this is a big day

You're leaving home today, Father says

and Asle doesn't say anything

You're only sixteen and you're moving out to live by yourself, he says

and Father says that he never did that himself, never moved away to go to school, and he regrets that, yes, except for the year at Agriculture School he's lived his whole life on this farm, he stayed here and tried as best he could to grow fruit and build boats, traditional Barmen pointed boats, yes, the way he'd learned to from his father, Asle's Grandfather, and now it must be something like ten years since he died, Father says, yes, it's a fine kind of boat, traditional Barmen boats, and he likes being a boatbuilder, it's not that, he says, but Asle had never seemed interested in building boats and he'd never wanted to put pressure on him to learn, he says and they stay standing there silently for a moment, and so, Father says, he kept on, growing and cultivating fruit, yes, he spent all his time building boats or growing fruit, he says

I should have gone to school too, Father says

So I'm glad you have the chance to do it, he says

and he says that after Asle goes to the high school, and gets good enough marks, he'll be able to do whatever he wants

You can become a doctor, or a minister, Father says

and he laughs

A minister, are you kidding, Asle says

You be a minister, he says

Well then a doctor, Father says

A doctor, me? Asle says

Yes, well, a doctor, a teacher, Father says

I don't even like school, Asle says

and then Father says that The Academic High School is totally different from the schools Asle's been to up until now so maybe he'll be happy at The Academic High School at least sometimes, he says

Maybe, Asle says

Yes who knows, Father says

But you need to go to class in any case, do as well as you can, he says

Yes, Asle says

Because you're a clever one, you're smart, he says

You must realize I know that, he says

and Father says that both he and Mother knew that his bad marks in school weren't because he lacked the ability, he says and he says that as long as Asle listens to his teachers and does his homework he'll graduate from The Academic High School just fine, he's sure of it, he says and Asle sees Mother come out with two shopping bags and she says it's the food she wants to give him to bring along and she puts the shopping bags in the boot

The boot's almost full now, Father says

Yeah, Asle says

Get in the back, Father says

and he points at the back seat and Asle suddenly remembers that he's packed all his other painting supplies but forgot the easel

I need to get the easel, he says

But we don't have any room for it, Father says

Well I need it, Asle says

and he says it can be folded up and he can hold it in his lap

And I need to bring my finished paintings too, he says

and he suddenly thinks he can put them in the old suitcase at his grandparents', up in the attic of The Old House, and Asle tells Father that and then Father unlocks the door to The Old House and Asle runs up the stairs to the attic and gets the suitcase sitting on a box there and then he thinks that he wants to bring the grey blanket Grandmother had covered herself with when she was sick, the grey blanket that she gave him and said he should have on the day they came to get her and drive her to The Hospice, and he goes into the main room and the blanket is sitting there nicely folded on the bench and he opens the suitcase and puts the blanket in and then he hurries outside and into the room that was his in The New House and he opens the suitcase and puts all the finished paintings in the suitcase and he tries to put layers of the blanket between the different paintings, and then he goes outside and puts the suitcase on top of everything else in the boot of the car

Well now it's full, that's for sure, Father says

and he pushes the lid of the boot closed and then Mother gets into the car, in the front seat

I can't forget my easel, Asle says

and he hurries into the room he used to have and he goes back out and while he's folding up the easel Father locks the front doors, both The New House's and The Old House's, and then Asle gets into the car, in the back seat, with the easel on his lap, and there's plenty of room for the easel if he holds it crossways on his lap and then he puts his shoulder bag on the seat next to him and then Father starts the car and it doesn't start right away but then it does with a little jolt forwards

Oof, Father says

What's wrong with you now, he says

and then the car stays still for a second before Father starts driving slowly forwards and turns the corner of The Old House, where Grandmother and Grandfather lived, and it's been many years since Grandfather died, Asle thinks and he thinks that he woke up and saw Grandmother lying in Sister's bed, since Asle and Sister shared a room, and Grandmother looks at Asle with tears in her eyes and he sees tears running down her cheeks and she says Grandfather's dead

Grandfather died last night, Grandmother says

and Father drives slowly down the driveway and Asle sees Grandmother lying there on the bench in her main room, there in The Old House, with the grey blanket spread out over her, and she can hardly move, her arms are all she can use the same as before, and she can talk a little, but not like before, and Asle sits there next to her a lot and talks to her a little and maybe she asks him to get her something or help her move a little or something like that and he does it and then one day an ambulance comes and when the men pick up the stretcher with Grandmother on it she hands Asle the grey blanket and he's a little surprised and then he says thank you and Grandmother tries to say that he should have it, Asle thinks and then they carry Grandmother out the door and into an ambulance and then they drive her to The Hospice, and The Hospice is in Aga too, not too far from The Academic High School, on a hill behind The Hotel, so they'll go visit Grandmother at The Hospice today, that's the first thing they'll do, Father said, Asle thinks, and then they'll drive to the house of the woman who's renting the room out to Asle, he said, he thinks, and Father drives out onto the country road and Asle looks at his home and he thinks it's good to be driving away, it's a deeply good feeling, he thinks

Yes so first we'll look in on my mother? Father says

Yes, Mother says

and it's like there's a kind of bad feeling in her voice

Yes, that's what we'll do, Mother says

And then drive to the apartment, she says

Yes, Father says

You know where it is, right? Mother says

Yes, she explained it all, the woman who's renting it, there are two green houses by the road before you get to the centre of Aga, on the downhill side of the road, just before a little river, and he could just turn in and park between the buildings, is what she said, Father says

Right, Mother says

And then ring the bell at her house, of course, Father says

And if we can't find it we have her phone number and there's a phone booth in the centre of Aga, next to The Co-op Store, he says

Yes, I remember, Mother says

and then they drive on and no one says anything

But first we'll go look in on my mother at The Hospice, Father says again

Right, Mother says gruffly

and they drive on and no one says anything and Asle thinks that he can't wait until they've left and until he has his things in the room he'll be renting and living in now and he can't wait to be alone there, and in the morning he'll start at The Academic High School, tomorrow morning is when he'll start at The Academic High School and from then on he'll be a high-school student, he thinks, but not until eleven o'clock, he thinks, and it's a bit of a walk from where his rented room is to The Academic High School, so he needs to leave in plenty of time, Asle thinks, and he looks at his watch, which Grandmother gave him as a confirmation gift, and Asle should never have gotten confirmed, he thinks, because it's hard to imagine anything more idiotic than all that Christian nonsense, he thinks, but he got confirmed anyway for some mysterious reason and the reason was probably the simple one that everyone else was doing it and had always done it in the village, but he doesn't want to think about that, not now anyway, no, it was just awful but he did get some presents and a little money, Asle thinks and as soon as he turns sixteen he'll officially withdraw from The National Church, he thinks, he's sure of that, because he saw it when he almost bled to death, he saw it then, yes, he saw that no National Church and no Minister knows anything about it, and The Minister just babbled on and on, Asle thinks, because reality, facts, that's something no Minister knows anything about, Asle thinks and it won't be long before he turns sixteen and the day he does he's going to write to The Minister and say straight out that he doesn't want to be a member of The National Church anymore, Asle thinks and he wants to say that out loud but he lets it go, because if he says it Mother will just start in with her nagging again, and then he says it anyway

When I'm sixteen I'm officially leaving The National Church, Asle says

Yes, you've already told us that, Mother says

You've said that lots of times already, she says

The day will come when you need God, you too, she says

I'm sure it will, Asle says

But God and The National Church have nothing to do with each other, he says

Yes, yes, Mother says

What they're doing there is an abuse of God's name, Asle says

and then it's quiet and Father doesn't say anything and Asle sees himself sitting on the swing outside the house and Grandfather is dead and Grandmother is standing in the door to The Old House and she's holding at arm's length a bundle of dead Grandfather's clothes and Asle sits on the swing and looks at her and Grandmother asks him if he could carry Grandfather's clothes down to the cellar and Asle can't say no, no matter how much he doesn't want to do it, no matter how creepy the thought is, he thinks, and then he goes over and takes the clothes and it's a whole armful and he goes down to the cellar and he opens the cellar door and he drops dead Grandfather's clothes right on the floor and he goes back up to the area in front of the house and sits back down on the swing and he sees that there's a grey wool sock right in the middle of the area in front of the house that must have fallen out of the bundle of clothes and he sees Grandmother come out to the door and she points at the sock and she's sobbing and she says can't he take the sock down to the cellar too and Asle goes over to the sock and picks it up between his thumb and one finger and holds it as far away from himself as he can and he carries the sock down into the cellar and drops it on Grandfather's other clothes, Asle thinks, and then he hears Mother say you need to let them pass and Asle turns around and the easel twists a little and he sees a long row of cars behind them

Yes as soon as I can, Father says

Yes, Mother says

There's a long row of cars behind us, she says

Yes I can see that, Father says

sitting there bent forward, his chest almost leaning on the steering wheel, and he's staring straight ahead and he's driving so slowly so slowly, and man how embarrassed Asle's always been about Father's driving, he always drives so, so slowly, he thinks, but now he's not embarrassed about it anymore, now he no longer has to care about it, he's not embarrassed anymore the way he was when he was young, Asle thinks and Father signals and pulls over and the car stops and the first car behind them speeds past with an angry blast of the horn and then a long row of cars drives past them

Yes, yes, Mother says

It's good you finally pulled over and let them pass, she says

and Father doesn't say anything and he just drives on and Asle dozes off and maybe falls asleep and then they're in Aga

So we'll go see my mother first? Father says

Yes, Mother says

and they drive up to The Hospice on the hill above The Hotel and Father parks the car and then they go in through a double glass door and Father goes over to the reception desk and the woman there tells him what room Grandmother is in, and on what floor, and then they go up some stairs and down a corridor and Father stops in front of a door and he knocks on it and there's no answer and then he opens the door and goes in and Asle goes in and he sees Grandmother lying in a bed and her lips have turned a bit blue and she holds out her hand and he goes and takes her hand and then sits down on the edge of the bed and he sits there holding Grandmother's hand and Father asks how she's doing and Grandmother tries to say something and Mother says that she seems happy, here at The Hospice she's probably getting the best care she could get anywhere, Mother says, and she says that she's bought a little fruit for Grandmother and a little choc-olate, she says and she puts a white paper bag on Grandmother's bedside table and Father stands there and Asle sees that he doesn't know what to do or what to say, it's like he doesn't want to be taking up any space at all, Asle thinks, sitting there holding Grandmother's hand and Mother says that Asle is starting at The Academic High School in the morning and that they've rented a room for him, they put an ad in *The Hardanger Times* and got a phone call the day the ad was printed, there was a place for him in the attic of an old shoemaker's workshop, the husband of the woman who called had had a workshop, but he was dead, and whoever the shoemaker's apprentice at the time was used to live there but since he'd died no one had lived there, so the apart-ment had been empty for several years, but now she'd realized that maybe someone going to The Academic High School and who needed a rented room to live in could live there, she'd said, Mother says, and Father accepted right away, she says, so now both Grandmother and Asle will be living in Aga, Mother says and Grandmother nods and Asle feels her gently squeeze his hand

I'll come and visit you every day, Asle says

and he looks at Grandmother

I'll come every day when school gets out, he says

And if you want me to buy you anything I'll do it, he says

and Grandmother shakes her head

But maybe sometimes? he says

Yes well now that you're living in the same town you can go see Grandmother a lot, Father says

Yes, Mother says

and then they say take care

I'll come back tomorrow morning, Asle says

and Grandmother nods at him and Asle lets go of her hand and he sees that Mother and Father are already out in the hall and I look at the white road and I'm driving south and now it won't be long till I get to Bjørgvin, I think, and that's good, because then I'll drop off the paintings and then I'll go see Asle at The Hospital, I think and I look at the white road and I see Asle sitting in the car that's parked between the two green buildings, one big house and next to it is what must be The Shoemaker's Workshop, Asle thinks

I think this must be the place, Father says

and he gets out and stretches and then goes up the steps to the house and he stands there and looks at the nameplate and he knocks and then an old grey-haired woman comes out and she stands and talks to Father and then she goes back inside and then comes out and she's put on a coat and Asle can see that she's carrying a keyring and Mother says they should probably get out of the car and then she opens the car door and gets out and Asle opens his door and gets out and then he just stands there in his black velvet jacket with the brown leather shoulder bag on his shoulder and he's holding the easel in his hands and he doesn't really know what to do with himself and he hears Mother say hello and he looks down

Hello, yes, The Landlady says

Welcome, she says

Here he is, Mother says

Ah that's him, The Landlady says

and Asle stands there and he looks up and he sees The Land-lady walking up to him taking little steps and Asle holds out his hand and she holds out her hand and they shake hands

Hello, Asle says

Hello, The Landlady says

Welcome, she says

and Asle sees Mother standing there squirming and he thinks that she's standing there embarrassed about him, about his long hair, his long brown hair, about him standing there holding an easel, that everything about him embarrasses her, Asle thinks

Yes so here he is, Mother says

and it's like she's saying it into thin air, without any connection to anything, Asle thinks

So, you're starting at The Academic High School, The Land-lady says

Yes, Asle says

and they stand there silently

Are you looking forward to it? she says

Yes, Asle says

But it'll be a real change now, won't it, The Landlady says

Leaving home and living on your own, I mean, she says

Yes, Mother says

It's hard to believe he's already big enough to move out and live on his own, she says

That he's already so grown up, she says

Yes, it used to be that you were considered grown up once you'd gone to the minister and been confirmed, The Landlady says

Yes, Father says

And then you had to just take care of yourself, The Landlady says

and it's like she wants to tell them something, but she stops herself and doesn't and Asle thinks that she was almost certainly going to tell them something about how it was when she was a girl and about having been in service somewhere or another and then The Landlady says that for a few years before she was married she was in service for the minister in Barmen at his house and ever since she got married she's lived in this house, she says

Yes, Father says

I've lived all my adult life in this house here, The Landlady says

and she raises an arm slowly and she points at the green house they're standing next to

And my husband was a shoemaker, yes, she says

Yes, Father says

It was good steady work for many years, she says

Before the shops started selling shoes from foreign factories, she says

After that it was mostly patching and repairs, she says

Yes, that's how it goes, Father says

That's what happened, The Landlady says

and they stand there and no one says anything

There's a bed and everything else you need, a table and chair, both a toilet and a shower, The Landlady says and she points at The Shoemaker's Workshop

Let's go take a look, she says

Yes, Asle says

So, now you'll be living on your own, she says

That's how it is, Father says

And since you're from Barmen you need to rent a room since The Academic High School's in Aga, she says

and Father says that that's how it is, and it's not just people from Barmen, people from Stranda need to rent rooms here, he says and The Landlady nods

Yes there are lots of young people living in rented rooms in Aga, she says and there's silence

Yes, she says

Thank you for answering the ad I put in *The Hardanger Times*, Father says

Well I'm a subscriber, The Landlady says

and she's started walking over to the door of The Shoemaker's Workshop and she's holding a key up to Asle and she says that this key, the biggest one, is for the front door, she says and then she unlocks the door and walks in and she turns on the light

There's the light switch, she says

and she looks back to see if Asle is there and he goes over to The Landlady and she points to the light switch and she says that when he's not at home it'd be nice if he turned out the light, to save a little on the electricity, she says and then she goes down a hall and there are whitewashed walls on both sides, and she points to a door

Here's the shower and the toilet, she says

Yes and let's keep looking, she says

and she points to a door farther down the hall

In there's the actual workshop, the shoemaker's workshop, where my husband made shoes, she says

And later just repaired shoes, she says

But through all those years he had a boy as an apprentice, she says

It was like he felt it was his duty, she says

and she looks at Mother and Father and she says he, the apprentice boy, always had lodgings up in the attic, and that's where Asle will have his rented room now, The Landlady says and she starts slowly climbing the stairs with Asle right behind her and when she gets to the top she unlocks a door and she goes in and she turns on the light and Asle goes in after her

Yes so here's your new home, The Landlady says

The room looks great, Asle says

It's nothing special, but it's a place to live anyway, she says and Asle sees a bed and next to the bed there's a nightstand and there's a lamp mounted on the wall over the head of the bed

Yes you'll have light to read by too, as you can see, The Landlady says

And there's a table and chair in front of the window, she says

So you can do your reading there, she says

Yes, Asle says

Asle, that was your name, right? she says

Yes, my name's Asle, he says

and Asle sees that next to the table, in that corner, is a wardrobe and The Landlady says that he can keep his clothes in that wardrobe, or anything else, whatever he needs to keep there, she says and then she goes over to a door next to the hall door and she opens it and it's a little room with a bench and she says now this here's a little room but you can use it as a little kitchen, and Asle sees that there's a small window in the room and he says he's brought with him a studio stove with one burner

Yes, when you cook you can let the smoke go out through that window, The Landlady says

and she says now it's nothing special, no, it's old and run-down and it hasn't been used in all these years, but lots of people have lived in this apartment before and no one ever complained, she says

Yes, Asle says

It all looks great, he says

So that's it, The Landlady says

and she stands there

You'll have to come over to the house and have a cup of coffee with me sometime, she says

and Asle says thank you thank you and then he puts the easel down on the floor, in front of the window, and then The Landlady takes out a pad of notepaper as though out of nowhere and Asle sees that it says Rent Book on top and The Landlady says that on the first of every month, if it's not a holiday and he's not back home at the time, he can come pay the rent and Asle nods and then they just stand there

Yes well there's probably not much more I need to show you, The Landlady says

and Father thanks her, thanks her very much for renting her home to Asle, it's not so easy to get a room in Aga so he really has to thank her, he says and The Landlady says it's nothing and then she goes over to the door and she leaves the room and goes downstairs and Father and then Mother and then Asle follow her and The Landlady stops outside The Shoemaker's Workshop and then she holds out the keyring to Asle and then she says to him welcome, and that she hopes he'll like it there and that everything goes well for him at The Academic High School, she says and Asle takes the keys

So I'll just go back inside then, it's a little chilly, The Landlady says

Yes, thank you again, and take care of yourself, Father says

Yes, take care of yourself, Mother says

and they see The Landlady go up to her house and up the steps to the front door and then Father says yes well they should probably just carry the things in now, he says

Yes, Asle says

and then Father goes and opens the boot of the car and picks up the studio stove with one burner and Asle takes the bag with the paintings and the sack of bed linens and Mother takes a box of plates and other kitchen things and they carry them inside and no one says anything and then Father goes and gets another two boxes and Asle and Mother go and get some shopping bags

We can help you unpack, Father says

No I'd rather do it myself, Asle says

But, Mother says

I want to unpack it myself, Asle says

and he goes and sits on the edge of the bed and Father and Mother stay standing there in the middle of the room and Asle rolls himself a cigarette and lights it and Mother says he probably doesn't have any ashtrays and then she takes a saucer out of one of the boxes and hands it to him and Asle says thanks and then he thinks that as soon as his parents leave he'll go to The Co-op Store in the centre of Aga and buy himself an ashtray and then Father says that they did bring some food with them but he'll need to buy himself some milk anyway, he says, and Asle says he'll go for a walk and go shopping, because it's not far to The Co-op Store, Asle says and he gets up and leaves the room

And then you'll go visit my mother in the morning? Father says

I'll visit her every day, Asle says

That's nice of you, Father says

And there's a phone booth next to The Co-op Store, and if anything comes up you should just call home, he says

and then it's silent and then Father says well he and Mother will just be driving back home then, he says

Okay, Asle says

But you really don't want us to help you unpack? Father says

No I'll do it myself, Asle says

and Father takes out his wallet and he says that now and every month until he's done at The Academic High School he'll get some money from him, for the rent, for food and clothes and whatever else he needs, schoolbooks and all that, it's not all that much money, nothing special, he's hardly a rich man, Father says, but he'll have the money he needs to get by, and today he needs a larger amount because the schoolbooks he needs will cost a good chunk of money, but books are so expensive, yes indeed, Father says and he hands Asle several notes and Asle takes them and says thank you

You have your wallet with you, right? Mother says

Yes, of course, Asle says

You can leave now, he says

Okay we will, Mother says

Yes, Father says

Now take good care of yourself, you hear, he says

Yes, Mother says

and Father holds out his hand to Asle and he says well good luck then Asle and Mother holds out her hand to him too and she says good luck and then Asle sees Mother go over to the door and she leaves and then Father is in the doorway and he stops and turns around and looks at Asle

Take care, he says

and then Father closes the door behind him and then Asle goes and sits down on the edge of the bed and then he lies down on the bed with his hands folded behind his neck and he puts the saucer he's using as an ashtray on his belly and Asle thinks that he'll be sixteen soon and finally, finally, he's being left in peace, he thinks, and the day he turns sixteen he's going to write to the minister in Barmen and withdraw from The National Church, he thinks and Asle smokes and he feels a lightness come over him and I'm sitting here in the car and I'm driving south and the main road is cleared and good to drive on, and I've seen some cars on the road but not many, and I think that the first thing I'll do when I get to Bjørgvin is park the car in front of The Beyer Gallery and then I'll give the pictures to Beyer and then I'll take a taxi to The Hospital to see Asle, and if I can't see him today either, yes, then I don't know, I think and I feel drowsy, yes, sleepy, because I didn't sleep much last night either, so that means both of the last two nights I didn't get much sleep, yes, maybe almost none, I think, and I think that before I go to The Beyer Gallery I need to drive past the block where Asle's apartment is, in Sailor's Cove, where I was the day before yesterday to get his dog, Bragi, and when I left Dylgja earlier today Bragi was still in my bed and I thought I didn't want to bring him to Bjørgvin, because it would just be a short trip, I think, I was just going to drop off my pictures, see Asle, and then drive back to Dylgja, I think, and I think that now I don't want to even look at the building where Asle's apartment is, I'll just look straight ahead and drive past it, I think and I drive steadily, confidently on south towards Bjørgvin and now I'll drive straight to The Beyer Gallery and then

I'll drop off my paintings and put them in the side room, The Bank, as Beyer calls it, and I can do that whether Beyer is there in person or one of those young women he always has a new one of, the university girls, as Beyer says, he's gotten another new university girl to sit in The Gallery, he says, so it doesn't matter if I've arranged a fixed time with Beyer, there's always someone in the gallery, and that's what we've done for all these years now, I think and Beyer has called me on the phone, the same way he does every year, just for form's sake, as he says, we've arranged to have a Christmas exhibition this year too, and he says it with a little laugh, Christmas exhibition, because he knows I don't like to use that word, because the word Christmas, yes, Christmas itself, all the Christmas festivities, I don't like them, I think, but never mind that, because now I'm almost there and I'll be able to park my car in front of The Beyer Gallery, I think, because now, yes, now I'll drive straight to The Beyer Gallery and drop the paintings off and then take a taxi to The Hospital and visit Asle, I have to, I think, because, yes, maybe I should bring him something? or maybe he wants me to buy him something? anyway I'll take a taxi to The Hospital to see how Asle is doing and afterwards I'll take a taxi to St Paul's Church and sit there for a moment, because I'll be too late for morning mass and it'll be too long a wait until evening mass, and then I'll take a taxi to The Country Inn, even though it's not so far to walk and I know the way, I think and at The Country Inn I can get something warm to eat, yes, that's what I'll do, and then I'll go back to The Beyer Gallery and then I'll drive back home to Dylgja, because I don't need to do any shopping, I already bought everything I needed to buy yesterday, I think and there's not much traffic, it's been a while since I've seen another car, and I think that I like driving, it's like it calms me down, like I fall into a kind of daze, sort of, like I'm collected and focused just on driving, nothing else, yes, it's a little like when I paint, except then I basically always have to be listening for something new the whole time but when I'm

driving I just listen without listening to the same thing the whole
time, and while I'm listening it's like my whole life becomes calm
and peaceful, everything that's happened, I think, and I think
that it's not good to drive if you're too tired, if you're about to fall
asleep, and I feel that I'm still tired so before I drive back home to
Dylgja I should get a little sleep, or if nothing else I need a lot of
coffee, I think and I've reached 1 High Street and there's a car in
just one of the parking places in front of The Beyer Gallery, and
it's Beyer's car, and I park my car next to his and I think so I'm
here and I look at the whitewashed walls right in front of me and
I think that if I just sit here a minute Beyer will probably come
out, I think, and I stay sitting in the car, but no Beyer comes out,
and I get out and go to the front door of The Beyer Gallery and
I see a scrap of paper hanging on the door and it says Be right
back, and that's not really so surprising, it's happened plenty of
times before when I've come to The Beyer Gallery without arranging a set time that there's been a scrap of paper like that on
the door, and it's never when one of the university girls is in The
Gallery but only when it's Beyer himself, I think, because Beyer
sometimes puts up a sign like that when he has to run an errand
or something, I think, and I think that in that case the first thing
I'll do is take a taxi to The Hospital to visit Asle, but I'm so tired,
so sleepy, so maybe I can just rest a little in the car, maybe even
sleep a little too, I think and I get back into my car and I look at
the white walls and I lean the front seat as far back as it can go,
and I close my eyes, and now I'll just rest a little, I think, and
then I want to pray, yes, I haven't prayed yet today, I think and
I close my eyes and I breathe evenly in and out and then I make
the sign of the cross and then I take out the brown rosary I have
hanging around my neck under my black pullover, the rosary I
got from Ales once, and I take the brown wooden cross between
my thumb and index finger and I think now I need to get a little
sleep and I think I need to pray and I see words before me and I
say inside myself Pater noster Qui es in cælis Sanctificetur nomen

tuum Adveniat regnum tuum Fiat voluntas tua sicut in cælo et
in terra Panem nostrum quotidianum da nobis hodie et dimitte
nobis debita nostra sicut et nos dimittimus debitoribus nostris Et
ne nos inducas in tentationem sed libera nos a malo and I move
my thumb and finger up to the first bead and I say Our Father
Who art in heaven Hallowed be thy name Thy kingdom come
Thy will be done on earth as it is in heaven Give us this day our
daily bread and forgive us our trespasses as we forgive those who
trespass against us And lead us not into temptation but deliver
us from evil and I think over and over again Let thy kingdom
come and then I think that maybe I'm getting tireder because
I'm saying Salve Regina and I move my thumb and finger back
down to the cross and then I see words and I start to say inside
myself Salve Regina Mater misericordiæ Vita dulcedo et spes
nostra salve Ad te clamamus Exsules filii Hevæ Ad te suspiramus
Gementes et flentes in hac lacrimarum valle Eia ergo Advocata
nostra Illos tuos misericordes oculos ad nos converte Et Iesum
Benedictum fructum ventris tui Nobis post hoc exsilium ostende
O clemens O pia O dulcis Virgo Maria and I repeat again and
again Nobis post hoc exsilium ostende and I hold the brown
wooden cross and then I say, over and over again inside myself
while I breathe in deeply Lord and while I breathe out slowly
Jesus and while I breathe in deeply Christ and while I breathe out
slowly Have mercy and while I breathe in deeply On me

IV

AND I SEE MYSELF STANDING and looking at the picture with the two lines that cross near the middle, one brown and one purple, and I see that I've painted the lines slowly, with a lot of thick oil paint, and the paint has run, and where the brown line and the purple line cross the colours have blended nicely and dripped down and I think that I have to get rid of this picture, but I want to keep it? anyway I don't want Åsleik to get it, I think and I think I'll carry the picture upstairs to the attic and into the storeroom on the left and put it with the other pictures I keep in boxes there, the other paintings I don't want to sell, I think, and there's always one painting out leaning on a chair between the two small windows on the short wall in the same room, under the gable, in the middle, and the one I've had there for a long time now is the portrait I painted of Ales, I think and I look at the picture with the two lines that cross and I see myself sitting in my car in the parking space outside The Beyer Gallery and I look at the white walls in front of me and it's Wednesday today, I think, and it's already been such a long day, I think and won't Beyer come back to the gallery soon? I think and it's a little chilly and I put the seat back up the way it usually is when I'm driving and I wonder if I should start the engine and turn on the heat, but I decide not to and then I wrap my black coat around me better and I knot my scarf tighter around my neck and Beyer'll be back soon, I think and then I think that painting isn't something I've done for myself, it wasn't because I wanted to paint, but to serve something bigger, yes, maybe, I do sometimes dare to think things like that, that I want my paintings to do nothing less than serve the kingdom of God, I think, yes, and I thought that way before I was confirmed too, and that might have to do with the fact that I've always felt God's closeness, yes, whatever that is, I think, and call it whatever you want, but now, for one reason or another, it suddenly feels like I've said what I have to say, yes, like I don't have any desire to paint anymore, that there's no more to see, no more to add, but if I do stop painting then what'll I do with myself? maybe read more? because actually I like reading, and maybe I'll get a traditional Barmen pointed boat and start going sailing, when the weather's good, because I've always liked being out on the water, and I always thought I'd get a boat someday, yes, a boat and a dog, that's what everybody needs, I thought, but it didn't work out that way, I never got a boat or a dog either, I think, because I've always lived completely inside my painting, in a way, it was like there was no room for anything else, not a boat, not a dog, no matter how many times I thought that I'd like that, a boat or a dog, yes, that's something a person needs if they want a good life, I would think, and now I have a dog at my house, yes, Bragi, and I like that a lot, I think and I think that now I also feel like I want to get rid of all the paintings I still have, yes, the paintings I've kept all these years, including two of the first pictures I ever painted, yes, painted myself, not from photos of houses and buildings but from what I felt and saw, and those are two of the best pictures I ever painted, yes, I really think so, I think, and that's why, because they came right at the beginning, so to speak, I've usually had one of those two out leaning against the back of the chair, but now I've had the portrait I painted of Ales there for a long time, I think, and I have no desire to take it down, I don't want to take it down, yes, it's sort of found its permanent place there on the chair, but I do sometimes go into the storage space and take out a painting from there, and then I stand and look at it for a little while, I

think and there are so many times I was sorry I'd sold my other
earliest paintings, yes, I practically gave them away, they sold for
so little or nothing, I think, and that was at an exhibition I put
on myself at the Barmen Youth Centre, I think, yes, it's pathetic,
and in the other room in the attic, the one I get to by taking the
door on the right when I come up the stairs, I have my storeroom
with tubes of oil paint, canvas, brushes, cans of turpentine, and
wood for making stretchers, I think, and there's a storage space
in that room too, but I rarely go into that one, and I don't really
want to think about it because that's where I put Ales's clothes
and other things, because when she died I couldn't bear to get
rid of anything so I took it all, folded her clothes up as neatly as
I could, her trousers, skirts, underwear, bras, all her clothes, and
all the rest, her toiletries, her make-up, what little she used, no
I don't want to think about that, not now, no, not now, I think
and I think that Åsleik and I wrapped up the nine big paintings
and the four small paintings in blankets today, thirteen paintings
in all that I'd finished, and then we carried them out to my car
and put them carefully in the back, because when I bought a
new car, many years ago, when the one I'd bought with Ales and
we'd used to move to the old house wasn't usable anymore, the
most important thing for me was to make sure that my finished
paintings could fit in the back, so I bought a large car, almost a
small van, and it had to have a roof rack so I could tie lengths of
wood for making stretchers to the roof, I think, and now I put
the pictures nicely stacked in the back of the car, wrapped up
well in blankets, and I'm happy to be getting rid of these pictures,
yes, bringing them to Beyer, I think, but where is Beyer? where
has he gone? I've been waiting a long time now, I think and I
think that it'll be nice to get back home, it always is, whenever
I'm away I'm constantly looking forward to getting back to our
good old house there in Dylgja, because I always think of it as
our house, even though I've been living there alone for so many
years, I still think that it's our house, but soon it'll be time to

learn to think about it as my house, not our house, yes, like that instead, my house, I think and I look at the white wall and now I see snowflakes falling one by one and landing on the windshield and I look straight ahead and I see Asle lying there in bed in The Hospital and a doctor opens the door and goes over to him and takes his pulse and his body is still shaking, still trembling

I hope it stops soon, The Doctor says

and the man sitting there keeping watch on him says that it keeps changing, sometimes he's almost not shaking at all but then he starts shaking again, he says and The Doctor says that's good to hear and then he goes over to the other bed and The Doctor puts his hand in front of the mouth and nose of the man lying there and takes his pulse and he says that he's gone and the man on the chair says he hadn't noticed anything unusual and The Doctor says he's dead and I see two people come in and then wheel the bed with the dead man out of the room and then Asle is lying there alone and the man sitting there gets up and goes over to the window and stays standing there looking out and then he looks at Asle and he sees that his body has started shaking again, up and down his body jerks, he sees, and I think that I don't understand why I suddenly decided I had to drive back into Bjørgvin to visit Asle and that was when I found him lying in the snow in The Lane, partly up on the stairs to a front door, lying there covered in snow, I think and I don't want to think about Asle anymore, I think and then I think that I'm a good driver, the only thing is I don't like driving in cities, because then I get flustered, yes, I get so confused that I could easily hit someone, I think and that would be pretty much the worse thing that could happen, I can't imagine anything worse than hitting someone with my car, being responsible for someone being killed or crippled because I hit them, no, even thinking about it is totally unbearable, I think and I sit in my car in the parking space in front of The Beyer Gallery and I look at the white wall in front of me and one snowflake after another lands on the windshield

and I look at the white wall and I see Mother come running up
and she calls Father and he comes and then they go to the room
where Asle and Sister sleep and Asle is behind Father and he sees
Father stand there and shake and shake his sister Alida and Asle
hears Father say he doesn't know what's wrong, but Sister seems
totally lifeless, yes, it's like she's dead, he says and Asle just stands
there and then Father goes and calls The Doctor and Asle just
stands there, and he thinks what happened? he doesn't understand a thing, he thinks and Mother and Father just stand there
next to his sister Alida's bed, he thinks and then The Doctor
comes and he goes in to Sister and he says he can only tell them
the truth, he says, that she's dead, it doesn't happen often but
sometimes children just die suddenly, and when is happens when it
reason is most often a congenital heart defect, The Doctor says,
but the best thing would be if Sister had an autopsy, he says, because then they might find out the cause of death for certain, The
Doctor says and then he leaves and I look at the white wall and so
many snowflakes have landed on the windshield by now that the
white wall is barely visible, and the snow is falling so thick that
it's impossible to tell one snowflake from another, and I look at
the white wall and I see Asle sitting in church, and everything is
just horrible and awful, he thinks and he thinks that his sister
Alida was carried away on a stretcher that was put into an ambulance, and that was the last he ever saw of Sister, he thinks, because she was put in a white coffin that was sealed up again and
now it's at the front of the church and all the kids from school are
there and some adults and everything's horrible and unbearable,
Asle thinks and he hears The Minister say something about it
being hard to find meaning in sister Alida dying so suddenly, it is
hard to understand what the almighty God could have wanted to
achieve with that, but still there is a meaning in it, even if we
can't understand the meaning, The Minister says, and then he
says that Christ died for our sins and because he rose from the
dead we too will do the same one day, he says, someday Sister

will rise up from the dead, but for now she's with God, now she is living in God's peace, so we shouldn't grieve, because Sister is happy now, she is in a good place, what Sister really was is there, what Sister is, her soul, her spirit, is gone now and only her body remains here, and that's not Sister, that is just a dead body, The Minister says and Asle thinks that he has to agree with The Minister about that, because his sister Alida's body lying there stiff and white and with no movement at all in it that isn't Sister, that is something else, something totally different from Sister, because sister Alida was a life in the body that's now lying there lifeless, up there in the white box, and when the life was gone Sister was gone too, that's how it was, none of sister Alida was there anymore because the corpse that lay there in the bed and that's lying here now in the white box isn't his sister Alida, just something stiff and cold, Asle thinks and he thinks that there's no meaning in the fact that his sister Alida died and it's not something that God could have possibly wanted, so it must be that something God didn't want to have happen happened, Asle thinks and I look at the white wall and the snow is now covering the whole windshield and I can't see the wall and I look at the windshield covered with snow and I think that it was to share in the human condition, our sorrows, that God became man and died and rose up again, because with him, with the resurrected Christ, all people were resurrected too, I think and I think that this is just a meaningless word, I think and I look at the windshield that's now totally covered with snow so that I can't see the white wall anymore and I think that since God is eternal and outside of space and time everything is simultaneous in God, yes, in God everything that has happened and is happening and will happen are all simultaneous, so that's why all the dead have already awoken, yes, they live, yes, they live the way they were and simultaneously as part of God, I think and I look at the snow covering the windshield and I see Asle sitting there in church and he's thinking that everything that idiot Minister up there is reeling off, about how there actually is meaning in the meaningless death of his sister Alida, is an insult, that's how he sees it, because Sister is dead and there's no meaning in it and so there's no meaning in life and you have to just live with that and that means you might as well be dead, Asle thinks, and if he wants to be able to live with meaningless suffering he needs to stop listening to the kind of meaningless talk that The Minister is reeling off, Asle thinks, because the meaning The Minister is talking about is a kind of torment while meaninglessness gives you a kind of peace, you might say, Asle thinks and he thinks that he doesn't want to be confirmed and I sit in my car parked here in front of The Beyer Gallery and I look and look at the snow covering the windshield and I think that one of the most important things when it comes to painting is being able to stop at the right time, to know when a picture is saying what it can say, if you keep going too long then more often than not the picture'll be ruined, yes, I knew that even when I was painting my very first picture, I think, sure you can scrape it off and repaint it, or paint over it, but then the picture kind of no longer gives itself, and that's what a picture should do, it should come to you on its own, like something that just happens, like a gift, yes, a good picture is a gift, and a kind of prayer, it's both a gift and a prayer of gratitude, I think and I never could have painted a good picture through force of will, because art just happens, art occurs, that's how it is, and once I've gotten as far as I can with a picture I stand back and look at the picture in the dark, yes, look at it when it's as dark in the room as I can make it, I think, and in the summer it never gets really dark so that's why the autumn and winter are the best time to paint for me and the pictures I paint in spring and summer have to wait until autumn or winter before I can really see them, yes, in the darkness, yes, I need to see pictures in the dark to see if they shine, and to make them shine more, or better, or truer, or however it's possible to say it, anyway the picture has to have the shining darkness in it, I think and I think when I get home later today I should start painting again, because I have a bad feeling that something has stopped in a way, that I'm not going to be able to paint any more, that I don't have any desire to paint anymore, that I don't want to paint anymore, so I need to start painting something new today, I think, and I should get home as soon as I can so if only Beyer would show up now, I think, because what Beyer always wants is to open the show a little before Christmas, he thinks that's the best time to open a show if you want to sell as many pictures as you can, and then you can keep the show going until New Year's and then, at New Year's, is often when most of the pictures get sold, I think, and during Advent once I've driven down to Bjørgvin, like today, and delivered the paintings to Beyer it's like I'm finishing something so that I can start something new, I think and I think that I don't have any desire to start any new pictures, the desire I usually always have after I've delivered the paintings, yes, I usually feel a strong need to start painting again that same day, because it's like I'm starting a new picture after I've delivered the paintings because all the pictures in an exhibition go together in a way, yes, it's as if they're all one picture, I think, and this need to paint that I've had ever since I was a boy can't just suddenly disappear? yes, from the first time I painted I wanted to keep painting since I was so good at it, but after a while being good at it was totally unimportant, yes, it was a mistake, I didn't want to be good at it, I wanted to paint just so that I could say something that couldn't be said any other way, yes, paint from a faraway closeness, that's how I think about it, I think, yes, make the blackness shine, yes, paint away the shining darkness, I think, and how often I've thought these thoughts, I think, because I always think the same thoughts over and over again and I paint the same picture over and over again, yes, it's true, but at the same time every single picture is different, and then all the pictures go together in a kind of series, yes, every exhibition is its own series, and finally all the paintings I've ever painted go together and make up a single picture, I think, it's like there's a picture somewhere or other inside me that's my innermost picture, that I try again and again to paint away, and the closer I get to that picture the better the picture I've painted is, but the innermost picture isn't actually a picture of course, because the innermost picture doesn't exist, it just is in a way, without existing, it is but it doesn't exist, and somehow it's as if the picture that isn't a picture sort of leads all the other pictures and pulls them in, kind of, I think, but maybe I've now painted everything I can paint from this innermost picture of mine? I think, maybe I've now in a way entered into this innermost picture and thereby destroyed it? I think, but this going into your innermost picture, yes, seeing it, well that's probably the same thing as dying? I think, yes, maybe it's the same thing as seeing God? and whoever sees God has died, as is written, I think and I look at the snow that's covering the windshield and I see Asle standing there in the room and I see Mother standing there looking at him

You don't want to be confirmed? she says

and she plops down on the sofa

I've never heard of anyone not getting confirmed, she says

What kind of talk is that? she says

and she says that it's the old custom, confirmation is when you stop being a child and become a grown-up, she says

It's true what your mother is saying, Father says

and look he's said something for once, he hardly ever does, Asle thinks

You have to get confirmed, Father says

and he says that Asle'll get presents, and he and Mother will throw a party for him, and he'll get a dark suit and white shirt and tie, yes, the same as all the other boys his age, and all the girls will get a traditional dress for confirmation, Hardanger embroidery, that's just how it is, Father says and Asle thinks well then he'll get confirmed, that's easy enough, and he thinks that as soon as he's old enough, when he's sixteen, he'll write to The

Minister and withdraw from The National Church, because
Christianity the way it's preached is nothing but a way to torment people, and it's only getting worse, Asle thinks and I sit in
the car and I shiver a little and I'm waiting for Beyer to come
back to his gallery and I look at the snow that's covering the
windshield and I see Asle sitting at the table in the rented room
in Aga on the day he turned sixteen and he's writing a letter to
The Minister in Stranda and he writes that he wants to withdraw
from The National Church and I look at the snow that's covering
the windshield and I think that it was only when I met Ales that
I started thinking that only God was with sister Alida when she
died, and that she was now with God in peace, in his peace, in
God's light, I think, because God doesn't want us to die, he came
down to Earth because people and God were separated and because God is love and free will is a prerequisite for love, and
therefore also for sin, or death, yes, because that's what separates
human beings from God, I think, and God and humanity were
reunited in Christ, in and through and with his death on the
cross, so now neither people nor God have to die, but does that
mean anything? does it make sense to think things like that? I
think, but that's how Ales used to think, I think and I think that
Ales was born into The Catholic Church because her mother
Judit was Catholic, she was from Austria and she'd fled to Norway, and Ales and I used to talk and talk together and eventually
I understood that what she was saying was true, it was true in its
way, because Ales and I went to mass together, and the Eucharist,
as they say, means that both Christ and the people who take part
in the ceremony together with him offer themselves up, in and
through Christ's body in the trans- substantiated host, as they
say, and in that way they died together for dead they loved every
time they went to mass, and in that way they rose up again with
the dead they loved every time they went to mass, Ales said and
it felt true, it felt real, I think and I think that it's obviously not
the only truth but it's a truth, it too, I think, yes, it's almost like

a language, because every language gives you access to its share of reality, and the different religions are different languages that can each have its truth, and its lack of truth, I think and it's foolish to think that God is anything defined, anything you can say something about, Ales said and of course she was right, I think and I think that people can't have free will if God is eternal and everything is in God, past, present, future, or actually of course it's possible, because God can know everything, can have everything in him, even if it isn't he who willed it, who set it in motion, I think, but thoughts like that don't mean much and really its only art, maybe, in the best case, that can say anything about the truth that belief contains, or not say anything about it but show it, I think and I think that Ales also said that God is not all-powerful, he is powerful in his powerlessness, it is God as Jesus Christ hanging powerless, nailed to the cross, who is powerful, it's his powerlessness that gives him power, that makes him all-powerful, for eternity, yes, God is powerless, not powerful, I think, any- way that's what Ales thought, I think and I think that maybe these are just empty thoughts but I think them anyway, that it's powerlessness that gives power, but whatever I think or don't think there's little or nothing to say, I think and I look at the snow covering the windshield and I think that I stopped at the turn-off near the brown house the day before yesterday and from there I could see two lovers together in a playground playing like children on the swings and seesaw and in the sandbox, and it was nice to see them, I think and I look at the snow covering the windshield and I think what ever happened to them all, well Sigve died many years ago, he dropped dead one morning while going to work, I know that, but what happened to Geir and Terje and to Olve who I played in the band with when I was going to middle school? and to Amund, who took over for me? I think and someone or other said that Olve went to prison after that, and that he'd been in various dance bands, I think, because after I moved to Aga I almost never went back to Barmen, I got anxious whenever I went, and I don't know why but it was like I was filled with unease and I would drive home the same day I went to visit, I never once spent the night in Barmen since the day I moved to Aga to go to The Academic High School, I think, and it's incredible that I started at The Academic High School because I was, well, to tell the truth I was really terrible in school, I was downright slow, and especially bad at maths, it was impossible for me to understand numbers, they just didn't mean anything to me, they gave me nothing, and honestly they still don't, I think, and that was why when I was going to primary school I used to sit and draw in my maths books and I drew so well that The Schoolmaster told my parents that I had a gift for drawing, and maybe for painting too, and so maybe they should buy me some painting supplies, and they did, but I was still just as bad when it came to maths, The Schoolmaster eventually managed to teach me the most basic things and after a lot of struggling I could do what I was asked to do, I learned that what mattered what not to try to think about it but just to do what I was told I should do, I had to keep every last thought out of my mind strictly in order do what The Schoolmaster said I needed to do, and that's how I got through maths problems, I think and I sit and look at the snow convering the windshield and I think that once I've dropped off the paintings I'll take a taxi straight to The Hospital, I have to go see Asle today, don't I? I think and if Asle wants me to run any errands for him I'll do it, and I still feel tired, sleepy, actually I'm exhausted now that I come to think of it, to tell the truth, because I'm not young anymore, no, to tell the truth I'm an old man, I think and I'm all alone in the world, yes, I'd have to say, there's almost no one besides Åsleik and Beyer that I'm in touch with, yes, really it's just the two of them, and then Asle, I think, because Ales and I lived pretty much entirely on our own, it was like we didn't need any other people besides each other, we shared our world, that was it, and naturally I also knew Åsleik and talked to him when Ales was alive but it was mostly after she died that we started seeing more of each other, and I've known Asle all these years, and I've known Beyer all these years, and Beyer and I are probably friends in our way, but we're probably mostly friends in art, to put it that way, or business partners, that's probably closer to the truth, Beyer would probably put it that way, I think and I look at the snow covering the windshield and I see Asle standing in front of Father listening to Father say that he thought Asle could try to put on an exhibition of the paintings he's painted, because that might make him a little money and that would come in handy in the autumn when he moved to Aga and started at The Academic High School, Father says, well it's not that he's sure someone would buy something, he's not, but it wouldn't hurt to try, Father says and then he says Asle could maybe show his paintings in the Barmen Youth Centre over the summer, since, well, people buy all sorts of things so who knows, maybe Asle can sell a picture or two, anyway it's worth trying, Father says, because there were so many people in town, both in Barmen and sometimes in Stranda too, who'd had him paint a picture of their house and farm and at least some of them would want to come see a show and now, over the summer, there were lots of city people too, especially from Bjørgvin, who drove through Barmen and maybe some of them would feel like stopping to take a look at the pictures, Father says and he says that he could ask the manager at The Co-op Store if Asle could put up a sign in the window saying that there's an Art Exhibition at The Barmen Youth Centre, no less, but in that case Asle would have to make a sign to hang in the window of The Co-op Store so that everyone in Barmen who went shopping at The Co-op Store would know about it, about there being an Art Exhibition at The Barmen Youth Centre, yes, Father says and of course people'll start to talk about it, yes, news of this art exhibition of Asle's will get around, so he's sure people will come look at the pictures at least, but as for whether anyone will want to buy one, no, he's not as sure about that, he has his doubts about that one, but, as they say, it's worth trying, Father says, and for all he knows maybe there are some folks who could see themselves buying one of these paintings of his even if they didn't look like anything, after all people are different, people like different things, he says, but if no one sees the paintings and they're just piled up in Asle's room then definitely no one will buy them, that's for sure, Father says, you need to show people the pictures if you want anyone to buy them, Father says and Asle can surely get permission to show his pictures in The Barmen Youth Centre, Father says and Asle thinks that's not such a bad idea, even if he doesn't sell a single painting well at least he'll have put on a show, so he should definitely go ask The Man in Charge of The Barmen Youth Group if he can put on an exhibition in The Barmen Youth Centre this summer, in July, and then he'll paint a sign that Father can hang up in one of the display windows at The Co-op Store, Asle thinks, and then people might come look at the pictures, people from Barmen who've already bought pictures from him and maybe some from Stranda, and maybe one or two people from Bjørgvin who happen to be driving through will stop in, who knows, Asle thinks, and then maybe he'll sell a painting, because these are so much better and truer than all the other pictures he's painted from photographs, he thinks, yes, he should definitely exhibit the art, yes, Asle thinks and I sit here in the car and I look at the snow covering the windshield and I think that for all I know it's still snowing and I think that now Beyer really needs to get back to his gallery soon and I look at the snow that's covering the windshield and I see Asle standing there in front of the sign hanging in the window of The Co-op Store and written on top is Art Exhibition and underneath Asle has painted a picture of The Barmen Youth Centre and under that he's written that there's an exhibition at The Barmen Youth Centre and it'll be open between two and five o'clock through the whole month of July, because the same day Father thought of the idea of this exhibition he's now looking at the sign for, Asle thinks, he, Asle, had gone to The Man in Charge of The Barmen Youth Group and asked if he could use The Youth Centre to put

on a show of his paintings this summer and The Man in Charge
had said yes of course, why not, he said and then Asle got the keys
to The Barmen Youth Centre and I sit here in the car and it's cold
and I think that now Beyer really needs to come soon so I can
deliver the pictures and I look at the snow that's covering the
windshield and I see Asle sitting there at a table in front of the
stage in The Barmen Youth Centre and he's thinking he's chosen
nine paintings for the show and then brought them over to The
Barmen Youth Centre, it took several trips, but it wasn't more
than a mile or so to walk so it was easy to do, and once he finally had all the paintings in The Barmen Youth Centre he took a
hammer and nails and started hanging up the paintings, nine of
them, he had more but there were two he didn't want to sell, that
he wanted to keep for himself, and then there were some that he
wasn't totally happy with, or else not totally done with, and he
thought that these nine made a pretty good number to put up in
the auditorium, and that these nine paintings made up a nice
picture all together, but the painting at the back of the little stage,
the scene of the village with the high cliff and the blue fjord and
the blossoming birch trees kind of ruined things for the other
pictures, they were kind of ashamed of it, Asle thought and then
he went home to Mother, he thinks, sitting behind the table in
The Barmen Youth Centre, and he asked if he could borrow four
white sheets and he could and he took the sheets and went to The
Barmen Youth Centre with them and by standing on a table that
he found behind the set onstage he'd managed to drape the sheets
over the stage set until finally it was entirely covered with white
sheets and actually it looked a little like a ghost, Asle thinks, and
that didn't matter, that didn't do anything to the paintings, he
thinks and then the exhibition was ready and now he just has to
wait to see if people will come look at it, Asle thinks and then he
somehow got the table down off the stage into the room and
found a chair behind the stage too and then he sat down behind
the table, he put it right in front of the stage and now he's sitting

there, he thinks, yes, he's sitting there looking at the paintings and now everything's ready, now people just need to come, he thinks and then he hears footsteps and the door opens and then The Man in Charge of The Barmen Youth Group comes in and he sees Asle sitting there behind the table and Asle stands up and goes over to The Man in Charge

I see you've hung up your paintings, he says

and The Man in Charge looks at a box of nails and a hammer that Asle has put down on the floor

Yes, Asle says

It went fine, I carried the pictures from home, it took a few trips but it went fine, it was easy, he says

And you hung them up today? The Man in Charge says

With nails, he says

Yes, Asle says

You didn't think about whether you'd be leaving marks on the walls? The Man in Charge says

And the auditorium's been painted pretty recently too you know, he says

But the pictures couldn't just sit on the floor, Asle says

No I suppose not, The Man in Charge says

But maybe you could've put them on chairs, each one on its own chair? he says

We take the chairs out whenever there's a dance, otherwise they're stacked up in the side room there, he says

and he points at a door

Well what's done is done, The Man in Charge says

and then he goes round and looks at the pictures and then stops and he looks at Asle and he says that these pictures were different from what he'd expected, Asle used to paint differently, he painted so that you could see what it was in the picture, sometimes you could even see that it was your own house he'd painted, but now, well, now it was impossible to tell what any of the pictures was supposed to be of, he'd just smeared paint around, no, why had he painted pictures like this? he'd painted so many good pictures before, yes, they were hanging in practically every house in Barmen and some in Stranda too, pictures Asle had painted of houses, people's homes, of the barn, the farm, the fruit trees in bloom and the fjord and the cliff, but these paintings, no, they don't look like anything, if he'd known that Asle was wanting to show paintings like these at his exhibition he doesn't know if he'd have given him permission to show them at The Barmen Youth Centre, no indeed, The Man in Charge of The Barmen Youth Group says and he says he doesn't think any of the village folks are going to like these pictures at all, probably some'll come to look at the exhibition but once they start telling their friends how the pictures are painted probably not many more people will come to look, he says

No, no, I thought these pictures would look different, he says

That they'd look like something, the way your other pictures do, he says

and Asle thinks that The Man in Charge of The Barmen Youth Group doesn't understand pictures and art any better than a cow and maybe the other people in Barmen don't either, they probably don't understand pictures and art any better than a cow either, Asle thinks and I sit in my car that's parked next to Beyer's car in one of the parking spaces outside The Beyer Gallery and I think that now Beyer really has to come back to his gallery soon, I think, and I look at the snow covering the windshield and I see Asle sitting there behind a table in front of the stage in The Barmen Youth Centre and there's a sketchpad on the table in front of him and he's holding a pencil in his hand and Asle thinks that now there've been some people at the exhibition, people he's painted pictures for before, and they all say the same thing, he thinks, they say that this wasn't what they were expecting, they don't understand these pictures, and he, Asle, can paint so much better than this, because anyone can paint pictures like these, they say, you just smear some paint around, or however they put it, and then Asle sits there longer and no one comes and it doesn't really matter, he thinks, because he has his sketchpad and pencil and so he can sit there alone in the middle of all these paintings he's painted and sketch, he can sketch out new pictures he's thinking about painting, yes, he has nothing better to do anyway, does he? Asle thinks and every single sketch is something Asle thinks he'll paint in oil on canvas someday, because he's sketching out pictures he's seen and that are stored up in his head and that he wants to paint away, Asle thinks and then he thinks that Father, after he hadn't sold a single painting after several days, told him that maybe it'd be a good idea to thumbtack a slip of paper saying Sold under a couple of the pictures, because people are like that, once one person wants something other people want it, Father says

Yes that's how people are, he said

Once one person has something other people want it too, he said

and then Asle put up a slips of paper saying Sold, with thumbtacks, under five of the paintings and as soon as he'd done that, Asle thinks, someone comes in who'd been by to look at the exhibition before and he starts going from painting to painting and he looks at each painting for a long time and Asle stands up and goes over to him

Do you like the pictures? Asle says

and he thinks that this man had come and looked at the pictures once before already, there haven't been so many visitors to the exhibition that Asle can't remember every one of them, he thinks, and this man is especially easy to remember because he takes up so little space, he's so quiet, so short and slim

Are you from Stranda? Asle says

No, the man says

and Asle can hear right away that the man is from Bjørgvin and the man from Bjørgvin nods and then he says that he's from Bjørgvin, as Asle could probably hear, he says and he holds out his hand and Asle shakes it and the man says Beyer and Asle says

Asle and then the man named Beyer says that he might like to buy a picture, he was here and he looked at the paintings a few days ago too and ever since then he couldn't forget them, he says

Yes, it's strange, Beyer says

There's something about these pictures that sticks in my mind, he says

and it was especially one of the pictures that stuck in his mind, and he really wanted to buy that picture, but now there's a slip of paper under it saying Sold so he guesses he'll just buy a different one, he says, but the question of course is how much Asle wants for the picture, he says and Asle thinks that he wants to make back what the picture cost him in any case and then he can maybe add a few kroner on top of that but not too much, because otherwise he probably won't sell a single picture, he thinks and then he says what he wants for the painting and Beyer says that he can certainly afford that much and so it's settled and then he walks around the room and looks at the pictures one after another and then he stops in front of one and looks at it for a long time and then he goes over to one of the picture with a Sold sign tacked up under it and then he goes over to Asle and says that he's found a painting he wants to buy, but he really regrets that not coming back out here sooner so that he could've bought the picture he saw so clearly in his mind, saw it again and again too, he says and Asle says that he can ask the person who bought that picture if he'd consider buying another one instead, so if Beyer could come back tomorrow maybe he'd be able to work things out so that he can buy the picture he'd rather have, Asle says

Thank you, Beyer says

Thanks very much, he says

Thank you, Asle says

and he says that not too many paintings have sold, he can see that for himself, and then Beyer leaves and now I'm tired of sitting and waiting, now Beyer really needs to come soon so I can drop off the paintings, I think, and I look at the snow that's covering the windshield and I see Asle sitting behind a table in

The Barmen Youth Centre and he sees Beyer come walking up
to him and Asle says that he got the other buyer to pick another
picture instead so Beyer can have the picture he wants, Asle says
and then Beyer says then he'll buy it and also the other one he
liked, so two pictures, if they both cost the same, he says and
Asle says that they do and then Beyer hands him the money and
he says that since he has to drive back to Bjørgvin soon he'd ap-
preciate it if he could take the pictures with him now and Asle
says that's easy enough and then he writes Sold on two sheets
of paper in the sketchpad and tears them out and then goes and
takes down the two paintings Beyer's bought and puts them on
the floor and then he hangs the sheets of paper saying Sold on
the nails the paintings had been on and then Beyer takes the
paintings and he says pleasure doing business with him and that
he hopes they'll meet again, and that Asle needs to keep painting,
he has a talent for painting, yes, he's very talented, he says, and
then Beyer leaves and then Asle sits there and sketches some more
and three more people come and say pretty much the same thing,
that now that they'd thought about it there was something about
these pictures after all and now they want to buy one, says each
of the three people one after the other, they all say pretty much
the same thing, and the strange thing is that Asle doesn't know
any of them, but maybe that's not so strange, because they're all
from Bjørgvin, and each of them chooses a painting and they ask
how much he wants for it and Asle sticks to the same price for
every painting, the price he'd told Beyer, and one after the other
the people from Bjørgvin hand over the money and pay Asle and
they ask if it's all right for them to take the painting with them
right away and Asle says that's fine and after they've left he goes
and takes down the signs saying Sold from under the pictures because there are signs under every one of the four pictures left, but
none of them have really been sold, and he puts them up on the
nails where the paintings that really did sell had been hanging,
and now Asle has sold five pictures, so now it says Sold in five

empty places on the wall and there are just four pictures left that haven't been sold, and now there's no sign saying Sold under any of them, Asle thinks, but it's not bad to have sold five paintings, he thinks and he sits down behind the table in front of the stage and then he sits there and sketches and he thinks that this is probably as good as it gets for him, he thinks, but he realizes he misses the pictures that were sold, that are gone, Asle thinks and before long he's filled a sketchpad with designs for pictures that he has stuck in his head and he thinks that he'll paint all these sketches at some point, or maybe not all, but most of them anyway, yes, some of the sketches anyway will turn into oil on canvas, he thinks, will turn into paintings, Asle thinks and then he sees Beyer, the man who's already bought two paintings, come back in, and it's really about time someone came, Asle thinks, because there hasn't been anyone in to look at his exhibition for a while and he has only four paintings left to sell, so he thought what's the point of sitting here anymore, but he did write down an opening and closing date for the exhibition so he has to stick to it, Asle thinks and Beyer nods at Asle and says hello and then he goes and looks at the four paintings still hanging there, he goes from one painting to the other and he takes his time, he looks at painting after painting for a long time and Asle thinks it's strange that Beyer as he's called came back, and then Beyer comes walking up to Asle and he says that he likes Asle's pictures so much that he wants to buy all four that are still left, yes, if he can get them for the same price as before, he says

Yes your pictures really have something, Beyer says

Something all their own, he says

But of course I need to ask what you want for the pictures, he says

and Asle says that he can buy them for the same price as before and Beyer says that in that case it's a deal and he takes out his wallet and he pays for the paintings and he says that the price is perfectly reasonable and Beyer says that he was on his way to

Stranda where some friends of his have a cabin and he stopped at
The Co-op Store and saw the sign for The Art Exhibition in the
window there, yes, the sign was actually a painting, and even if
the motif on the sign wasn't quite as interesting still The Barmen
Youth Centre was painted well and that's why he thought he
should go back to the art exhibition, he says

Yes you have a real future ahead of you, he says

I can see that, he says

And I really know about paintings, he says

and then he says again that his name is Beyer and then he asks
again what Asle's name is and then he says that if he remembers
correctly there were signs saying Sold under at least two of the
pictures he just bought, he says and he looks at Asle who doesn't
say anything and then Beyer says goodbye and he takes two of
the paintings with him and Asle says that he can help him carry
the other two out and then Beyer walks to his car and he puts the
paintings in the back and lays a blanket between each painting
and then Asle stands there and Beyer gets into his car and drives
off and Asle goes back inside and he looks at the empty walls and
he feels sad that all the painting are gone now, because actually
he would've liked to keep all the paintings himself, Asle thinks,
and he'd felt so calm and peaceful when he was sitting in The
Youth Centre surrounded by his paintings and sketching out pictures that he was going to paint some time in the future, some
of the sketches would turn into paintings anyway, and now, now
there are no pictures left, so now it's become kind of empty and
sad, Asle thinks and he thinks that the pictures he's painted of
people's homes, yes, he's always been glad to get rid of those, the
sooner the better really, but he likes these paintings more, and he
feels sad and in a way heavy when he thinks about how they're
gone now, he thinks and then Asle goes and rips all the signs
saying Sold off the nails and throws them out in the litter basket
outside The Youth Centre and he goes back in and pulls all the
nails out of the walls and goes and throws them out in the litter

basket too and then he takes down the sign saying Art Exhibition from the front door of The Barmen Youth Centre and throws it in the litter basket and Asle goes back in and puts the table and chair back behind the stage where he found them and then he takes down the sheets in front of the horrible set painting of Stranda in the blazing sun with a glittering blue fjord and a black cliff with white snow on top against the horizon and then he puts the sheets back in the shopping bag he'd brought them in, and he puts the hammer and the box of nails on top and then he puts his brown leather shoulder bag on and then Asle turns off the light and he leaves and he thinks he needs to put up a sign on the front door saying Sold Out and then he takes out the sketchpad and writes Sold Out on a page of it and then he takes out the thumb-tacks that were holding up the earlier sign and uses them to put the sign saying Sold Out up on the front door of The Barmen Youth Centre and then he shuts the door and he goes to The Man in Charge of The Barmen Youth Group and gives him the keys

You're giving up? he says

Yes, Asle says

It's not so easy to sell paintings, is it, The Man in Charge says

No, Asle says

But thank you for letting me use The Youth Centre, he says

and then Asle walks home carrying the shopping bag and Mother asks why he's home already and Asle says that he's sold all the pictures, but actually he's sorry he sold them, because now he misses them and now he'll never get them back

No I don't believe it, Mother says

and she says no she just doesn't understand people, she can understand how he can sell his usual paintings, but that someone would pay good money for incomprehensible smears that don't look like anything, no, she can't understand that, Mother says and she says so the sign saying there's going to be an art exhibition hanging in the window of The Co-op Store, that'll have to be taken down

Yes, right, Asle says

and he takes the nails and the hammer out of the shopping bag and says that he'll just go put these back in the basement of The Old House and then he hands the bag with the white sheets to Mother and says thanks for the loan

I'll wash them now, she says

and then she says that Asle should go right now and take down the sign in the window of The Co-op Store

Yes I'll do that now, he says

No I never thought you'd sell those paintings, Mother says

Whoever bought them must have something wrong in the head, she says

and Asle says that there's one person who's sick in the head, who has something wrong with her mind, and that's her, Mother, and she says imagine saying something like that to your own mother and she says that he can't have gotten much money for his paintings did he and Asle says he sold them for the amount it cost him to make them plus a little extra

No, it's unbelievable, that you sold those pictures, I wouldn't have thought you'd sell a single one, Mother says

and she asks who bought the pictures and Asle says that a man named Beyer who lives in Bjørgvin bought most of them

Yes of course it had to be a Bjørgvinner who'd buy pictures like that, Mother says

No, well, Asle says

and then he goes into town to The Co-op Store and he takes the sign, or rather the painting that says Art Exhibition, out of the window and then he goes home with it under his arm and I sit here in the car and I look at the snow covering the windshield and then I turn on the windshield wipers and they sweep the snow away and I can see to the white wall and now raindrops are falling on the windshield, so now it's already started raining, I think, and I've been sitting in the car a long time now, and it's really cold and I'm shivering a little, I think, so now Beyer really needs to come back to his gallery soon so that we can carry

the paintings in and put them in the gallery's side room, The
Bank, as Beyer calls it, I think and actually I don't want to do
that, I don't want to get rid of these paintings either, I think, it's
like saying goodbye forever every time, and it's like I'm giving
myself away bit by bit, I think, but I need something to live on
too and I live on the sales of the pictures I paint, that's what I've
lived on my whole life, I think, so it just has to be done, I have
to just bring the paintings to Beyer's Bank, I think and I open
the car door and I get out and the rain and cold hits me and I
think anyway I can go check if the door to The Beyer Gallery is
open, because maybe Beyer's come back to the gallery without
my noticing it, that might very well have happened, I think and
no sooner am I out of the car than I see Beyer standing in the
gallery door holding the door open and he shouts that it's good
my pictures are here, it's like it's not really Christmas without
them, Beyer says and he says he has to admit he's been waiting
for the pictures, he says and I jog over to the open door and Beyer
holds out his hand to me and we shake hands and I see that the
sign that was hanging on the door is gone and I think Beyer must
have been in the gallery the whole time, he just didn't want to be
disturbed, or else the sign on the door was a mistake, I think and
Beyer says I should come in and Beyer is sort of beside himself
with happiness at seeing me and he again says it's good to see me,
because to tell the truth it's been almost a year since the last time
we saw each other and I say it sure has

We're both getting old, you and me, he says

and I look at Beyer and I see that he has a cane in his left
hand and I've never seen him with one before, but he has been a
little unsteady on his feet for a few years, his walk has been kind
of halting, but this is the first time I've seen him with a cane and
then Beyer raises his cane into the air

Yes just look, he says

and he holds up his cane a little higher

I can get by without it but it's good to have it, he says

and I think that Beyer has aged a lot in just a year, I think and I see that you couldn't call his hair grey anymore, it's turned white, and Beyer has sort of gotten a little crooked and he lets go of my hand and then he says I look good

You haven't aged much since the last time I saw you, he says

and I don't know what I should say, and I just stand there

Yes you and I have been doing business together or whatever I should call it for many years now, Beyer says

Yes, I say

A generation at least, Beyer says

No much longer than that, he says

and he says that it must be getting on fifty years if you count the first time, when he bought six pictures from me when I was a boy putting on my first exhibition in The Barmen Youth Centre, Beyer says and then he stands there and doesn't say anything and then he looks right at me and then he asks if I remember the first time we met and I say of course I do, yes, I remember it like it was yesterday, and I was thinking about it just recently, I say and I think that Beyer has brought this up so many times, yes, this too has turned into something we do just to do it, something we talk about to kind of show how connected we are to each other

Yes, there in the Barmen Youth Centre, Beyer says

Yes, I bought five paintings from you then, he says

Six actually, I say

and it doesn't seem like Beyer hears what I'm saying

And I got my family and friends to buy the others you were selling, he says

and he says that he's heard that none of them regretted it, he says

And clever you had put up signs saying Sold under a few of the paintings even though they weren't sold, he says

and Beyer laughs and shakes his head

Yes I must admit I've used that trick lots of times myself, he says

And it works too, it works well, he says

and then there's silence

So I knew that not only could you paint, and that you had a great future as an artist ahead of you, but also that you understood how to sell things, Beyer says

Yes, good business sense, he says

It was my father who thought of it though, I say

Yes well then he has good business sense, Beyer says

You're descended from a real businessman, he says

and he says the word businessman in a way that clearly implies that this is really something I can be proud of

A businessman, yes, he says

My father built boats, traditional Barmen boats, and grew fruit, I say

Yes I know, Beyer says

and I don't say anything else and it's quiet for a moment and then I say that Father worked hard, both building his Barmen boats and then he kept working in his orchard, but no matter how much he worked he didn't make much money, we weren't rich in our house, so I wouldn't say Father was a real businessman exactly, I say

No, maybe not, Beyer says

But you, you have a sense for making money, he says

and I say that I need something to live on too, and for me it was living on painting these pictures, something you'd hardly believe was possible, at least where I grew up, there people lived so far apart that even if every last one bought a picture every now and then I wouldn't have sold many pictures, I say and Beyer chuckles and says very true, very true, yes, very true

I don't entirely understand it myself, how I managed it, I say

and then I say that it's thanks to him, thanks to Beyer, that I could do it, without his help it never would've worked, and that's precisely because I'm not a businessman at all, no, but it's also because I haven't thrown a lot of money around, I've scrimped and saved actually, I spend as little money as I can, I only have two pairs of shoes, one for winter and one for summer, and then one pair of dress shoes, and then a pair of big rubber boots that I cut down to shoes, for example these, I say, but when I do buy shoes I always buy expensive shoes, the best brands, I say, and those shoes last a long time, and sometimes I need to take them to the cobbler and eventually they're worn out and have to be thrown away but it's years between each time, I say and Beyer says now that I mention it he's noticed for a long time that I'm always wearing the same shoes, he says, just like I always wear black clothes, a black pullover of one kind or another and I'm always in black trousers and always in a black velvet jacket, and he's barely ever seen me without a brown leather shoulder bag on my shoulder, and then in the winter I wear the long black overcoat that I have on today, he's never seen me in a suit, but my shoes are always black, and then often, though not always, I have on some scarf or another

Yes I need my artist's scarf, I say

and I use those words because I know that if I don't Beyer will, if I don't say artist's scarf Beyer will, I think and I don't entirely like it when he says that because it's almost like he's looking down on me a little when he says those words, artist's scarf

Yes you allow yourself that much, Beyer says

and he says that even if I'm constantly wearing a new scarf, some of them are silk, he noticed that a long time ago, so I must have quite a big collection of scarves, he says and I think that I always asked Ales for a scarf as a present, and most of the time I got one too, either for my birthday or for Christmas, and that's why I have a lot of scarves, some of them nice scarves, and when I go out and see other people I usually like to wear a scarf, it's true, that's how it is, I think and it's quiet for a moment and then Beyer again says that it was very clever of me, sneaky even, to put up a sign saying Sold under pictures that weren't sold, yes, that means that I have a real business sense, he says, and that too is one of those terms I don't really like, but for Beyer like for most Bjørgvin people it's a compliment

A real business sense, yes, Beyer says

That was a good idea, he says

I never remember if it was me who thought of it, I say

It might have been my father, I don't exactly remember, I say

Yes, clever, I'd say sneaky even, whoever came up with it, Beyer says

and then I say, as I stand there, that I still think those nine pictures I sold back then are some of the best ones I ever painted and I say that I regret having sold them all, and that was a lesson for me, I say, because now I set aside pictures I don't want to sell in the attic of my house in Dylgja, in one of the crawlspaces, in a crate up there, and Beyer says that's interesting, hearing about the pictures up in the crate, and I say that I always have one of those paintings out on display, on a chair between two small windows in that same attic room, which painting it is changes but there's always one out, and I switch them sometimes but it's always a painting from the collection up there in the crates, I say and I say that it's probably to sort of remind myself that not everything I've done in life has been totally meaningless, I say

No, you've hardly done things that are meaningless, Beyer says

On the contrary, he says

and he says that he discovered me, it's surely fair to say that, and that his discovery of me is the most important thing he's done for Norwegian art, because now my pictures still aren't appreciated properly but that'll change, it just takes some time, the best artists aren't appreciated like they deserve until long after they're dead, Beyer says, yes it's almost always like that, he says

Quality, quality and truth always win out, he says

But it can take a while, he says

It takes a long time but in the end truth will out, as the Bard says, Beyer says

and he says that it might take a long time before my pictures are sold at the price they deserve, most likely neither he nor I will live to see it, in any case he won't, but I have to believe what he says even if neither of us will live long enough to confirm the truth of his words, he says, but I, my pictures, a day will come when they are recognized as the most important works of Norwegian painting, nothing less, he says

Oh now I don't know about that, I say

You know it perfectly well, he says

and Beyer's voice is firm

Yes, deep inside I probably do know something like that, I say

and then we're standing there in silence and Beyer says that I've already achieved a lot, I've had my work bought by the National Museum of Art in Oslo, I have several paintings there, and several public institutions have bought pictures, and I mustn't forget that The Bjørgvin Museum of Art has bought several paintings, still, most of my pictures, almost all, have been bought by ordinary people who really liked my pictures, and that's also because he didn't price them too high, a little high but not too high, since actually not a single one of my pictures has been sold for too high a price, he says, so you can't complain, he says, there's no reason to be dissatisfied, when I sometimes have even had shows at the Arts Festival in Bjørgvin, I've been an Arts Festival Artist, which is maybe the greatest honour a Norwegian visual artist can be given, he says, admittedly there were some people who weren't happy about the show, there's always someone who feels the need to act all big and important, and the person who was, and still is, the art critic for *The Bjørgvin Times* wrote that choosing me as The Arts Festival Artist was extremely strange, there were lots of people who painted better than me, he wrote, that idiot, Beyer says, but the art critic for *The Bjørgvin Times* has never understood art and it's strange, Beyer says, that so often the people with the least feeling for what's good art and bad art are the ones who decide to study art and become art critics, so in a way it was just as well that *The Bjørgvin Times* doesn't even review my shows anymore, they did for the first few years, because back then Anne Sofie Grieg was the critic and she always wrote good, thorough reviews, but then the guy who thinks my pictures are too airy, too wispy, yes, too mystical, started writing for them and he only stopped recently and the newspaper started reviewing my shows again, and that's good too, really, maybe that's the best thing, despite everything, Beyer says and then he says that I probably won't come to the opening this year either, will I, no of course not, he says

No, I say

and he says that I've never been to a single one of my openings, and I don't agree to interviews anymore, he says, it was better when I did every now and then, and that was before I stopped drinking, no, I don't exactly make it easy for him to sell my pictures, I don't go to openings and I don't give interviews, Beyer says, and he says that even so, despite that, my pictures usually sell well, usually all my paintings sell, or almost all, and the ones that don't he keeps and when there are enough for a show of their own he sends them to The Kleinheinrich Gallery in Oslo, and they're sold there, yes, almost all of them, and the pictures that don't sell there he takes back, and sooner or later they'll be exhibited in Nidaros, he says, but my best paintings stay in Bjørgvin, Beyer says and he gives a good laugh and now, yes, now there'll soon be enough paintings that didn't sell either in Bjørgvin or in Oslo for a show in Nidaros, the exhibition planned for a long time at The Huysmann Gallery in Nidaros, yes, he and Huysmann have known each other for all these years, it's planned for this spring, so next year that'll be no fewer than three exhibitions, one in Oslo, one in Nidaros, and of course the yearly show at The Beyer Gallery, he says, next year I'll sell more paintings than ever before, Beyer says and he says that we can't just stay standing around like this chatting away, it's stopped raining so now we need to get the pictures inside, and then he puts a doorstop under the front door to hold it open and I go and open the door to the back of the car and then I say that I can carry the pictures inside on my own and Beyer says thanks thank you and he says that he's so eager to see the pictures that he can barely wait, he says and then I go and get two pictures and Beyer goes into the gallery and he opens the door to The Bank and I go in there and I carefully put the paintings down on the floor and then I go back out and get more paintings and carry them inside and then I get the last two and carry them in and put them down in The Bank and then I go back into the gallery and Beyer shuts the door to The Bank and he says that it's good to have the paintings safe and sound in The Bank, and he says that he's looking forward to taking what I call the blankets off the paintings like a child looks forward to Christmas presents, yes

That's how I like to do it, Beyer says

and I have to bring in the paintings wrapped in blankets, he says, and I say yes, right, and then we don't say anything

Yes, well, typical Bjørgvin weather today, Beyer says

As soon as we get some snow the rain starts, he says

Yes, I say

But it's good that it lets up every now and then between the showers, he says

And it feels good to have gotten the pictures in here, he says

and then Beyer says that he always waits to look at the pictures, to unwrap them and look at them, until he's about to hang the exhibition, and since that's what we always do he'll do it alone this year too? Beyer says and I nod and I've painted the pictures' titles on the back same as always, haven't I, on the top edge of the stretcher, and then signed the picture itself with a big A in the lower right corner? he says and I nod and then Beyer says so everything's as it should be and after he's unpacked the pictures and hung them the way they're going to be in the show he'll take a photograph of each picture and then he'll price the pictures and prepare a list of pictures with the title and price of each one, in the order they're hung in, he says

We'll do it the same way we've always done it, I say

Yes, this isn't our first time, is it, Beyer says

and he says it's my annual Christmas show, and I think I've never liked that expression, Christmas show, it's really a marketing term, but that's exactly what Beyer is like, in large part, he's a huckster, a businessman, and he likes words like that, and in a way it's good that he's like that because I need to make money and if Beyer wasn't a huckster I'd probably be in bad shape when it came to money, I think, and then I think that even though I like Beyer a lot there's something about him that makes me uncomfortable, so we've never truly become friends, we're too dissimilar for that, maybe it has to do with me being a country kid and he a city kid, maybe it's because his family are big city people and mine are more humble, just ordinary country people, I think, and I think Beyer's a good person, I like him, but I do get tired of him pretty quickly, he gets on my nerves, there's something about his eagerness that gets to me, so whenever we see each other it's always a pretty short meeting and a bit forced and I tell Beyer I have to leave, I have some errands I need to run, I say, and then I ask Beyer if he'd be so kind as to call me a cab and Beyer says of course of course and then he goes to the telephone and calls for a taxi and then he comes over to me and says that a taxi'll be here right away and then we stand there by the door to the gallery and look out at the rain and slush and neither of us says anything and then Beyer says just to say something that he's really looking forward to these pictures, he's as excited to take them out of their blankets as a little boy is to unwrap his Christmas presents, he says and he says that he has to wait, and not look, not peek, no, he'll wait until three days before the opening and only then will he take the blankets off the pictures, one by one, and then he'll look at each picture for a long time before carrying it into the gallery and putting it on the floor where he thinks it should be hung, and then he'll go and get a new picture, one by one, until all the pictures are standing against the wall on the floor of the gallery and then he'll stand and look at each picture for a long time one by one and think about how each

picture goes with the next one and so on and then he'll move the
pictures around until they're in the order he sees in his mind, and
most of the time, when it comes to my paintings, he can feel sure
of it pretty quickly but it doesn't always go so well with other artists, but it's important that the whole show is like a single picture,
because as soon as someone comes into the room they should feel
like they've kind of entered into a picture, the room itself should
be like a picture, a picture you can enter into, Beyer says and I
think that it's obvious that the picture all my pictures come from
would in a way fill the room, I think and Beyer says that he doesn't
know what exactly makes it that way, it's not something to put into
words, because you can't put what a good picture says into words,
and as for my pictures the closest he can get is to say that there's an
approaching distance, something far away that gets closer, in my
pictures, it's as if something imperceptible becomes perceptible and
yet still stays imperceptible, it's still hidden, it is something staying
hidden, if you can say it that way, my pictures kind of talk to the
person looking and at the same time it's impossible to say what the
picture says, because it's a silent kind of talking to you, yes, that's
what it is for him, Beyer says and then he says that he's just blabbing
away and I see a taxi pull into one of the parking places in front of
The Beyer Gallery and stop next to my car and Beyer holds out his
hand to me and says thank you thank you and we'll talk again soon
and I say thank you too and then I go out to the taxi and I open
the rear door and I get in and I say I want to go to The Hospital

I think I just drove you to The Hospital yesterday, or whatever day it was, The Taxi Driver says

It's possible, I say

and even though he recognizes me I have no memory of him
at all

Yes I do believe it must've been you, he says

May well be, I say

Are you going in for a checkup or something? The Taxi
Driver says

and he turns his head a little to look at me

No I'm visiting a friend, I say

and The Taxi Driver drives and doesn't say anything and then he says that it's always like this in Bjørgvin, as soon as it snows it starts raining, he says, and that's all well and good as long as it doesn't get cold enough for the sludge to freeze to ice, yes, then you're risking life and limb to walk or drive in Bjørgvin, he says, but life must go on, even in icy conditions, The Taxi Driver says and then he sits there silent for a moment and then he signals and pulls over in front of The Hospital and stops by the entrance and he says how much it'll be and I pay and then I say thank you for the ride and then I go into The Hospital and I go over to the reception desk and the woman sitting there slides the window open and I say who I am and the person I'd like to see please and the woman sitting at the reception desk flips through some pages and then says that Asle has to rest, it's written here that no one can disturb him, no one can go see him, the doctors have decided that, he needs his rest, he needs to get his rest, he needs peace and quiet, she says and I ask when she thinks I'll be able to visit Asle and she says that she can't say and then she says that I can call The Hospital and ask when I can come

I guess you're saying he's seriously ill? I say

Yes that's what that means, she says

But is his life in danger? I say

It's possible, she says

and I stand without moving and without saying anything

I'm a close friend, it was me who brought him in, I say

and she nods

First we went to The Clinic and then they sent him here to The Hospital, I say

and she nods and says yes if someone is seriously ill then they're transferred at once from The Clinic to The Hospital

Yes, I say

But I just wonder if he needs anything? if there's anything I can bring him? or buy for him? I say

129

and the woman sitting at the reception says that I don't need to worry about that, he doesn't need anything besides what he has now, he's just lying in bed and sleeping most of the time to regain his strength, she says and I say thank you and I stare blankly straight ahead into empty space and nothingness and I see Asle lying there with lots of tubes connected to his body, and there's another bed in the room with someone lying in it, and then there's a man in a white coat sitting on a chair, and Asle's body is shaking and shaking, he's trembling the whole time, shuddering, and then he suddenly stops and is calm and the man sitting on the chair looks at Asle and then he gets up and goes over and shakes Asle by the shoulder

Asle, he says

Yes, Asle says

and it's as if he's saying it from far far away, but he says yes and then the man who shook him by the shoulder goes back and sits down on the chair again and then the woman sitting at the reception desk asks if everything's all right and I say yes and then I ask her if she can call me a taxi and she says that she can see a taxi sitting outside The Hospital, it's probably free, she says, so I could go ask if that one's free first, she says, and if it isn't free then of course she'll call a cab for me, she says and I say thank you thank you and then I say that I'll call tonight to ask if I can come in the morning and the woman sitting at the reception desk says that it's fine for me to wait until the morning, because they'll only decide in the morning if he's able to receive visitors or not, she says, and I say thanks very much, thank you for your help, I say and she says it was nothing and then I go out to the taxi that's stopped there and it's the same car that drove me to The Hospital still parked outside The Hospital and I look at The Taxi Driver and he nods and I open the rear door and I get in and The Taxi Driver says that was a short visit and I say that I couldn't see the person I wanted to see because The Doctor had said that he needed to rest, to sleep, and no one could visit him, I say, that was The Doctor's decision, I say

Yes that's how it is sometimes, The Taxi Driver says

Is that why you didn't drive away, because you thought that might happen? I say

No, The Taxi Driver says

and then he says that there's often someone in front of The Hospital who needs a taxi, so once he's driven here, if he's not called of for another ride, then it's just as good to wait here, more often than not someone comes out before long who needs a taxi, he says, and now and then it's like what happened with me, that someone a person wants to visit isn't allowed to have visitors, for whatever reason, and then whoever took the taxi to The Hospital needs another taxi right away, he says

And where would you like to go now? he says

To The Country Inn, I say

Yes I thought so, he says

and then The Taxi Driver says that he's sure I've ridden with him before, he recognizes me in any case, and he thinks that he's taken me to The Country Inn before, but he also thinks it was The Hospital, he doesn't exactly remember, but there's something familiar about me anyway, yes, now he remembers, his memory is so bad, he's driven me home to my apartment lots of times, yes, that's it, he's driven me lots of times from The Alehouse back to my apartment in Sailor's Cove, he says and I wasn't entirely sober then either, no, he says, far from it, he's driven me home from The Last Boat, that's it, The Taxi Driver says, yes, there's no doubt about it now, but no matter how drunk I was I've always behaved well, and I've always paid, given a good tip, yes, he remembers now, and then, many years ago, he also saw a picture of me in *The Bjørgvin Times*, I'm a painter and the article had something to do with an exhibition at The Beyer Gallery, so that was why he picked me up there, outside the gallery, he says, and my name is Asle or something like that, isn't it? The Taxi Driver says and I say yes, that's my name, yes, and I say I recognize him, The Taxi Driver, I recognize him too

So you're an artist? he says

Yes, at least I try, I say

But you make enough to live on from that? he says

More or less, I say

Well then, The Taxi Driver says

and then it's silent

Selling your pictures brings in enough for you to live on? he says

Yes, I say

Yes, aha, he says

and then he says that the kinds of pictures I paint must be really expensive, not for the likes of him, just for rich people, he says and I don't say anything

Or is that not true? he says

All kinds of people buy my pictures, I say

I don't believe it, The Taxi Driver says

and there's silence and then he asks if I'm going to have another show at The Beyer Gallery soon and I say yes, that a show of mine will be opening there soon

Then I think I'll go look at your pictures, he says

But they probably don't look like anything? he says

Anyway it probably costs a lot to get in, right, to your exhibition at The Beyer Gallery? he asks

and I say that it doesn't cost anything, anyone who wants to can go look at the paintings, I say and The Taxi Driver says well then he'll definitely go take a look since now it's like he knows me a little, the artist himself, yes, so he'll go look at my pictures because he likes paintings well enough, yes, even if they don't look like anything, the most important thing is for the picture to say something, kind of, that it's not just scribbles and smears but painted to really say something, yes, that's when he likes the painting, The Taxi Driver says and he turns around and looks straight at me before turning back forwards, he likes a painting if it has something to say, yes, he says, so he might really like my paintings, and since he's driven me home so many times he's now pretty interested in seeing how I paint, and now that he thinks about it he feels like he's driven me when I was sober too, yes indeed, he says and I see The Country Inn up ahead and The Taxi Driver pulls over and stops in front of The Coffeehouse

Yes well here we are, he says

and he turns his head to look at me and says how much it is and I hold out the money and he says yeah of course he remembers me, he's driven me home from The Alehouse, The Last Boat, so many times, how could he not have recognized me at once, no, he says, and Asle or something, that's my name, right? he says and I say yes and I pay and then The Taxi Driver says that this year he'll go look at my paintings, for sure, he says

Because they are paintings, right? he says

Yes, I say

Good, paintings are what I like, he says

and I say take care and he says thanks you too and then I open the door and get out and then I go right into The Coffeehouse and there, at the window table nearest the door, a woman with medium-length blonde hair is sitting, and her hair looks like the hair of the woman I met the day before yesterday, the one who showed me the way to The Country Inn when I somehow managed to get lost in the snowstorm here in Bjørgvin and who watched Asle's dog, who lived in The Lane, who was apparently named Guro, but then again there are so many women with medium-length blonde hair, and there's a suitcase and a couple of shopping bags next to her, so it can't be the woman I met the day before yesterday, but the woman sitting there does look like her, she really does, so it might be her, I think and I walk into The Coffeehouse and it's empty inside and I pick a window table as far back as possible and I take off my brown leather shoulder bag and put it down on a chair and then I take off my black coat and put it on top of the shoulder bag and I go over to the counter and I pour myself a coffee, and I take milk in my coffee, and then I go to the cash register and I see that they've hung up the lunch menu, so I can buy lunch now if I want, and I look over the menu and I see that there's nothing there I want, they sell homemade meatballs every day at The Coffeehouse but I don't feel like that today, or like any of the other dishes either, because I'm not that hungry, just a little hungry, it's like I have to eat just a little something, I think, so I'll probably get the usual then, I think and I say I'd like bacon and eggs please and the woman sitting at the register says that's fine, I can just find a table and sit down and she'll bring me my food, she says, I just need to get my own knife and fork, she says and then I get a knife and fork and napkin and I go put them on the table and then I go and get *The Northern Herald*, which is on a pole along with *The Bjørgvin Times*, and *The Northern Herald* is a good paper, every so often there's the rare good review of an art exhibition, sometimes of mine, not always just sarcastic criticism like in *The Bjørgvin Times*, I think and I cautiously peek over at the woman with the medium-length blonde hair and she looks exactly like the woman who helped me the day before yesterday, so it must be her, but surely it's just someone who looks like her because otherwise she'd surely have recognized me and said hello, or said something like wasn't I going right home yesterday? or had I driven back into Bjørgvin from Dylgja again today? she might have said, but she's just sitting there with a cup of coffee reading a news- paper, or looking at a newspaper anyway, and there's a suitcase on the floor next to her, and a couple of bags, so she's someone who's visiting town and is about to go home again, or maybe someone who's about to catch an express ferry either north or south, since the ferryboats are docked not far from The Coffeehouse, you just need to go a few hundred feet along The Pier and then there you are, and that's why there are often people who are about to take an express ferry sitting and waiting in The Coffeehouse, and if they need to spend the night in Bjørgvin they like spending the night at The Country Inn, I think and the woman's probably someone visit- ing town and most likely she's spent the night at The Country Inn and now she's sitting and waiting for an express ferry, you can say speedboat so why can't you say speedferry? and it'll go express, of course, to somewhere north or somewhere south, I think and then I realize that she's looking at me in a way that seems to mean she knows who I am and then she looks back down at her newspaper and then she looks up again and I think she definitely recognizes me, or at least knows who I am, I think, but even if I can't see any difference between her and the woman from the day before yesterday, because I can't, it can't be the woman from the day before yesterday, so she must be recognizing me from something else, maybe she's someone who saw a picture of me a long time ago in *The Bjørgvin Times*, when I was the Arts Festival Artist or something, and there were also some interviews in *The Northern Herald* before I totally stopped giving interviews, because if she was the woman from the day before yesterday she would absolutely for sure have said something to me, no, you again? hello, nice to see you again, something, she would have said something like that, but the woman sitting there now is just shyly looking down at a newspaper and sitting as if she's just thinking her thoughts, and I've found a window table all the way at the back of The Coffeehouse, and there's no one else here, just me and the woman with the medium-length blonde hair sitting at a table near the front door with a suitcase and a couple of bags next to her, and I'm sitting at a window table looking out, down at The Pier, at The Bay, and I think that even though there are two newspapers you can read for free at The Coffeehouse I always read only *The Northern Herald*, never *The Bjørgvin Times*, because *The Bjørgvin Times* is full of stupidity and foolishness and nothing else, I think and it looks like that's the paper the woman with the medium-length blonde hair is sitting there reading while I sit here paging through *The Northern Herald*, and it's really unbelievable how much she looks like the woman who helped me the day before yesterday, no, I don't want to think anymore about that, because it's eerie, almost uncanny, I think, and then there's the fact that I can't go see Asle, that must mean he's seriously ill, yes, maybe even dying, anyway it's possible that he'll die, and it was mostly to visit Asle that I came to Bjørgvin today, and also to deliver the pictures, but that could've waited a few days, and then I was thinking I'd go sit in St Paul's Church but that totally slipped my mind, yes, after I'd gone to The Hospital and hadn't been allowed in to see Asle I thought that all I wanted to do was go to The Coffeehouse and then drive back home to Dylgja, but there was no big hurry to take the pictures to Bjørgvin, actually I could've waited a few days before taking the paintings to The Beyer Gallery, I didn't need to drive to Bjørgvin until next week, so it was really only to look in on Asle that I drove to Bjørgvin again today, because maybe he needed something? maybe I could get him something from his apartment? something he wanted, maybe a sketchpad? a pencil? yes, everything's kind of run together a bit for me, I think, it's all a bit mixed up in my mind, but the day before yesterday I drove to and from Bjørgvin and then back to Bjørgvin again because I suddenly decided I needed to go see Asle, and I found him lying in the snow, he could have easily frozen to death, it was so cold, so it was certainly good that I came back, yes, no matter how much driving I'd just done, I think and then I see a woman come over and she has a plate with bread and eggs and bacon in her hands, the bacon is nice and crispy, the bacon at The Coffeehouse is always cut in thin slices and then almost charred, and then I feel how hungry I am and this'll be good, I think, because crispy bacon and eggs at The Coffeehouse, no, there's nothing better to eat than that, not in Bjørgvin anyway, unless it's the potato dumplings they serve at The Coffeehouse every Thursday, I think and I start eating right away, and I certainly was hungry, that's for sure, and it tastes good, and the reason I like bacon and eggs so much probably has something to do with always thinking it was so good when Grandmother made it for me when I was young, she fried the bacon and then fried the eggs with onions, and that might have been the very best thing in the world when I was little, I think and I eat and I take a sip of coffee and then I hear footsteps and I look over and I see the woman with the medium-length blonde hair, the woman named Guro, walking over to me and she says no, I'm back in Bjørgvin again? wasn't I going to drive straight home? she sure was surprised to see a man with a grey ponytail sitting there in the back of The Coffeehouse, and she thought it must be me, she was sure it was me, she says and I think that it must be the woman who was by the door who's come over, and that she seems to be the woman I talked to the day before yesterday, who took the dog to sleep at her place, and I look at the front door and the woman who was sitting by the door is still sitting there and looking down at her newspaper, and the suitcase and bags are still on the floor next to her, and the woman talking to me now, yes, this is Guro, and she looks exactly like the woman sitting by the door

What a surprise, she says

I thought you had to drive home, after you picked up the dog, she says

and I nod and chew and swallow the food in my mouth and then I say that I did drive home but then I thought it was time to bring the paintings for my next show to The Beyer Gallery, I say and the woman named Guro says that I usually have one exhibition a year at The Beyer Gallery, during Advent, it opens a little before Christmas, she says

Yes, I say

And I've seen, yes, well, I think I've seen every one of your exhibitions, she says

and I don't say anything

And I've bought two paintings, too, she says

and she says that she's probaby already told me but it's been many years since she could afford to buy pictures, now she can't, it was back when she lived with, yes, The Fiddler that she could afford paintings, but he'd cleared out to East Norway and moved in with some woman or another

And then I got some from you too, she says

and I look at her

You remember that much, don't you? she says

and I don't understand what she means

Since you've been in my place so many times, she says

and she smiles and winks at me

And spent the night lots of times too, she says

and I don't understand what she's saying, what she's talking about

But you probably don't remember that, you were probably drinking too much back then? she says

and she asks if she can sit down and I say of course she can, yes, please do, I say and she says that after she buys a cup of coffee she'll come and sit down and have a chat, she says and I see her go over to the counter and I eat the rest of my bacon and eggs and I think that now I'll again never get away from this Guro, I think, because, no, there's not something wrong with her, but I can't exactly say that I enjoy her company, I just wanted to sit by myself for a while, I think and I pick up my coffee cup and I drink up all the coffee and Guro comes back with her coffee cup and she puts it down on the other side of the table and she says she comes by The Coffeehouse almost every day

Yes, The Coffeehouse is like a second home for me, she says

and we don't say anything

And it's good that you can't buy beer or wine at The Coffee-house, she says

and she says that otherwise she might all too easily do that, but in the morning, yes, during the day, it's better to avoid alcohol, she says, when he couldn't do that anymore was when it started to go wrong with The Fiddler and even then she didn't touch alcohol until late afternoon at the earliest, but sometimes she gets tired of sitting in the apartment with her Hardanger embroidery and then

she likes walking over to The Coffeehouse, she says, yes, to see
people, and run into people she knows sometimes too, sometimes
there are people from back home there, people she knows from
when she was growing up, visiting town on holiday, because nowadays almost everyone from the country comes for a visit at some
point, well, no, not everyone, there are lots of people she knows
who never leave where they're from, she says, it just never seems to
happen, the same way they sort of never seem to do anything, yes,
Hardanger was where they were born and Hardanger was where
they stayed, and some of them have probably never seen anywhere
else besides where in Hardanger they were born and raised, she
says, it was like a rule in earlier times, for many of them, to stay
where they were born, Guro says and I realize that I don't want to
say anything and I think that I have to say that I have an appointment, something I need to do, that I have to go

    Sorry, I have to go, I say

    What? Guro says

    Why? she says

    I don't have much time, I say

    You have to go? she says

    Yes, I say

    That wasn't much of a chat, she says

    But you really should look me up next time you're in Bjørg-
vin, she says

    and I say I will

    You promise? she says

    and then she smiles

    You used to do it a lot, she says

    and we don't say anything

    But you don't really remember do you? she says

    And I got a bunch of small pictures from you, she says

    And then I bought two big ones, she says

    Yes, my apartment's like a little gallery of your paintings,
she says

I don't have much time, I say

Yes, I understand, she says

See you around, I say

Yes, see you soon, she says

and I get up and put on my long black coat and I drape the brown leather shoulder bag over my shoulder and I say bye and she says bye take care and then I go and now I should go straight to my car that's sitting parked outside The Beyer Gallery and then I should drive home to my good old house in Dylgja, and it'll be good to get home, it'll be so good to have a little peace and quiet, I think and now I shouldn't look at the woman sitting alone near the door, the woman who looks exactly like Guro, yes, there is no difference at all between them, I think, so now I just need to get outside and then I'll walk to my car that's sitting outside The Beyer Gallery, and then I'll drive home to Dylgja, and it'll be good to get home, I think, and I get outside and I go up the pavement and then I take a right and I walk for a bit and then I take a left and then I go up The Lane and it was 3, The Lane, where she lived, right? the woman who says her name is Guro and who says that I've been to her place so many times, and that I've given her paintings, but just small ones, and that she bought two paintings herself, and that her apartment there in The Lane is like a little gallery of my paintings, I think and it's grey nasty weather, it's been raining, and I walk through slush, the street's pretty slushy, but luckily it hasn't gotten cold enough for the slush to freeze into ice, otherwise it would be hard to walk on this steep Lane, but now it's fine, except just a little slippery, but if you have good shoes on it's fine and I do, I think, and I get to the top of The Lane and I turn right on High Street and I see my car parked in front of The Beyer Gallery next to Beyer's car and I go straight to my car and I get in and it starts on the first try and I turn the heat on full blast, because it's cold in the car, and I turn on the windshield wipers because the front windshield is totally covered with rain and sludge and then I pull out of the parking space and then I drive the roads I know, that I've driven on so many times, the way Beyer taught me to drive back in the day so that I could get out of Bjørgvin, and I realize that I'm not thinking about anything, it's like there's been too much for me, and it feels good to be driving, I notice, and the car just needs to warm up and then everything'll be good, and now I shouldn't think about anything, I think, and I realize that I don't have any desire to paint, and it's been a long time since I haven't wanted to paint, and then there's the picture with those two lines that cross, I don't want to see that picture again, I have to get rid of it, I have to paint over it, because it's a destructive picture, or maybe it's a good picture? but in any case I don't want to sell it, but maybe I can take it up to the attic and keep it with the other pictures I don't want to sell? I think and I reach the country road and the car is more or less warm now and I drive steadily and calmly, almost slowly, north and I feel something like happiness inside me, almost joy, because now I'll be home soon, now I'm going back home to my house in Dylgja, and if I don't want to paint anymore then I don't have to and it does me good to think that, to think that if I don't want to paint anymore I don't have to do it, I think and I drive north and I don't think about anything, I try not to think about anything and I don't look at the building where Asle's apartment is, in Sailor's Cove, and I won't look at the brown house where Ales and I used to live, or at the turn-off where I stopped the day before yesterday and saw the two young people in the playground there, I think and it's raining but the roads are clear and it's not slippery driving on them and I feel so tired and that's not so strange, because I drove to Bjørgvin today despite everything, and I brought my paintings to Beyer, and now I'm driving home again, and I went to The Hospital, and I wasn't allowed to see Asle, and I went to The Coffeehouse and got some food and talked with Guro there and also saw someone who looked exactly like her, a woman sitting near the front door with a suitcase and two bags next to her, so no wonder I'm tired, I think and I fall into a kind of daze, and it's nice driving a car when I don't think about anything and just pay attention to the driving, yes, there's something about it I really like, just driving along not thinking about anything, I think and now I'm at Instefjord and I take a left and I drive out along Sygne Fjord and now I won't look up at the grey house where Asle's sister lives, in Øygna, the woman who's also named Guro, I'll just keep driving, I think and I drive slowly and steadily along Sygne Fjord and I think that I don't want to look at Åsleik's house and farm when I get to them either, I think and I keep driving, and I drive past Åsleik's farm and I just keep driving, and I really like driving, because even if the roads are small and winding I really like it, I think and all the snow is gone now, the roads are clear, I haven't noticed any ice anywhere, and I see my house, my beautiful old house, and I'm filled with happiness and I turn into the driveway and I drive up and stop the car in front of the house and when I get out of the car I hear Bragi barking, poor Bragi, I wasn't thinking about you, I totally forgot about you, I think, poor you, you must be hungry and thirsty, and you must need to go out too, I think and it's so terrible, Bragi's barking, I think and I go into the house and I hear Bragi scratching at the door to the main room and I open the door and Bragi comes to me and he's jumping up at me and he's barking and wagging his tail and I pet his back

Poor dog, Bragi, I say

Poor doggy, you had to be alone for so long, Bragi, I say

and I realize it's a little cold in the room, so I need to start a fire in the stove, I think, and then I'll lie down on the bench and rest a little, I think, but first Bragi needs to get some fresh air, I think and I go out into the hall and I open the front door and Bragi runs outside and over to the grass as quick as he can and as soon as he gets to the grass he lifts his leg and he stays there pissing for a long time and then he walks around sniffing a little and I call Bragi but he keeps on sniffing and I call Bragi lots of times but he doesn't listen and then I see that the dog is hunching up, with his rear end out, and his tail in the air, and he takes a good long shit and when he's done he comes running up towards me

Good doggy, I say

What a clever dog you are, Bragi, I say

and then I pet him on his back and we go in to the kitchen and I hear a clattering noise and I see Bragi bumping his empty water dish

No, you don't have any water, I say

and I pick up the bowl and I fill it with water and put it down for Bragi and he slurps and gulps his water

Oh you were really thirtsy weren't you, I say

and Bragi gulps his water down until the bowl is totally empty and I refill it and put it down for him and he slurps just a little water and I see that the food bowl is empty too and I crumble a slice of bread into pieces and I put them in the bowl and Bragi goes over and eats some of the pieces of bread and then he looks up at me and I think that he must want something else to eat, and that's understandable, I think, and later, later I'll find something else for him, I think and with Bragi at my heels I go into the main room and I go hang my shoulder bag up on the hook and I go over to the stove and I put some kindling and a few wood chips in and put two good logs on top, good dry birchwood, and I light the kindling and the fire starts right away and I think that it's good Åsleik gave me all the wood I need for a fire, the chips, the kindling, the logs, I think and I stay standing there and I look at the logs and I don't think anything, I just feel empty and tired, and I feel a lightness, and I don't exactly know why, and then I think that it must be because I thought that there was no need for me to paint anymore, I think, because I don't feel the slightest desire to paint, I feel almost an aversion to it, and I can't ever remember feeling like that before, I think and then I shut the stove hatch and I go out into the hall and take off my coat and hang it in its place and I hang the scarf on its hook and then I go

into the main room and put my velvet jacket on my chair next to
the round table and I sit down in the chair and Bragi comes over
and hops up and lies down in my lap and I stroke his back and I
think that it's nice to have a dog, yes, I need to get myself a dog,
that's what I actually want to do, and then I need to get a boat, a
sailboat, I really want to do that too, I think, and I've been thinking about getting a dog and a boat for years and years but it never
happened, I've been too busy painting, I think and I look at my
fixed spot in the water, at my landmark, the tops of the pines in
front of the house need to be in the middle of the middle right
pane, because the window is divided in half, and can be opened
from both sides, and each side of the window is divided into
three panes, and the middle one on the right side is where the
tops of the pines need to be, I think and then I look at my landmark, and at the waves out there in the Sygne Sea and I cross
myself and then I take out the rosary I have around my neck
under my pullover, the brown rosary with the wooden beads and
a wooden cross, and I hold the cross tight and then I pray a silent
prayer for Asle, that he'll get better, or if God wants to then he
should take Asle back to himself and let him find rest in God's
peace and I stay sitting there holding the cross at the bottom of
the rosary with the brown wooden beads that I always have
hanging around my neck and that I got from Ales once, I got lots
of rosaries from her, and I've taken good care of all of them, and
I got lots of scarves too, and I've also taken good care of those,
because when Ales asked me what I wanted for Christmas or as a
birthday present I always said I wanted either a rosary or a scarf
and then she said didn't I have enough rosaries and scarves too
and then I would answer yes, well, I did have a lot of rosaries and
a lot of scarves but there's nothing wrong with that and then Ales
would say that still I always used the same rosary, the brown one,
yes, the one I still have on, and I said I have a collection of them
and she said yes, yes, she knows, she can see that, because on the
wall behind the head end of the bench in the main room I had

put up a hook and I hung all the rosaries I had on it, and all of
them were from Ales, I think and I look at the rosaries hanging
there on the wall and I think that every so often I take them
down and sit and look at one or more of them, especially at the
ones Ales had, and she had only three, and I hung them up together with mine after she died, and when I sit with one of Ales's
rosaries in my hands we kind of talk to each other for a long time,
about anything and everything, before we say goodbye to each
other and say that it won't be long before we meet again and then
I hang the rosary back up on the hook, and I miss Ales so much,
and why did she have to die and leave me, so young, so suddenly?
I think and I hear Ales say that even though I always wear the
same rosary I do change the scarf I wear, and I say that I'm absolutely sure I've worn all the scarves she's given me, and she says
that I certainly have and then I hear Ales ask if I'm doing all right
and then I see her sitting in her chair, there to my right, there
next to the round table in front of the window, and I say I am,
but I miss her so much, and also I'm so scared about Asle, I say
and Ales says I shouldn't be, either he'll get better or God will
take him back, so I shouldn't be scared for him, Ales says, and
even though it's impossible to say anything about how she is,
now that she's dead, because in a way she's not like anything, well
yes she'd have to say that she's doing well, because there's kind of
no other way to say how she's doing, and when we talk together
we do have to use words, but words can say so little, almost nothing, and the less they say the more they say, in a way, Ales says
and she says she's always near me and then I say that I can't always
tell if it's God or her who's near me and Ales says that I don't need
to think about that, and I sit there holding tight to the cross at the
bottom of the rosary and I pray that things are good for Ales
where she is now, that God is good to her and Ales says don't I
understand that things are good for her and I say yes, yes, I can
feel it inside, I say and then I say that I have the feeling that I
don't want to paint anymore, and Ales says she can understand

that, I've painted so many pictures, I've done my part, maybe I've
painted my paintings, what I needed to paint, she says and even
if I don't paint anymore I'll get by, I'll have enough to live on,
Ales says and I say yes and then she says that maybe it won't be
long now before I too come back to God, come back to where I
come from, to where she is now, Ales says and I think that that's
how it is, a person comes from God and goes back to God, I
think, for the body is conceived and born, it grows and declines,
it dies and vanishes, but the spirit is a unity of body and soul, the
way form and content are an invisible unity in a good picture,
yes, there's a spirit in the picture so to speak, yes, the same as in
any work of art, in a good poem too, in a good piece of music,
yes, there is a unity that's the spirit in the work and it's the spirit,
the unity of body and soul, that rises up from the dead, yes, it's
the resurrection of the flesh, and it happens all the time and it
always happens when a person dies because then the person is
washed clean of sin, what separates the person from God is gone,
because then the person is back with God, yes, the innermost
picture inside me that all the pictures I've tried to paint are at-
tempting to look like, this innermost picture, that's a kind of soul
and a kind of body in one, yes, that's my spirit, what I call spirit,
it goes back to God and becomes part of God at the same time as
it stays itself, I think and Ales says that it is like that, insofar as it
can be thought and said in words that's what it's like, but it can't
be said in words, she says and I say no of course not and I say that
all religions and faith say, or try to say, something about that, and
they all do say it but in different ways, they're like languages, I
say, and actually they all say only the tiniest little bit about reali-
ties, yes, as I've so often said myself, just think if all the colours
had names, yes, how infinitely many names that would be, I say
and Ales says it wouldn't have been any better without language
and it's because we have the same belief, the same language, yes,
that we can talk together now, and it's our angels who let us do
that, Ales says, because actually it's her angel and my angel that

are talking to each other now, and for an angel to exist you have to believe it does, and you have to have a word for it, the word angel, and if you don't believe that God exists, well then God doesn't exist, neither in life nor when you're dead, so we need the word God, but deep down inside all people believe in God, they just don't know it, because God is so close that they don't notice him, and he's so far away that they don't notice him for that reason either, and it's just the same with the angel, with angels, but the dead are all still with God too, they've gone back to God, but they just don't know it, Ales says and I don't exactly know if I understand what she's saying and I don't exactly know what to say and then I say that I miss her and Ales says she misses me too, but even if we aren't together visibly on earth anymore we are still invisibly together and of course I can feel that, she says and I say I can, and she and I can talk sometimes together, I say and Ales says that we can but only because our angels are there and because I say or think her words, it's not she who's saying them, because now she is everything that exists in language, because God is the pure, the whole language, the language without division and separation, yes, something like that can be said too, Ales says and then she says that it won't be long before we're indivisibly together in God, the two of us together, like we were on earth, but in God, Ales says and she can't tell me what that's like, because people can't picture it, Ales says and I say that I'm tired and Ales says I can go lie down, yes, I need to, she says and I sit in my chair and I look at my landmark in the water, near the middle of the Sygne Sea, look out at the waves, and Ales's voice goes away and I hold the cross on the rosary tight and I see words before me and I say inside myself Pater noster Qui es in cælis Sanctificetur nomen tuum Adveniat regnum tuum Fiat voluntas tua sicut in cælo et in terra Panem nostrum quotidianum da nobis hodie et dimitte nobis debita nostra sicut et nos dimittimus debitoribus nostris Et ne nos inducas in tentationem sed libera nos a malo and I slide my thumb and finger up to the first bead between the cross and the group of three beads on the rosary and I say inside myself Our Father Who art in heaven Hallowed be thy name Thy kingdom come Thy will be done on earth as it is in heaven Give us this day our daily bread and forgive us our trespasses as we forgive those who trespass against us And lead us not into temptation but deliver us from evil and I slide my thumb and finger down to the brown wooden cross and I hold it and then I say, over and over again inside myself while I breathe in deeply Lord and while I breathe out slowly Jesus and while I breathe in deeply Christ and while I breathe out slowly Have mercy and while I breathe in deeply On me

V

AND I SEE MYSELF STANDING and looking at the picture with the two lines that cross near the middle and it's morning and today's Thursday and I've lit the stove and the room is starting to get warm, and yesterday I drove to Bjørgvin and delivered my paintings to Beyer, I think, and I feel exhausted and I stand in front of the easel and I look at those two lines that cross near the middle, one brown and one purple and I think that I don't like this picture, because I can't stand pictures that directly paint feelings even if I'm the only one who knows it, that isn't the kind of thing I paint, it's not the kind of thing I want to paint, because a painting can certainly be filled with feelings but you shouldn't paint feelings themselves, like screaming and weeping and wailing, I think, and I think that this is a truly bad painting, that's what it is, but at the same time it is what it needs to be, what it's going to be, it's done and there's no more to do on it and I hear Åsleik say St Andrew's Cross, emphasizing the words, he says the words with pride, emphasizing them, it's revolting, and it is a St Andrew's Cross, I think and I think that I need to put the picture away, or maybe I should just paint over it with white? I could do that, and once I've done it and the paint dries I can start painting a new picture on top of the St Andrew's Cross, but I don't want to do that, I don't have any desire to paint over this picture, in fact I have no desire whatsoever to paint anymore at all, I think, and the only thing I considered painting was painting over this picture in white, the same as I've done with so many other pictures, but I didn't do it, and maybe that's because there's something in this picture after all? maybe it's a good picture even though I don't like it? I think, because that often happens, that the pictures I dislike most are the best ones, and the ones I like best are the worst ones, strangely enough, that's the way it often is, how good or bad something is doesn't have anything to do with how much I like it or don't like it, only with how good or bad it is, whether it's good art or bad art, because art is about quality, not about liking or not liking it, not at all, and it's not about taste either, quality is something that just exists in the picture whether it's beautiful or ugly, and anyway for something to be beautiful it has to also be ugly, that's how it is, and of course good and evil exist in the same way, and right and wrong, and true and false, of course it can be hard to say whether something is good or evil, or right or wrong, or true or false, but most of the time it's clear enough, so it's usually easy to see if a painting is good or bad, if it's bad it's bad, and in that case it's just bad and there's nothing more to say about it, but if it's good it can be hard to say how good it is, and it's often the pictures I paint that I don't like, or don't entirely like, that are the best, that are my experience, they're a bit embarrassing for me in a way, it makes me feel a little queasy to look at them, I think and I don't want to look at this painting with the two lines crossing anymore and since I don't want to look at it I might as well put it aside with the other pictures leaning against the wall with the stretchers facing out, in the stack of pictures I'm not done with yet, there between the door to the side room and the hall door, I think, and my brown leather shoulder bag is hanging on the hook above them, because yesterday I drove all the paintings I was done with down to Beyer and dropped them off there, yes, after Åsleik had chosen the picture he wanted to give Sister for Christmas I drove the finished paintings down to Bjørgvin yesterday, so the place where the finished paintings usually go is empty now, I think, but I can't stand this picture with the two lines that cross, it makes me feel sick to look at it, I have to get rid of it, and maybe it's not even a picture at all? but at the same time I don't want to paint over it with white paint, and I don't want to set it aside in the stack of pictures I'm not totally satisfied with, and there are a lot of pictures there, and all of them are big paintings, or bigger, none are that big, and it's good they're big, I think, because I've realized I don't want to paint anymore at all, maybe I've painted enough, painted myself out, maybe I'm done, I'll give up painting, and the unfinished pictures actually are finished in their way, they're surely not that bad the way they are, I think and in that case I have, as I thought, enough pictures for three more shows aside from the ones I delivered yesterday, I think, so that's one exhibition at The Beyer Gallery, and then one in Oslo, which Beyer already has enough pictures for, and then finally the one in Nidaros, the exhibition at The Huysmann Gallery that's been planned for years, and that Beyer now thinks he has enough pictures for, out of the pictures that didn't sell either in Bjørgvin or in Oslo, so I can just bring all the pictures I have in my house to Dylgja, the unfinished ones over there plus the ones I have stored in crates, take them to Beyer and then he'll probably start in again talking about how I just never stop, I keep going like a roman-fleuve, he's said that over and over again, yes, it's just like with Åsleik, Åsleik feels proud of himself when he can use an unusual word and Beyer feels proud in the same way when he can use a French word or expression, roman-fleuve, Beyer says and he glows with pride and he says that every exhibition has a unity of its own, its own totality, or entirety, as if it's not completely ended or finished, as if there's something still fragmentary about it that as it were looks forward to the next one, that's also true, and so that's how one exhibition follows the other, like a river, yes, a picture-river, Beyer says and I think that with three exhibitions I'll probably make a decent amount of money, plus I have a little in the bank, and soon I'll be able to collect a pension and

then I'll be set, I'll get money every month whether I do anything or not, I think, and it'll be good to get a fixed amount of
money every month because to tell the truth that's never happened in my whole life, I've painted pictures to sell them and
that's how I've made the money I need, I think, and if I stop
painting and don't have to buy what I need for painting anymore
then I'll hardly have any expenses, because I already have what I
need, yes, my car is fine, I bought it just about five years ago, so
I'll have that car for as long as I live, or as long as I'm able to
drive, I think, but this painting here, the one with the two lines
that cross, yes now what should I do with that? it was so wrong
not to let Åsleik take it, he wanted it to give to Sister, but maybe
I can put it up in the attic with the pictures I want to keep and
not sell, and that I'm now kind of tempted to just get rid of, yes,
that's probably what I'll do, but not right now, I think and I feel
sure in my whole body that I have no desire to paint anymore,
none at all, and I don't understand why this feeling has come over
me so suddenly, I've always liked painting, ever since I was a boy,
and I don't understand it, I think and I think that even if I don't
like the picture of the two lines that cross each other it might still
be a good picture, that may be, but I don't know if it's bad or
good, I only know that I don't like it and that I don't want to
paint over it with white paint and that anyway I probably need to
put it away, I think and I think again that it was stupid not to let
Åsleik have the painting to give to Sister for Christmas, but I
didn't want to give it to him, still, that was the picture he wanted
as a gift for Sister, and then he picked another one and took it
instead, probably the best of the big paintings I'd finished for the
show at The Beyer Gallery, the one called Silent Boat, yes, Åsleik
knows whether a picture's good or bad, so now probably the best
picture I've managed to paint since my last show at The Beyer
Gallery hasn't gone to Bjørgvin, and there's a kind of floating
boat in the picture Åsleik chose, and the picture is brown and
purple, but what really makes the picture good and makes it

shine is the thin layer of white paint white brushstrokes I added
when I looked at the picture in the darkness, when I glazed it, as
they say, and of course that's just the picture Åsleik wanted, the
best picture I'd painted in a long time, and I couldn't say no,
because he's always gotten his choice of paintings, he could
choose freely, but only a small painting, this year was the first
time I let him pick a big one and then of course he had to pick
the best one, I think and I look at Bragi who's standing on the
floor looking up at me and I say Bragi and he comes over to me
and I rub his fur and I think I need to go get him a little food and
see if he still has water, I think, and then do I need to walk him?
since he is standing there looking at me? yes he's both hungry and
thirsty and he needs to go, I think, but it's probably better if I let
him outside first so that he can go, I think and I go out into the
hall and I open the front door and I think that outside it's about
as light as it's going to get this time of year, and I see Bragi run
around in circles in the snow, because it snowed a lot again last
night, snow one day and rain the next and then snow again the
day after, I think and it's like Bragi is washing himself in the
snow before he stops and raises one leg and his piss leaves a yellow
hole in the snow, and he pisses for a long time, yes he sure needed to go, I think and then Bragi jumps around in the snow some
more and spins and rolls around in the loose white snow and then
I call him

Bragi, Bragi, I call

and he comes running up to me and he stops in front of me
and he shakes himself, shakes from side to side, so that most of
the snow falls off him, and then I say let's go inside now and Bragi comes inside and I shut the door and we go back into the main
room and I feel how tired I am, so tired, and I think I'll just sit
down and I see my chair there next to the round table, the one
on the left, and I go sit down in the chair and then Bragi comes
and jumps up and lies down in my lap and I take my bearings, the
tops of the pines outside my house need to be in the middle of

the middle pane on the right of the div- ided window, and then I look at the sea, at the place in the water I always look at, near the middle of the Sygne Sea, at the waves and I see Asle sitting on his bed upstairs in The Shoemaker's Workshop and Mother and Father have just driven off and Asle lies down on the bed and he lies there and he stares straight ahead and he thinks that tomorrow he'll go to The Academic High School, and he thinks he knows the way there, and he'll leave for school nice and ear- ly, Asle thinks, and he'll be wearing his black velvet jacket and leather shoulder bag, the same as he always wears, he thinks, be- cause he saw a black velvet jacket at a shop in Stranda and bought it on the spot, and in another shop he found the brown leather bag, and ever since then he's always had his black velvet jacket and brown leather shoulder bag on and Mother said that it looked so stupid, going around in a black velvet jacket, and then with his brown hair so long, down his back, and then with a shoulder bag too, Mother said and Asle told her she can say whatever she wants but he'll dress however he wants and have his hair how he wants it too, he says and then he walks away from Mother in his black velvet jacket and he has a sketchpad and a pencil in his brown leather shoulder bag, and now he'll have his schoolbooks in it too, Asle thinks and he sits up on the edge of the bed and he thinks he might as well take a walk outside and maybe go to The Co-op Store and buy himself something or other, because he's the one who has to go shopping for his own food now, he thinks, and then he needs to unpack the things he's brought with him and try to set them up as nicely and cosily as he can in this room he's rented in The Shoemaker's Workshop, Asle thinks and he gets up and then he stands there in his black velvet jacket and he feels his pockets to check if he has his tobacco pouch and matchbox, and if his wallet is in his inner pocket, and then he drapes the brown leather bag over his shoulder and he sees the keyring lying on the table and he picks it up and then Asle leaves and he locks the door to his room behind him and then he goes downstairs and goes outside and then he locks the front door and then he puts the keyring into the pocket of his velvet jacket and he takes the tobacco pouch out and rolls himself a cigarette and lights it and then he starts walking towards the centre of town, of Aga, and he thinks he'll go to The Co-op Store and buy himself an ashtray, that's the first thing he'll buy, he thinks and then he doesn't think anything else but he feels so light, yes, it's almost joy he feels, because now, now he doesn't live at home with Mother anymore, Mother who he's constantly getting into fights with, and he's done with seeing Father work and toil from dawn to dusk, either he's in The Woodshed building boats, he does that all winter, or else he's with the fruit trees in the orchard, constantly working there, and it doesn't bring in much, Asle thinks and he walks slowly down the road and then he hears someone calling Asle and he turns around and who should he see there walking behind him but Sigve, and Sigve is carrying a black bag in one hand and he raises his other hand and Asle raises his hand and he stops, because look at that, he hadn't thought of that, but Sigve, a few years older than Asle, yes, he recently moved to Aga too, to work at The Furniture Factory here, Asle thinks, Sigve's been working here for a few months now, he knew that, Asle thinks, because the day he went to Stranda and bought both the velvet jacket and the shoulder bag he'd taken the bus from Barmen with Sigve, Sigve had a couple of days off and was home visiting his parents, as he said, but then he had to go back to Aga, back to work at The Furniture Factory there, he said, and he liked it all right there, the days went by quickly, and Sigve had rented a little house, a little old house, almost right in the centre, Sigve had told him, and that was sure different than living in an attic in a boathouse, the way he'd had to live throughout his whole childhood, Sigve had said, and now Asle sees Sigve coming closer and closer and he stops and stands there and Asle looks down and he looks up and he hears Sigve say it's nice to see him, he's probably come to Aga now to go to The Academic High School and Asle says yes, he's just arrived

Your parents drove you, Sigve says

Yes, Asle says

Where are you living? Sigve says

There, Asle says

and he points at The Shoemaker's Workshop

In the green side building? Sigve asks

Yes, Asle says

and Sigve says that he walks past that house every day because The Furniture Factory, well, it's right there, he says and Sigve turns and points and there's a big long white building in a little dip on the other side of the road a few hundred yards behind them and now Asle sees that it says Furniture Factory on the front of the building

That's where I work, Sigve says

Aha, Asle says

So every single day I go past the building where you have a room now, and I've often wondered what kind of building it is, Sigve says

and he says that he can see it's now an outbuilding, but it doesn't exactly look like an normal house, he says and Asle says that there used to be a shoemaker's workshop there, and Asle even thinks of himself as living in The Shoemaker's Workshop and says he lives in The Shoemaker's Workshop, he says

So that's what it is, Sigve says

Yeah, Asle says

and then they stay standing there and neither one says anything and then Sigve says yes, well, so that's where he's living now, he says, and Asle says yes and he says that Father put an ad in *The Hardanger Times* and an old lady answered, it was the lady who lives in the green main house, she's really old, and she walks taking little bitty steps, Asle says, and Sigve says that he's noticed her, sometimes she'd be walking home after going shopping when he was going home from work, and she walks so slowly that almost as soon as he's seen her he's walked past her, he says and then he says that Asle was lucky to have found a whole house of his own and not to have to live in a room in someone's house where other people live, he says

Yeah, Asle says

It's much better to live by yourself, Sigve says

Of course, he says

I was lucky too, to get a little old house, and in the centre of town too, not far from The Co-op Store, he says

and Sigve says that The Boss at The Furniture Factory had told The Labour Office about the house so he was placed there, someone who'd worked at The Furniture Factory had quit and he'd been renting the house, so it was available

Aha, Asle says

and he and Sigve started walking towards The Co-op Store

The house is in a strange spot, Sigve says

Right between The Co-op Store and The Hospital, yes, all by itself kind of, he says

Yes, I've noticed that house, Asle says

It's hard not to, isn't it, Sigve says

Yes, it's in a strange spot for a house, Asle says

and Sigve says that that's probably why he was able to rent it, because with his history he wasn't really the first person someone would want to rent to, and definitely not if they knew he'd grown up in a boathouse

Is it a nice place? Asle says

Yeah, it is, Sigve says

and Asle says that he just got here, his parents just now drove him and his stuff to the room in the top floor of The Shoemaker's Workshop, and he said hello to The Landlady, and she looks really old, Asle says and Sigve says he's really lucky he found somewhere he can live by himself, in his own house, most of the other people who come from Barmen or Stranda or wherever to go to The Academic High School have to live with housemates, there are young people from towns and farms across half of Vest-land coming to The Academic High School, and some of them go home only for Christmas and summers, and over Easter, so the ones from Barmen or Stranda are lucky because they can go home every weekend if they want

I don't want to, Asle says

Go home every weekend? Sigve says

No, Asle says

Well then you don't have to, Sigve says

and he says that he doesn't go home to see his parents much either, but then again he's quite a bit older than Asle, he says

Yes, Asle says

and they get to The Co-op Store and Sigve points to The Hotel down by The Fjord, a nice old hotel, and Sigve says that he likes to go there every now and then for a beer and he says Asle should come with him sometime and Asle says that he's not old enough to buy beer and Sigve says that they're not so strict about that there at The Hotel, and if they do ask for proof of age well then it's easy enough to change his ID, yes, he did it at the post office when he got his red post-office savings- account book, Asle has one of those doesn't he? he says, and Asle says he does and Sigve says they can just change the ID card, the date of birth, he says and Asle says that he has one of those cards and a bankbook too and Sigve says everyone does, don't they, he says and you just need to make a little change to the last number, then he'll be eighteen just like that and be able to buy beer at The Co-op Store and The Hotel

But I can't just do that, can I? Asle says

Sure you can, Sigve says

It's not hard, he says

You just need to find a ballpoint pen that writes the same, because the date of birth is always written with a totally normal ballpoint pen, and then it's just about making sure the colours match, and then a one can be turned into a seven no problem, or a nine into a four, and other things are even easier, four to nine, you can change any number without it being noticeable, just take your time and be careful, because sometimes you need to carefully scrape away a little of the number that was there before, that happens sometimes, and it's easy enough with a needle, an ordinary pin, but usually you don't need to, Sigve says, and he says that Asle can come home with him and he'll change his birthdate on the ID right now, it doesn't take long, and then maybe they can go to The Hotel tonight and get a beer or two or three to celebrate that Asle's a free man now, Sigve says

Because you're a free man now, he says

You've left home and neither your mother nor your father can go chasing after you whatever you do anymore, he says

Yeah, it feels good, Asle says

I'm sure it does, Sigve says

and he asks if Asle wanted to buy something and he says he was thinking of buying an ashtray

An ashtray? Sigve says

Yes, Asle says

You're starting School tomorrow? Sigve says

Yes, Asle says

and Sigve asks if he's still painting and Asle says that he is, he paints and he draws, wherever he goes he has a sketchpad and pencil with him at all times in his shoulder bag, he says and then Sigve asks if he can hire him to paint a picture of the house he lives in and Asle thinks that he doesn't really want to, no, he really doesn't, but he can't really say no either, Asle thinks and he doesn't answer and Sigve says he'll pay for it of course and Asle nods, or maybe I can pay for it by buying you a few glasses of beer? Sigve says, does that sound good? he says and Asle nods and he says that if he's going to paint Sigve's house he needs a photograph to paint from and Sigve says he has one hanging on the wall, there was an old photo of the house hanging above the sofa when he moved in, and in that photo the house is in such a pretty location, because where The Co-op Store is now there used to be just a little shop, and The Hospital wasn't there yet either, so all you can see in the picture is the little shop that's been torn down, but he doesn't need to paint that, it's fine if he just paints the house and then a little bit of the hills around the house, he says

Grandma's in The Hospital, Asle says

Your grandma? Sigve says

Yes, Asle says

and Sigve asks if she's seriously sick and Asle says that she had a stroke, one day she didn't come outside like she usually did and the front door was locked so Mother couldn't get in and then she found Father and he broke down the door and went in and then he saw Grandmother lying in bed and she was just looking at Father, he'd said, and then she tried to say something but she couldn't, Asle says, and then Father called The Doctor and he came right away and he said that Grandmother had had a stroke, and Father tried to sit her up in bed, and she helped as much as she could, and then Grandmother was sitting there in bed and then Father and The Doctor tried to pick her up and Grand-mother stood up, but she just stood, and she tried to walk and she did put one foot forward but it was like she couldn't move the other one

Were you at home? Sigve says

Yeah, Asle says

We were on winter break or whatever, he says

and he says that Grandmother couldn't really walk, so Fa-ther and The Doctor supported her and they walked slowly into the main room, because when Grandmother was holding Father with one arm and The Doctor with the other she could manage to move the other foot a little too without losing her balance, and they led Grandmother into the main room and sat her down on the bench there and then Grandmother managed to lie down herself on the bench and then she looked at Asle, he says

Yes, she's a good person, your Grandmother, Sigve says

Yes, Asle says

And I'm going to go see her every day, he says

You should, Sigve says

and he says that he and his parents drove to The Hospital to
see her before they dropped his things off at the room he's renting, so he's already been to see her today, he says

Grandma and I have always been close, he says

Yes, Sigve says

While Mother and me argued pretty much all the time, he says

and Sigve doesn't say anything

And Father just kept his mouth shut, he says

No your father's never been much of a talker, Sigve says

He almost never says anything, Asle says

and he says that when Mother was arguing with him, which
she did constantly, she used to say that Father needed to say
something and then he'd mumble something about how Mother
was right, something like that, Asle says and Sigve says that Father's a good man

I was thinking I'd buy a few beers, Sigve says

And some bread, he says

and then Sigve and Asle walk into The Co-op Store and
Sigve goes and gets some bottles of beer and then a loaf of bread
and he says they should look for an ashtray for Asle and then they
go to the part of The Co-op Store where they sell various house-
wares and Asle sees an ashtray with a cover and a little bar stick-
ing up on top and when you pull the lever the ashes and butts
disappear, and there's something like a belt of brown fur around
the ashtray, and he wants to buy it, Asle thinks and he tells Sigve

That one's not so cheap, he says

I'm buying it anyway, Asle says

and he takes the ashtray off the shelf and Asle says it's a pain
they don't sell painting supplies at The Co-op Store and Sigve
says yeah in that case he'll still have to take the bus to Stranda,
to The Paint Store there, but there's a bus to Stranda about every
hour, and there's a hotel there too, The Stranda Hotel, and now

and then he sometimes takes the bus there to get a glass of beer
or two at The Stranda Hotel, and sometimes he starts talking
to someone there, yes, a painter lives there in Stranda, a picture
painter, and he's usually at the hotel there, and Sigve's talked
with him a lot, he's a smart guy, but dead broke, and he likes beer
but he almost never has any money for more than a cup of coffee
so he's always extremely happy when Sigve wants to buy him
a pint, one day Sigve had asked him if he was hungry and he'd
nodded and then Sigve had bought him an open-faced ground-
beef sandwich and he'd thanked Sigve over and over and said he
was really hungry, and he, the picture painter, yes, as a matter of
fact his name is Asle too, and he can't be much older than you,
Sigve says

  And it's really strange, he says

  Because he reminds me a lot of you, he says

  Yes, Asle says

and Sigve says that the picture painter there, the one who's
named Asle too and is about the same age as Asle, maybe a couple
of years older, and who looks like Asle, yes, he gulped down that
ground-beef sandwich practically in one bite, and then he'd said
that that was the best meal he'd ever eaten in his life, yes, he was
so hungry, so unbelievably hungry, Sigve says and then they walk
to the cash registers and Sigve puts the bottles of beer down in
front of the woman sitting at the register

  Back again today, are you, she says

  I don't come in that often, Sigve says

  Yes you do, she says

and she rings up the price of the beer on the register and
Sigve puts the bread down in front of her and she rings that up
and says the total and Sigve takes out his wallet and pays and then
he opens his bag and puts the bottles and the bread into the bag,
and Asle had been wondering why Sigve was carrying that big
black bag around and now he knows why, he thinks and Asle
puts the ashtray down in front of the woman sitting at the register

So, you're buying yourself an ashtray, she says

I am, yes, Asle says

and she rings up the price and Asle takes out his wallet and pays and then he opens his shouldebag and puts the ashtray in and he sees Sigve walk towards the door

Goodbye, the woman at the register says

Goodbye, thanks, Asle says

and he follows Sigve and when they're outside Sigve says that that he always carries his big bag with him when he goes to work in the morning and at The Furniture Factory they say that they can't understand why he brings such a big bag to work, all he has in it is lunch and coffee, they say and then they laugh, but let them laugh, because the reason he always has this bag with him is that it means he can buy a few bottles of beer on the way home, and a little something else, Sigve says and he asks if Asle wants to come over? then they can have a beer and maybe a sandwich, if he feels like it? and then Asle can take the photograph he's going to use to paint the house Sigve is renting, he says and Asle says he'd be glad to, it'd be nice to go over to his house, he says and Sigve says well then they should go straight there, it's not far, he says and they walk to Sigve's house and he unlocks the door and then asks Asle to come in and Asle goes into the hall and Sigve says that the door on the right is to the toilet, because they'd had a toilet and a shower put into the house, and the door to the left goes to the kitchen, Sigve says and then he opens that door and goes through it and he puts the bag down on the little kitchen table and then he opens another door and points and says that's the living room and Asle should go inside and Asle goes inside and there's a table there in the middle of the room with four chairs around it, one on each side, there's a chessboard on it, and then there's a big bookshelf and it's chock full of books all jumbled together, some standing up and some on their sides, some slanted to the side and others straight, and then there's a sofa along one wall and above it there's the old photograph of the house that Sigve was talking about, and there's one window on the short wall and in front of it's an old armchair, and then there's a door on the right and Sigve comes in with two glasses of beer and invites Asle to sit down and he nods at the table and Asle sits down and Sigve puts a glass down in front of Asle and then he puts the other glass down on the other side of the table, next to the chessboard, opposite Asle

Yes this is sure not like living up in the attic of a boathouse, Sigve says

and Asle doesn't say anything and then Sigve goes back out to the kitchen and he comes back in with the bottle of beer that's now a little less than half full and he puts it down on the table between them and then he sits down and raises his glass and says cheers and Asle raises his glass and says cheers and then he drinks, and well he's never thought beer tastes all that good but even if it doesn't taste good it works, it calms him down, yes, when he drinks beer he feels that life is good, yes, better than it feels any other time, Asle thinks and he takes out his tobacco pouch and he rolls a cigarette and Sigve does the same and there's already an ashtray on the table and Asle lights his cigarette and then holds the match across for Sigve and lights his cigarette too and then they sit there and they're silent for a moment

So, today you left home, Sigve says

I was supposed to go to The Academic High School too, he says

and he points to the books and says that he reads a lot, all kinds of books, on every topic, now and then he reads poetry too, that may be what he likes to read best of all, he almost always gets something out of modern so-called incomprehensible poetry, not that he understands it either, in the usual way, but he does kind of understand it, in a different way, yes, it's like it's something you have to understand with something other than intelligence, or your mind, Sigve says and he takes a big sip

It's like those poems are incomprehensible the same way life is, he says

Yes, Asle says

and he says that he hasn't read that much, just what he's had to read for school and Sigve says that in that case he's missed out on a lot, but he can borrow a book or two and he should read them and then he'll understand what he means, he says, but he'll need them back, because the books he wants to lend me are two of his favourite books, Sigve says and he gets up and he starts rummaging around on the bookshelf

I can never find the book I'm looking for, he says

and Asle smokes and drinks his beer

Yes well here's one of them at least, it's stories, or something, by Samuel Beckett, he says

and Sigve hands Asle the book

Have you ever heard of him? Sigve says

No, Asle says

and Sigve keeps looking

Yes, these are good too, poems by Georg Trakl, he was from Austria so he wrote in German, but these are translations of course, he says

and you probably haven't heard of him either, Sigve says and Asle shakes his head and Sigve hands Asle that book too and he says that he should read both books and then he, Sigve, needs them back of course, he says, and Sigve says that he's bought all these books himself but he never buys books at the regular price, that would be too expensive, but every other year the bookshops have their big sale, The Aga Bookshop has the sale too, Asle does know that there's a bookshop in Aga, doesn't he? it's not far from here, when you're looking from The Co-op Store or from his house the bookshop's hidden behind The Church, and in fact Asle will have to go there tomorrow or one of these days to buy his schoolbooks, and there, at The Aga Bookshop, there's a book sale every so often and that's when Sigve buys books, he says and he falls silent and then he says that it was when he moved to Bjørgvin that things really went wrong for him, there was too

I IS ANOTHER: SEPTOLOGY III-V

much drinking, and he was friends with the wrong kind of people, as they say, but actually his friends were good people, not the
wrong kind, no, but anyway it ended up with him getting fired
from his job at a warehouse in Bjørgvin because he didn't go to
work for several days, and because he'd never been totally sober
when he was at work, at that was true enough, and then it led
to more drinking and burglary and prison and the DT's, yes, if
he didn't know what those were then he wasn't going to be the
one to tell him, delirium tremems as they're called in Latin, the
shakes, and he wouldn't wish them on his worst enemy, and then
they had to transfer him from The Prison in Bjørgvin, the one by
The Fishmarket, to The Hospital, and when he was better they
sent him back to The Prison and when he'd served his sentence
he went and bought himself a black bag of all things, yes, the one
he still used, and the bag was black and plastic, with a zipper, and
he bought himself three half-bottles of spirits and then a chessboard of all things, with pieces, and then he took the bus home
to Barmen, yes, he and Asle saw each other the night he came
home didn't they, and he'd probably told Asle all this then, yes,
that was the same night that Asle had quit the band he was in,
yes, Sigve had probably said more than he should have that time,
that's for sure, he says, and he'd said that he had to go somewhere,
hadn't he, and he showed up at his parents' house totally drunk,
yes, it was shameful, and he'd probably said that he had to go
back and see his parents sometime, Sigve says and he had to go
home because he had nowhere else to go, nowhere to live, and in
spite of everything it was better to spend the night in the attic of
a boathouse than lying on the ground outside
    I remember that, Asle says
    I'm sure do you, Sigve says
    I probably said way too much that night, he says
    and Asle says that he remembers Sigve saying that he had to
go see his parents again sometime, and then he'd handed Asle
a bottle and Asle had taken a little sip of it and then Sigve had

slapped himself on his cheeks and said again that he had to go see his parents again sometime and so he had better keep going, carrying his bag in one hand and the half-bottle of spirits in the other, Asle says and Sigve says that it's true what he's saying, because he remembers it all, well, most of it anyway, he thinks, Sigve says

But I wasn't wanting to talk about all that, he says

No, Asle says

That was a long time ago, Sigve says

I was on the skids, by the end I was drinking day and night, he says

and he says that now he has only one or two glasses a couple of nights a week and then on weekends, but he never drinks in the morning, never, he says, not even on his days off does he drink in the morning, because when you start doing that then look out, yes, he's learned that lesson all too well, he says, so even if Asle does it he can't start doing that, he can drink in the evening but never in the morning, Sigve says and Asle finishes his glass and Sigve pours him another one and then he says that it's strange how much Asle looks like the painter who lives in a rented room in Stranda and Asle thinks that he needs to go back to his own room now, he has to unpack and make things as comfortable as he can there, he has to set up his easel and painting things, the other things too, but it shouldn't take long, and then he wants to get some sleep and so Asle says that he should probably be getting home

Next time we'll have a beer at The Hotel, Sigve says

Yes, Asle says

And your ID card, the one you got from the post office, yeah, we can do something about that, like I said, Sigve says

Do you have it with you? he says

and Asle nods and he takes out his wallet and his ID card and he hands it to Sigve and he looks at it and he says that he'll be able to turn the nine at the end into a four easily, because it's written with a totally normal blue ballpoint pen, and he has several ballpoint pens, and one of them will have to look the same, and then maybe he'll just need to scrape a little at the top of the nine with a nail, carefully, yes, so carefully that no one will be able to tell and then, yes, with that Asle will be old enough to buy beer, both at The Co-op Store and at The Hotel, and if anything goes wrong, well then it's no big deal, they don't care if it's fake, Sigve says

Yeah, Asle says

and then Sigve gets a bunch of ballpoint pens and a piece of paper and an eraser and a nail and then he makes a little line on the paper with each of the pens and he picks one of them and then he starts scraping with the nail, gently, gently, scraping ink off the semicircle at the top of the nine and he is just barely touching the ID card with the point of the nail and then he carefully rubs it, he picks up the ID card and looks at it and then puts it back down and picks up a pen and then he kind of goes over the lines running up and down so that the number turns into a four and then Sigve picks up the ID card and says well that was easy enough, there's no way to see that that isn't a four, well maybe someone could tell if they looked at it with a magnifying glass but no one in a hotel or a shop will do that, so now Asle can buy as much beer as he wants, Sigve says

Thanks, Asle says

and then Asle says he's going home to his room

I have to unpack, and set up my easel at least, he says

Of course, Sigve says

But someday, sooner or later, we can maybe get a couple of beers at The Hotel, he says

and then Sigve says that Asle mustn't forget the photograph of the house and he goes and takes it down

Yes it sure looks like it's been hanging there a long time, Sigve says

and he says that Asle should just come by and knock whenever he wants, and then they'll go to The Hotel, at least if it's anytime in the afternoon or evening, he says and Asle says yes he will

Thanks for the beer, he says

No problem, Sigve says

and then Sigve says that he mustn't forget the books and then he dashes back into the living room and gets the two books and Asle takes them and opens his shoulder bag and puts them in

The Asle who lives in Stranda has a brown leather shoulder bag just like that, Sigve says

and Asle doesn't understand why Sigve keeps talking about that other Asle he's never met, but maybe it's just something that comes to mind? something to say? Asle thinks and he and Sigve say see you later and then Asle leaves and under his right arm he has the old photograph of the house Sigve's renting and Asle thinks that he should have gone to see Grandmother, but now he smells like beer, and she'd notice, and she wouldn't like that, so it would be just as well if he looked in on her tomorrow, and he's already been to see her once today, with his parents, and from now on he'll go and see Grandmother every day after he gets out of The Academic High School, he thinks, but that was good, the beer, so maybe he should go buy himself a bottle or two, Asle thinks and he walks into The Co-op Store and gets a bottle of beer and he goes over to the cash register and the woman sitting at the register asks if he can prove that he's eighteen and old enough to buy beer, yes, that's what she says, prove it, Asle thinks and he takes out his wallet and ID card and hands her the ID and she looks at it and hands it back to Asle and then she rings up the price on the cash register and Asle pays and he opens the shoulder bag and he puts the bottle in the shoulder bag, and then it's sitting there next to the sketchpad and the ashtray and the two books he's borrowed from Sigve, and then the woman sitting at the register says goodbye and Asle says goodbye and then he leaves and then he walks up the road, in his black velvet jacket, with his shoulder bag, with his long brown hair hanging down his back he walks up the road and I sit at the round table in front of the window and I look at the same spot in the water, at my landmark, at the waves there, and I might have dozed off a little, I think and the fire in the stove must have burned out and I realize I'm a little cold and it isn't dark outside yet but it's always a little dark all day at this time of year, and if I were doing what I usually did I would have long since been painting by now, but I realize that I just don't want to paint, I have no desire to paint, and I've always liked to paint, yes, I've liked it since I was a boy, and now, I think, I'll go light the stove again and get it a little warmer in the room, I think, and I then I probably should eat something? I think, so I'll just go make myself a sandwich, I think and I still feel so tired so tired and now maybe I want to get a little sleep? lie down on the bench? or maybe I'll read a little first? because I do feel like reading, I think, it's been a long time since I've felt like reading, because painting sort of took over, yes, took up all my time, but he, Sigve, used to read a lot, but then he died suddenly while walking to work at The Furniture Factory one morning, he just fell over, and he wasn't that old, I think, and Ales read a lot, she read everything, and in the last few years after she started painting icons she read mostly about icon painting of course but she also read a lot in the last few years she was alive from the Christian mystics from the Middle Ages, and she especially read a lot by Meister Eckhart, and I read him too, and so maybe I'll read some more Meister Eckhart now, I think and I think that Ales often used to say that there was something in Meister Eckhart's writings that I was also doing in my painting, not directly, of course, but in a way I was kind of doing the same thing, she said and she was definitely right about that and it's cold, I think, so I need to light a fire in the stove, I think and I think that Ales often said that it was these so-called Christians, Catholics and other kinds, who were always constantly misusing God's name, again and again, yes, the people who took God's name in vain the least were the ones who never took the word of God into their mouths at all, because, as Ales said, der Mensch kann nicht wissen, was Gott ist, that's what Meister Eckhart wrote, Ales said, and she said that Was Gott für sich selbst ist, das kann niemand begreifen, she said, yes, Gott ist keinem Dinge völlig nichts, Gott ist für sich selbst nicht völlig nichts, Gott ist nichts, was man in Worte fassen kann, Eckhart wrote, Ales said and she said that when she heard how many Christians misused God's name she thought that if God was the way they thought he was then she couldn't believe in him anyway, she said, I remember she said that one of the first days we were together, I think and I've read nowhere near enough but I have read a little now and then in The Bible, and there are passages there that have given me a lot, maybe most of all where it says that the kingdom of God is inside you, inside us, inside me, because I constantly feel something like God's nearness, I think, and Ales said that maybe what I felt was an angel passing over me? or maybe The Holy Spirit was nearby? she said, I think, but those are just words, because what's the difference really? I think, and I think that The Bible has to be interpreted, has to be read metaphorically, yes, like it's not the real thing but a picture, like a painting, with its own truth, because The Bible is literature, and when it comes right down to it literature and visual art are the same thing, I think, and to understand The Bible you have to start from its own spirit, for the letter kills but The Spirit gives life, as Paul wrote, I think, because even if The Bible is literature it's also more than literature, I think, and even I'm only a borderline member of The Catholic Church, I think, or really I'm outside it, because of how I think, still I've found my place in The Church, I think, and seeing oneself as Catholic isn't just a belief, it's a way of being alive and being in the world, one that's in a way like being an artist, since being a painter is also a way of living your life, a way of being in the world, and for me these two ways of being in the world go together well since they both create a kind of distance from the world, so to speak, and point towards something else, something that's both in the world, immanent, as they say, and that also points away from the world, something transcendent, as they say, and you can't entirely understand it, I think, and then I again

think that the kingdom of God is within me, because a kingdom
of God does exist, I think, and I can feel it when I make the sign
of the cross, I think and I make the sign of the cross, and I do that
all the time, but only when I'm alone, except in Church, and I
sometimes do it many times a day, whenever the pain comes, and
also when gratitude comes, yes, then too, yes I make the sign of
the cross all the time and there's a power in doing it, yes, there
definitely is, even if it's impossible to say what kind of power it is,
because the power is outside of words, but it's there, the power,
and that's a fact, and it's impossible to understand why it's like
that since it's just not something you can understand, I think and
I look at all the rosaries hanging on the wall on the short side of
the room above the bench, because I do have a lot of rosaries, and
I got all of them from Ales, and now the ones I got from Ales and
Ales's too are there on a hook above the end of the bench, aside
from the one I always wear, I think and I think that there is also
a strange power in the Eucharist, yes, every time the priest holds
up the bread in the consecration, as they call it, to change it into
Christ's body a kind of light shines out from the host, yes, I see
it, I see it with my own eyes, the host gives off a weak light in all
directions, stronger or weaker, light comes from the host, or
from something like a halo around it, sometimes you can only
just make out the light, yes, it's like it's in a fog, but you can still
make it out inside the fog, or else it's more like a halo around it,
it's not something you can understand but I know what I know,
I've seen what I've seen, and of course I might be imagining it
but so what? I think and I think that words, yes, language, both
connect us to God and separate us from Him, I think, and now
it's gotten so cold that I need to light the stove, I think and I get
up and Bragi falls onto the floor, because I'd forgotten he was
lying asleep on my lap, that's too bad, again, I think and Bragi
looks at me with his dog's eyes and then I go over to the stove and
I put some wood chips and kindling and a log in and light it and
it catches right away and I put another log in and I look at the logs

and I think that I never would have become Catholic if Ales hadn't been Catholic, but I became one too, because I couldn't stop drinking so much, by the end I was drinking almost around the clock and I couldn't stop, and because to paint well I had to be sober, if I drank even a little I lost the concentration and precision you need for painting, so it was either alcohol or paintings, I think and when the alcohol was gone then the mass replaced it, because everyone needs something, in a way, I think and I think that near the end of when Ales and I were living in Bjørgvin I spent so much time in The Alehouse, I think, and Ales had to come get me more than a few times, I think, because sometimes I'd be drinking around the clock, and I never regretted converting, because becoming Catholic, not just feeling God's closeness all the time as I'd felt before I became Catholic too, was good for me, it's as simple as that, and Ales said everything so clearly, and I always think muddled thoughts, but now that I've realized I don't have any desire to paint any more should I maybe start reading more? because Ales read a lot, yes, she read and read, novels and plays and poetry, she read in all the Scandinavian languages and she read academic literature in English and German as well, so we were similar in that way, because even if I didn't graduate from The Academic High School I was on what they call the Modern Languages track but when I stopped going to The Academic High School and started at The Art School I could barely read a book in either English or German, and not at all in French, but I learned English and German gradually, by reading, it was just French, yes, the only French that stuck were a few expressions that I'll probably always be able to rattle off, and as I stand there looking at the logs I think that I know so little, for example I don't even know something as simple as why I've always signed my paintings with a big A in the right-hand corner of the painting itself and painted the title on the top of the stretcher on the back, always in thick black paint, why did I do it in that particular way? I think and I think that all the titles were either in Norwegian, Nynorsk, or in Latin, and the ones in Latin were always quoted from somewhere in the Latin mass, because I prefer it when the mass is celebrated in Latin, I think and I can't just stay standing here looking at the logs through the open hatch of the stove, I think, and it's been a long time since I've eaten anything, so even if I don't feel hungry I should probably go make myself a sandwich, I think and I shut the hatch of the stove and I go out to the kitchen and I see the leg of lamb hanging there, and there's almost no meat left on it and I think that I am hungry and still I don't feel like eating, I think, but I will get myself a little something to drink, I think and I pour myself a glass of nice cold water and I drink it down in one gulp and I still feel tired, so maybe I'll just go lie down on the bench for a bit? I think and I go into the main room and lie down on the bench and spread the grey blanket over me, the one Grandmother handed to me when they came to take her to The Hospice and that I've had with me ever since, wherever I've lived, and Bragi hops up onto me and lies down curled up against my feet and I close my eyes and I see Asle sitting at the back desk of the class-room and The Teacher is standing up front at the lectern and he says that he'll be teaching us English, as a main subject, and French, which we'll all be starting together, he says, and to find out a little more about us he would like us to read a little English out loud for him, and he's taken a text that, if he may say so himself, he personally wrote for this very purpose, and divided it up into sections, he says and now each and every one of us will read our own section, and we might as well start on the right, yes, with you, The Teacher says and he looks at the girl sitting at the front desk to his right, and it would be nice if you all stayed sitting at the desks you're sitting at now, and if you would first say your name and then read, one section each, and while we're doing that he will make a name chart for the class to help him remember all our names, there are so many names to keep track of when you've been a teacher for as many years as he has, The

Teacher says and then he gives a packet of sheets of paper stapled together to the girl sitting in the front desk of the row to the left of the row where Asle is sitting and she says her name and then she starts to read and as far as Asle can tell she reads English well, she pronounces the words nicely, and she reads with a nice flow to the sentences and then she's done and then she hands the packet of paper to the boy sitting at the desk behind her and he says his name and then he reads for a while and Asle can't hear if it's good or bad because he's suddenly filled with a kind of terror, the packet of paper is moving from desk to desk and getting closer and closer to him and soon it's going to reach him and then he'll have to say his name and then he'll have to read out loud and he's never felt terror like this before, and the terror gets stronger and stronger the closer the packet of paper gets and one person after another says their name and reads and never never in his life has Asle felt so scared, it's like his whole body has gone stiff and like the fear is a stake through his body, a stake paralyzing him, and he can't do this, he just has to get out, he can't do it, Asle thinks and he's breathing more heavily and he's afraid he'll fall off of his chair and his hands are all sweaty and he's clutching the desk and he bends forward over the desk and his hair hangs down in front of his face and his whole body is rigid and, and, he can't do this, he needs to run away, but he can't run away either, he thinks, because he can't, he can't move, he can't escape and the girl sitting at the desk in front of him turns around and looks at him and then she hands him the stapled packet of paper and Asle takes the packet and his hands are shaking so much that he's afraid the packet will fall to the floor but he manages to get it onto his desk and then he sits there and he starts reading, word by word, voice shaking, he stops, he skips over one word and then he hears The Teacher say thank you and Asle picks up the packet and his hands are shaking so much and then he turns and hands the quivering paper to the girl sitting at the desk next to him and she takes the paper from him and he turns back forwards and his whole body's shaking and the girl sitting next to him says her name and then she starts reading in a calm voice and it's nice hearing her read, her voice is so relaxed, and she reads in such a steady flow, Asle thinks and he realizes that he's starting to calm down, and it's like the voice of the girl reading now is making him calmer, and what just happened? he thinks, and he thinks that having to read out loud has never made him scared before and he was always having to read out loud in school, he thinks, and he thinks that he can't go to school if he's like this, so he'll have to drop out of The Academic High School, he thinks or else he'll have to talk to The Teacher and tell him, say that he's scared to death of reading out loud and ask if he can get out of doing that, he thinks, or else he'll just have to drop out of The Academic High School, and he can do that, he doesn't need to go to The Academic High School, there's nothing forcing him to stay, he had to go to primary school and middle school but he doesn't have to go to The Academic High School, he thinks and The Teacher says that today's time is almost up, it's breaktime, they got through about half the text this time and the rest of the class will say their names and read their sections next time, he says and Asle thinks that there's maths next period and even though he can't do maths and has never been able to do maths and will never learn how to do maths, and will never understand a thing in what they call mathematics, at least he won't have to read anything out loud, he thinks, and then the last period is history, and that's one subject Asle has always liked, and he won't have to read out loud then either, so he'll be spared today, but tomorrow there's French and then Norwegian, and he doesn't know a word of French so he won't have to read in that period, Asle thinks, but in Norwegian class he might have to read out loud and so he has to tell The Norwegian Teacher before then that he can't read out loud, that he's scared to death of that, yes, scared to death of hearing his own voice reading something out loud, so they'll have to let him get out of that or else he'll have to drop out of The Academic

High School, that's what he has to say, Asle thinks and The Norwegian Teacher is also the instructor in history, and he was the
one who wrote the weekly schedule up on the blackboard during
the first period and told everyone what teachers they'd have, and
what books they needed to buy, and he was dressed a little
strangely, in grey trousers and a blue-grey velvet jacket, and he
was wearing both a belt and suspenders, and both the belt and the
suspenders were narrow, and both were clearly visible, and his
trousers were wide, and his velvet jacket was too, and then he had
a thin red tie on, while The Teacher they would have for English
and French just wore trousers and a pullover, a grey pair of trousers and a white pullover with blue stripes and I lie here on the
bench with the grey blanket tucked tight around me and I open
my eyes and I scrunch my hands in Bragi's fur and I pull him
closer to me and I close my eyes and Bragi moves a little and I pet
him, I close my eyes and I see Asle standing there and he's telling
Beyer that he doesn't want to go to the opening and Beyer says
he's about to have his first show, doesn't he want to be there for
the opening? and also, Beyer says, well, if the painter doesn't
come then it's possible not a single painting will sell, he says, a
totally unknown painter, making his debut, yes, and still a student at The Art School or at least until just recently, and now he
doesn't want to come to the opening

No, unbelievable, Beyer says

You have to come to the opening, of course you do, all painters do that, Beyer says

I've never heard of anyone who doesn't, he says

and Beyer says no never before has that happened to him, of
course Asle has to be at the opening, he says, all painters have to,
that's just how it is, he says, because openings are when painters
meet their audience, the people who might be spending all that
money to buy a painting, and is it any surprise that they'd like
to say hello to, or at any rate set eyes on, the artist who made the
painting they're buying? Beyer says and Asle asks him to say hello

to the people who come to the opening for him and say that he's afraid of crowds like that

It can't just be me, you have to be there to meet them yourself, Beyer says

But I can't do it, Asle says

and Beyer says Asle's done it before, both at The Academic High School, even if he didn't graduate, and at The Art School, even if he's dropped out of there too now, he says, so it's not like this'll be the first time he's been in a crowd like that, Beyer says and Asle says that he can manage to be in a crowd if he doesn't have to say anything, because he's scared to death of speaking in public, yes, even in a classroom, someday Asle'll tell Beyer about how it was at The Academic High School before he quit, he says and he hears Beyer say yes, well yes, artists are their own special kind of people, but in that case it was extra important that there be a debut-artist interview with Asle in *The Bjørgvin Times*, newspapers don't always want to print interviews with debut artists but it does happen, and since the pictures are so good, yes, anyone can see that, he thinks that they'll agree to set up an interview, Beyer says and Asle says well then he'll give an interview, he says and Beyer says at last, a good answer, he'll try to set up an appointment and it'll probably be at The Grand Café restaurant, he says, and Asle says that he's never been there before and doesn't know where it is, and Beyer says that if he gets an interview set up then Asle can just come to The Beyer Gallery beforehand, in time to get to the interview, and he'll take Asle to The Grand Café personally, he says and Asle thanks him and I lie here on the bench and I think that I can't just stay lying here like this, I think, but the room's nice and warm now and I close my eyes and I see Asle standing in the brown house looking out the window and he thinks that he was recently interviewed in *The Bjørgvin Times* and it was a real takedown under the title 'Fear of Crowds', Fear of, Fear of, Asle thought when he saw it, that's what he thought, Asle thinks and he sees a car drive by on the road down below, and the car, a small van, is one he's seen many times, Asle thinks and he thinks that the article in *The Bjørgvin Times* appeared with a large and bad photograph of him standing in his black velvet jacket with a scarf around his neck and with his brown leather shoulder bag in place and he was looking down so that his medium-length hair almost entirely covered his face and in the interview the journalist, he was from Bjørgvin, wrote that there was serious disagreement among the critics whether these were good paintings, and the question, he wrote, was being asked whether The Beyer Gallery, usually so dependable, had made a mistake this time, but that remained to be seen, and whether anyone would want to buy the paintings in the exhibition remained to be seen too, the critic wrote in *The Bjørgvin Times*, Asle thinks and he thinks that the interview was all obvious questions that Asle gave obvious answers to and he thinks that Beyer did say yes well about that interview, Asle thinks, there's not a single honest critic, they only became journalists because they couldn't do anything else, that's true, Beyer said, Asle thinks, and he thinks that the opening went fine without him being there and the review of the exhibition in *The Bjørgvin Times* could hardly have been worse, every picture shows a total and complete lack of talent, something like that is what the review said, Asle thinks and Beyer said that the critic would be ashamed of his words someday, the newspapers' art critics were getting worse and worse over the years, it wasn't like it used to be back when Anne Sofie Grieg was the art critic for *The Bjørgvin Times*, she had never studied art history but she'd been to all the greatest art museums in Europe and she was a skilled pianist and she had a real eye for what was good art and bad art, but whether she'd gotten too old and didn't want to write anymore or for some other reason she didn't write about art in *The Bjørgvin Times* anymore anyway, now they had some whippersnapper as an art critic who'd gone to The University and who could only see concepts and theories instead of pictures, instead of art, Beyer said, but luckily, yes, luckily

ordinary people could see better than him, because all of Asle's
paintings had sold, and within two days, and that's even though
Asle wasn't at the opening, and despite that terrible interview
and photograph in *The Bjørgvin Times,* and despite the terrible
review, if you can even call it a review, Beyer said, Asle thinks,
and Beyer said to tell to the truth he'd said beforehand to everyone who usually bought pictures or who even sometimes bought
pictures that now they really had to step up and buy one because
the pictures he was showing now were by the greatest talent he
had ever come across in all his long years alive, he'd personally
said that to anyone and everyone, Beyer said and, as he said, all
the paintings sold in two days, he said, Asle thinks standing there
looking out the window and I'm lying on the bench and now the
room is nice and warm and then I say Bragi and he looks up at
me with his dog's eyes and then I pet him on the back and I tuck
the blanket a little tighter around him and I close my eyes and I
see Asle standing in front of the door to the little house where
Sigve lives, right between The Co-op Store and The Hospital,
and he thinks that he was just in The Co-op Store buying two
bottles of beer, and he has under his arm both the photograph
he'd taken with him of the old house where Sigve used to live
and the picture he's painted of the house, but it took him much
too long to finish painting it, now he's finally finished it but he
didn't paint it the way Sigve wanted him to paint it, Asle thinks,
and he thinks that, today, like most school days, the first thing
he did after his day at The Academic High School was over was
to go to The Hospital, to the room when Grandmother was, but
she was asleep, and he sat down on a chair in her room and he
looked at Grandmother's face, especially her lips that had turned
a little bluish, and her breathing was rapid and irregular and then
Asle thought that he didn't want to wake Grandmother up, he
would just come back later, Asle thinks and he knocks on Sigve's
door and nothing happens and then he knocks again and a little
harder this time and then he hears hurrying footsteps and Sigve

opens the door and his eyes are half-closed and he says no, it's you, and he doesn't seem so happy to see Asle and then Sigve says that he just lay down for bit, and then he must have fallen asleep, but it's good that Asle dropped by and woke him up because if he'd slept any longer his sleep tonight would be ruined, that's happened more than a few times before, Sigve says and he says that Asle should come in and he goes in and Sigve shuts the front door behind him and locks the door and then they go into the living room

Yes so the school day's over too, he says

Yeah, Asle says

It went well today? Sigve says

Yes I'd say so, Asle says

That's good, Sigve says

and then it's silent and Asle thinks Sigve must not have noticed that he has both the photograph and the painting with him and he hands Sigve the painting and Sigve looks at it and it doesn't seem like he thinks there's anything special about it, anyway he doesn't say anything and then he goes and puts the painting down on the floor in front of the bookcase and Asle hands him the photograph and Sigve hangs it back up in its place over the sofa

It's nice to get that photograph back in its place, he says

I didn't like not having it, it was like something was missing when the photograph wasn't there, he says

I really missed it, he says

and then it's silent and then Sigve says that he'll treat Asle to a meal and some beer in exchange for the painting, and Asle, who was sure he'd get paid, that they'd agreed on that or had an unspoken agreement at least, feels a little disappointed but he doesn't say anything and then Sigve asks if Asle's eaten and he says that he ate a little something back at his room and Sigve says that he doesn't eat dinner every day, not at all, to tell the truth he comes home pretty rarely, maybe once or twice a week, yes sometimes he makes himself a meal, he can cook pretty well, getting better at least, he says and laughs, but today he wasn't that hungry, Sigve says and Asle says that he isn't either, but he has brought over two bottles of beer, so if Sigve's thirsty he could always have a glass, Asle says and Sigve says a glass of beer's always good, and Asle opens his shoulder bag

That's a nice bag you have there, Sigve says

and he says he's thought about that bag a lot, oddly enough, he says

Real leather, it looks like? he says

Yeah, Asle says

That can't have been cheap, Sigve says

I bought it when I sold my guitar, Asle says

Yes, that was something wasn't it, didn't one of you punch out another guy's tooth? Sigve says

Yeah, Asle says

You'll have to tell me about that sometime, Sigve says

and then he says that first they need a beer and Asle takes the two bottles out and puts them on the living room table, next to the chessboard

Yes, one bottle each, he says

Sounds good, Sigve says

and he goes and gets an opener and two glasses and then Asle sits down and Sigve puts a glass down in front of him and another on the other side of the table, by his place, and then Sigve sits down, and then they each pour themselves some and then they sit there and they each roll a cigarette and light it and Sigve says it's good that the old photograph of the house is finally back where it belongs, he'd missed it, he'd been so used to seeing it there, Sigve says and Asle says that he's sorry it took so long to paint the picture and he thinks that Sigve's still not really happy with the picture he painted and it's quiet for a moment

I kind of thought the painting would be different, Sigve says

Yes, with colours, not just in black and white, he says

Yes it's almost all black and white, isn't it, he says

and Asle says that he's stopped painting houses and homes in beautiful spring weather with fruit trees in blossom and a smooth glassy fjord, and white snowcaps on the mountaintops, he doesn't want to paint any more sunny pictures like that, he says, but when Sigve asked him to paint a picture of the house he lived in he didn't want to say no, Asle says, and he thinks that now he's painted the house where Sigve lives but he truly did not want to paint it in colour, he thinks and Asle says that he painted the house in black and white just like the photograph

I'd been picturing more of a painting with colours, Sigve says

I thought all paintings had colours, actually, he says

But the house is white, and the roof is grey, there are big slate tiles on the roof that are grey, Asle says

But the hills are green, and the trees, you probably noticed the big tree next to the house? Sigve says

And the sky is blue, he says

and Asle says that, as he said, he's painted so many pictures of houses in colour and with a blue sky that he didn't want to paint any more of them and Sigve says he was thinking he'd hang the painting on the wall, it would kind of brighten things up a bit with a little colour, things are already kind of grey and black, he didn't need more of that, most of the year it's black and dark almost around the clock but the sun, the yellow sun, and the sky, the blue sky, he could use some more of that, he says and Asle says he knows all that but he's stopped painting pictures like that, he says

Yes well you need to paint the way you want, Sigve says

But let me take you out to a meal and a beer, you did paint it after all, he says

and Asle says that he'd rather be paid in money, and he says what he usually gets for painting a picture like that and Sigve says that that's not unreasonable so that's fine, he says and he raises his glass to Asle and says they should drink to their deal, their agreement, he says and they toast and drink and then Sigve says a little beer sure is good, that's for sure, yes, he says and he says he's glad he's finally living in his own place with a regular job, because that's what keeps a person from going crazy, yes, Asle knows what he's talking about now because he remembers the night Sigve arrived in Stranda on the bus from Bjørgvin to go home to his parents, because what else was he supposed to do? and then he ran into Asle, Sigve says and he was insanely worried about seeing his parents again, and that's why he'd been drinking himself blind drunk, to put it mildly, and then he'd gotten off the bus a long way before the closest stop and then he and Asle had run into each other and started talking and he'd probably told Asle more than he should have that night, but he probably knew it all already anyway, that his father had been a German soldier in Norway, that he was a so-called German baby, and how shameful that was, it was the worst shame possible, but to be honest no one in Barmen had ever teased him or bothered him about it, he had never heard anyone say a single insulting word about it, but still it was always there, in everything anyone said to him, it was there, in the ways people talked to him and looked at him, everything was kind of said in the way they talked to him and looked at him, or maybe he was just imagining it? that was possible, but a German baby was what he was and that was the truth and his father had most likely been taken out by some Barmen people and shot and tossed into The Fjord with a stone in a potato sack tied to his feet, yes, that's what people said at any rate, and his mother didn't want to talk about it, she wanted it all to be forgotten, but sometimes, and every time he was drunk, he'd question her and when she didn't want to say anything, the same as always, he'd sometimes grab her shoulders and shake her and then she'd say crying that his father had been shot and dumped in The Fjord and that the other Germans didn't know where he'd gone and they thought he'd just deserted, just snuck off like a traitor, that's what she said they'd said, something like that

But now we don't talk about it anymore, Sigve says

No, Asle says

and they drink and smoke and it doesn't take long before they've drunk all the beer since they've been smoking the whole time, as soon as one cigarette was done they rolled themselves a new one and Sigve says that they should either go to The Co-op Store and buy some more beer or go to The Hotel and get some beer there, Sigve says, no, actually, he says, they can take the bus to Stranda and go to The Stranda Hotel, they've talked about doing that so many times but they've never got around to it, and they'd definitely run into the other Asle there, his Namesake, the one who looks so much like Asle, even if he is a little older, or, damned if he knows, for all he knows they're the same age, yes, Asle must have almost met him before, Sigve says and if The Namesake isn't in The Stranda Hotel, because he usually goes there, and he never has money for beer so he drinks coffee, yes, if he's not already there at The Stranda Hotel then Sigve knows where he lives, he can tell him, it's in the basement of a house right up from The Stranda Hotel, yes, the other Asle, The Namesake yes, that's his name, he's found a house where he can live in the basement, Sigve says and he looks at the clock and he says that if they hurry they'll just catch the bus to Stranda in five minutes and Asle thinks why not, but he doesn't understand why Sigve isn't embarrassed to go to The Stranda Hotel since he'd robbed that exact place once, the first time Sigve had to go to prison, that's what he'd heard anyway, but he can't very well ask Sigve if it's true, and The Namesake, no, he probably doesn't look as much like him as Sigve likes to say, but if he's a painter too then it would be nice to meet him, Asle thinks and he gets up and Sigve picks up the glasses and empty bottles and carries them out to the kitchen and puts them down on the kitchen counter and says Ordnung muss sein in German and Asle drapes his shoulder bag over his shoulder and follows Sigve and then Sigve puts on some jacket or another, a kind of puffy jacket, and it has a zipper, it looks very strange, it's a weird blue colour that Asle could never have imagined painting, and Sigve pulls the zipper up and Asle goes out and Sigve follows him and he locks the front door and they walk over to the bus stop together and Sigve says that Asle won't believe it when he meets The Namesake, he says and a bus drives up and Sigve sticks out his hand and they get in the bus and Sigve pays and Asle pays and then they go to the back of the bus and sit down in the last row

I always like sitting in the back, Sigve says

Me too, Asle says

As far back as possible, he says

Yes, always, in the last row if it's free, Sigve says

and then they sit there next to each other in the last row and there are just one or two other passengers on the bus, an older married couple and an old woman, and they are sitting far away in the front of the bus and neither Asle nor Sigve says anything, they just sit there and Asle thinks that he still feels nervous and then Sigve says that Asle looks anxious, everything about him seems so anxious, he says, yes, like something really bad has just happened, he says and Asle doesn't answer and then Sigve says that Asle will feel a little more relaxed after he has a beer, yes, that'll do him good, Sigve says, after a few glasses he'll feel totally calm again, Sigve says and Asle asks how Sigve's day had been and he says that his day had been like every other day, his only bad days were the early days when he'd just started at The Furniture Factory, he says, because then he needed to say hello to The Boss and to this and that person working there and he really doesn't like having to talk to people he doesn't know, no, so that was really bad, Sigve says, and he didn't understand how to do the jobs he was told to do, they were actually super simple, just screwing the arms and legs onto a kind of chair they made there, but even that was something you had to learn, there's a knack to doing even that, and the guy who'd had that job before him and was leaving for a new and more challenging job taught Sigve what to do and he laughed and chuckled and showed Sigve where to place the chair leg before he attached it and where to place the armrests before screwing them on and where to put the finished chair down, and where to carry the chairs to, one in each hand, after he'd finished two chairs, and he had to avoid bumping into the doorframe of course, or whatever, yes, every job has things you have to do, Sigve says and in the early days he'd managed to make pretty much every mistake he could possibly make but after that everything went fine and the guy who'd told him what to do, and who was now off to do a bigger and more important task in the company, said that now he was up to speed, now he could do the job well on his own, but if he ever needed to ask about anything he should just ask, he said and then he left and then Sigve was there screwing legs and armrests onto chairs, and now he'd been there doing that for a couple of years, and it may not sound that nice but the truth is he likes that job, Sigve says, by this point what needs to get done happens by itself so to speak and while he's doing the job he can think about whatever he wants to think about, or can stop thinking and just space out, half go to sleep almost, yes, to tell the truth the lunch breaks had been the worst thing about the whole job, because obviously all the other people who worked at The Furniture Factory knew that he was a German baby, no one had said anything to him but he was sure they knew it, and he gradually stopped going to the cafeteria where the others ate, he just sat down on one of the finished chairs and ate the two sandwiches he brought with him every day, always brown cheese on bread, always, and drank the thermos of coffee he had with him, and that way he could avoid talking to anyone, except the guy who delivered the chair seats with the backs, and the guy who delivered the armrests, and the guy who delivered the chair legs, he exchanged a word or two with them, the first time anyway, but after a while the first guy would just come with the chair seats and backs and the second guy would just come with the arms and the third guy would just come with the legs and none of them would say anything, and that's how it was today, and he likes it like that, he's left alone, and every month he gets his pay, and the pay is pretty good, nothing you'll get exactly rich from but it's more than enough for him, Sigve says and Asle asks if it doesn't get boring and Sigve says it doesn't seem that way to him, and if it does get a little boring then he can always just think about the next chess move he's going to make

Chess move? Asle says

Yeah, I saw that you have a chessboard on your table, he says

Yeah, Sigve says

I taught myself chess when I was in prison, he says

and he says that when he got out the first thing he did was buy himself a black bag, black plastic, yes, the one he uses every day, and a chessboard with pieces, and since he didn't have any-one to play chess with he started playing something called postal chess, that means that every Friday he mails a letter with a chess move and every Wednesday he gets a letter from the guy he's playing against where the guy's written his move, and the corre-spondence continues until one of them wins or it's a draw, Sigve says and he has no idea who he's playing against, he just knows his name and address, yes well he doesn't even remember the guy's name, and definitely not his address, but as soon as he gets the letter with the other guy's chess move he starts thinking a lot about what his own next move should be, and before he gets the letter he thinks a lot about what move the guy he's playing against is going to make, Sigve says and then he's always reading a book, he says, and sometimes he thinks about what's written in the book, but then thoughts come to him about the times when he had the shakes, yes, as he'd said, and the times when he was in prison, but he was only in prison twice, people can say whatever they want, Sigve says, and then he says that the first time was when he and someone he used to drink with, yes, that was at The Stranda Hotel, where they're going now, they wanted something more to drink so badly when the bar was closed that they just broke down the door and went into The Stranda Hotel to find more to drink, yes, maybe even a bottle of spirits, and then The Policeman came of course and they were arrested and put in jail at The Police Station, but it was just a room with a bed and an ordinary door and by moving the bed so that they could press their backs against the end of the bed and their feet against the door they could put so much pressure on the door, because the guy he used to go drinking with was really strong, that they were able to push it out of the doorframe, yes, they broke down this door too and then they got as far as they could from The Police Station and they decided that the best thing to do would be go to Bjørgvin and then they started walking down the road that led to Bjørgvin, because sooner or later a bus would drive past, they thought, and then they tried to hitch a ride from every car that went by, but not many went by, since it was the middle of the night, and all the cars drove right past them and they walked and walked and they felt so tired, and then they sat down on a milk bench and they sat there and of course they nodded off every now and then too but every time a car drove by one of them stood up and walked out to the edge of the road and stuck out his hand with the thumb up and every single car kept driving and then they just had to wait until the next car, and a little eternity passed before the next car came by and none of the cars stopped so there was nothing to do but keep walking to the next bus stop, they'd get to it eventually, so they started walking down the road again and they were sobering up and they felt terrible all over and then, yes, finally a car stopped, and two men got out, and damn if it wasn't The Policeman and The Policeman's Partner and that was all right, he thought, that was fine too

So, here are our runaways, The Policeman said

They didn't get far, he said

and then The Policeman's Partner handcuffed them both and put them in the car and The Policeman said now he'd drive them straight to the prison in Bjørgvin, and then there'd be a trial and they wouldn't get out of there so easily, and if there was one thing he was sure of it was that this wasn't the only crime they had on their conscience, he said and then they were put in a real prison, this time, in separate cells, there was a bench and a writing desk with drawers and then somewhere to shit and piss, in the cell, and there were bars on the window, and then they were both found guilty and then they were sent to The Prison there in Bjørgvin, Sigve says, and then, yes, then you're sorry about all the stupid things you've done, he'll never be rid of these shameful marks, he says and he holds out his hands with the tattoos on them, three dots between thumb and index finger on his right hand, making a triangle, they call it a beggar's mark, he says, and in the same place on his left hand he has a heart, a cross, and an anchor, yes, a person does all sorts of crazy things when he's drunk, he says and the bus pulls over and stops in front of The Stranda Hotel and they get out and Asle says it'll be nice to get a glass of something now and Sigve says it sure will, that's the truth, and then the question is whether The Namesake will be there, he says, yes, he can go into The Stranda Hotel first and see if he's there and if not they can go up and knock on the basement door where he lives, because it has its own door, the basement, and he knows, as he said, where he lives, Sigve says, and now Asle should just stay there and wait and then he walks into The Stranda Hotel to see if The Namesake is sitting there and so Asle stands there, just standing around, in his black velvet jacket, and with the brown leather shoulder bag hanging over his shoulder, and with a scarf around his neck, and he rolls himself a cigarette and he lights it and then Sigve comes out and says yeah, his Namesake is in there, with *The Bjørgvin Times* and a cup of coffee, so they can just go on in, Sigve says and then Asle walks up the stairs and Sigve opens the door and Asle walks into the lobby, and next to the front desk there's a dining room, and Sigve goes inside and Asle follows him and there, at a table way at the back, with his back against the wall, by a window, there's a guy with long brown hair, and of course he's wearing a black velvet jacket, and a scarf around his neck, Asle sees and then Sigve says they need to go over and say hello to The Namesake and Asle walks towards The Namesake who looks up and Asle thinks that the guy sitting there looks like him, yes, Sigve was right, he thinks and Sigve and Asle go over to the table and Sigve says he thought the two of them should meet, because they're not all that different, he says and The Namesake gets up and holds out his hand to Asle and says Asle and Asle holds out his hand and says Asle and they shake hands

So we're both named Asle, Asle says

Yes, so we are, The Namesake says

and then he sits back down and Asle sits down in the chair opposite The Namesake and he looks down and Sigve says well then they'll just get a beer, yes, he says and he looks at The Namesake

You probably don't have enough money for a beer? Sigve says

That's probably why you're drinking coffee? he says

Yeah, it's like you're psychic, The Namesake says

and Sigve says he doesn't need to be psychic to know that much and then he asks hasn't The Namesake sold any pictures recently and The Namesake says that he hasn't been painting the kinds of pictures people want to buy for a while now, he just paints the pictures he's going to paint and wants to paint and needs to paint, but he has started on two paintings of a sailboat in a storm, Boat in a Storm is the title, yes, the same title that he gives all his paintings like that, he says and he's planning to finish them both quickly, since he needs the money, and then he'll stand in front of The Stranda Hotel like usual, at the bottom of the stairs with the paintings leaning up along the ground floor wall and see if anyone wants to buy a picture from him

You're still standing on the hotel steps selling pictures? Sigve says

Yes, The Namesake says

You said you'd stop doing that, Sigve says

I certainly did say that, The Namesake says

and then it's silence

But I need the money, he says

and then the woman who was sitting at reception comes walking towards to them and Sigve quietly tells Asle that her name is Gunvor and that she's the wife of the owner of The Stranda Hotel and she comes over to them and she asks what'll it be and Sigve says it'll be a glass of beer each, he says and she looks at Asle and she asks if he has proof of age and then Asle takes out his wallet and takes out his ID card and hands it to her and she looks at it and then she says three glasses of beer then and she gives Asle back his ID and she turns and walks away

I would never have thought you were eighteen years old, or well maybe I would, The Namesake says

and Sigve looks around and then says that Asle's not old enough, he's not eighteen, but they did a little something to his ID card and then suddenly he was eighteen and The Namesake says so that's how it is, he might have known, he did the same thing with his own ID, he says, and it was easy as can be, you'd almost think they made the IDs so that people could change the numbers on them, he says

Yeah, Sigve says

And if you work carefully no one can see that anything's been changed, he says

Anyway, you need to use a magnifying glass, he says

and then it's quiet and then Sigve sits down next to Asle and he looks at The Namesake and says that Asle is going to The Academic High School in Aga

So you're an advanced student then, The Namesake says

But he paints pictures, him too, Sigve says

Yes I thought so, The Namesake says

And he just painted a picture of the house I live in, well, you've been there, yes, from a photograph, the one hanging above the sofa in the living room, Sigve says

So you do that kind of thing, The Namesake says

I used to do it a lot, but I was so tired of painting houses and homes with a blue sky and a blue fjord and a white house and a birch tree just putting its leaves out and a black mountain with white snow on the top that I stopped that, so the picture of the house is in black and white, Asle says

and The Namesake says that he used to do that too

You painted pictured of people's homes for them too? Asle says

Let's not talk about that, The Namesake says

and Asle thinks that he doesn't want to ask The Namesake where he's from, but one thing's for sure, he's not from Barmen or Stranda, but he must be from some other town in Hardanger anyway, you can hear it in his voice, Asle thinks, and he thinks he'd rather not know exactly where The Namesake comes from, it's like he'd prefer not to know that

But lately I haven't wanted to paint any more happy little houses in happyland, it's just lies, The Namesake says

And then, he says

Yes, then I started thinking I'd rather make money painting pictures of boats in a storm at sea, and especially sailboats, but I've also painted steamships and you might say almost modern boats, wooden fishing smacks, that kind of thing, but those paintings are all just lies too, he says

Lies and fraud, he says

and again everyone stops talking

But you have to live on something, everyone needs a little money, he says

and he says, and he looks straight at Asle, that now he'll have two pictures like that done soon and then he'll set up outside The Stranda Hotel, in front of the stairs, with the pictures leaning against the ground-floor wall, he's already done that lots of times, and he always manages to sell the paintings, but it's no good to try to sell too many at once, he says, the best thing is to have just one or two to sell, because then you can get more money for each one, he says, and he says he hopes Asle's not getting any ideas into his head because this is his territory, he says, and he'd rather avoid any competition when it comes to selling paintings like this, he says and Asle hears what he's saying and he has suddenly started thinking about all the people who've sat in this hotel drinking beer, at one or another of these tables, and who are gone now, yes, the ones who are lying in their graves and the ones who've left nothing behind, and now he is sitting at a table in this old hotel, The Stranda Hotel, drinking beer, now it's his turn to be up on the earth, but not for long, and he doesn't know how long he has, no, and then he too will be in the ground, down in the dirt, and will there be anything of him left behind? yes well, aside from the remains lying down in the earth? no, nothing will be left, or maybe a few bones for a while, until they disappear too, so there's nothing left of all the many people who've sat in this old Stranda Hotel drinking beer, Asle thinks, but every single person is more than just bone and meat and fat, and hair and skin, there's a soul too, or a spirit, or both, or whatever you'd call it, whatever the difference is between soul and spirit, and the same way every single person looks different, yes well almost, yes, almost everyone but well it's basically impossible to see any difference between him and The Namesake, he and every other person also has a soul, or maybe a spirit, that's totally unlike other people's, so if he and The Namesake look exactly the same then their souls, their spirits, can't be as similar as their appearance, he thinks

Well you're off in dreamland, The Namesake says

What are you thinking about? he says

I was thinking about all the people who've sat and drank beer at one of the tables in this old hotel and are gone now, Asle says

Yes, The Namesake says

What I'm trying to paint has something to do with them, he says

Same with me, Asle says

But what we're talking about now isn't something that can be said, it can just be painted, maybe, yes, it can be shown in a way, The Namesake says

Yes, Asle says

and it gets quiet and then Gunvor comes over with a tray that has three bottles of beer and three glasses on it and she puts a glass and a bottle down in front of each of them and then she pours a little beer into each glass and she says enjoy and Sigve says thank you and that he'll be paying, but they might be having a couple more rounds probably so maybe he can wait until later to pay, he says and Gunvor says that's fine and she leaves and then Sigve says can't they talk about something else, because this is starting to sound like prayers at a meeting house or a sermon in church or something

Let's drink and be merry, he says

While we still can, he says

and he raises his glass

Yes, The Namesake says

and he raises his glass and then Asle raises his glass and they toast and they drink and then they bang their glasses back down on the table and then they each start rolling a cigarette and they light them and then Sigve says that it's good to be alive, just a glass or two of something and life is good, he says

Yes, Asle says

Yes, it feels good, he says

It calms me down, he says

and The Namesake nods and then none of them says anything

Well that was quite a silence, The Namesake says

Nothing wrong with a little silence, Sigve says

and then The Namesake says someone he knew has moved in with him, now the two of them are living together in one room there in The Basement, she'd started working as a maid at The Stranda Hotel and at first she lived in one of the ordinary

hotel rooms herself, but she didn't like that, so she moved in with
him, they agreed that she should move in one night when he was
sitting here having a beer and she came and sat down at his table,
he says and she's there at home in The Basement right now, he
says and then he says that he's going to try to get into The Art
School in Bjørgvin, one of these days he's going to bring some of
his paintings and take the bus to Bjørgvin and then he'll go up to
The Art School and show them his paintings and if he starts there,
yes, then he too will get an artist's stipend, The Namesake says,
so now if he just finishes the two paintings he's working on and
gets them sold and gets the money for the bus he'll go to Bjørgvin
and try to get a spot at The Art School, he says, and Asle says that
he thought you needed to have gone to an academic high school
to get into The Art School, that's why he was going to The Academic High School, not because he wanted to but because he
wanted to get into The Art School, he says and The Namesake
says that that is how it is but it's possible to make an exception to
the rule, if a painter's good enough he can get in even if he hasn't
gone to The Academic High School, he says and he wasn't clear
about that either, he says, but then he wrote to The Art School
and asked if that ever happened and got an answer and it said in
the letter that it was possible to get into The Art School without
having gone to an academic high school if you painted good
enough pictures, he says, and Asle thinks how about that, yes,
so maybe he doesn't need to slog through all of The Academic
High School, because the pictures he paints are good enough,
he's sure of that, or maybe that's just something he's imagining
and they aren't as good as he thinks they are and it'll be easier for
him to get into The Art School if he has his examen artium, so
it's probably better if he finishes The Academic High School after
all, he thinks, and he feels calmer now, the beer has taken his fear
away and The Namesake says that the woman who's moved in
with him is a few years older than him, her name is Liv and now
she's going to have a baby too, yes, they're going to have a baby

together, he's already about to become a father, young as he is, The Namesake says and Sigve says well he's going to be a young father and The Namesake says that it isn't something he wanted, so of course that's what happened, but what will be will be, and if he gets a spot at The Art School and gets an artist's stipend and they find a place to live in Bjørgvin it'll probably all work out, he says, because there must be cheap apartments to rent at what they call The Student's Home, maybe they can get a place there, he says and then he finishes his drink and Sigve says live and let live and both Sigve and Asle have a lot of beer left in their glass and The Namesake says that he should probably get home to Liv, she must be waiting for him, because he said he would just go out for a little walk, he says and he gets up and he says that he needs to finish painting those two sailboats, and he signs all these pictures of boats in a rough sea in the lower right corner, he writes Helle Halle there, and so unclearly that it's illegible and whenever the buyers ask him what his name is he says Helle Halle, The Namesake says and he puts his shoulder bag on and then he says see you and he leaves and then Sigve and Asle are sitting there and Sigve moves over to the other side of the table where The Namesake had been sitting and he moves the empty coffee cup and the empty beer glass that The Namesake left behind over to the side of the table and then he takes his own beer glass and puts it in front of him and Asle takes a sip of his beer and then he looks out the window at The Fjord and it's almost totally still, it's not entirely calm but almost, because there's a light wind making small waves on The Fjord, and every single wave is different, if you look closely you can see that there isn't a single wave that's exactly like another, the same way there's not a single cloud that's exactly like another cloud, all the waves are different, and all the clouds are different, Asle thinks and that's how they are in a good painting too, no wave is just a wave and no cloud is just a cloud, they're like that only in pictures of a sailboat in a storm, as The Namesake puts it, and that's probably why he thinks these paint-

ings are so bad, and that he paints them quickly and badly just
to make money, since those are the kinds of painting that people
want to buy, Asle thinks, and then he thinks that it's strange that
people like so much to buy bad paintings but no one wants to buy
the good ones, no, it's impossible to understand, Asle thinks and
then he hears Sigve say that he needs to drink, too, not just think
or dream or whatever it is he's doing and Asle sees that Sigve
has finished his glass and Asle sees that his is only half drunk so
he takes a good sip and Sigve says that as soon as Gunvor shows
up, because she's always checking to see if the customers want
anything, they'll order another drink, Sigve says, yes, he's been
to The Stranda Hotel so many times that he even knows that the
woman who was sitting at the reception desk and who's serving
them now is named Gunvor and that her husband, who owns
the hotel, is named Stein, they're both named Stein, The Stranda
Hotel has been in the same family for generations, Sigve says and
no sooner has he said it than Asle sees Gunvor appear and Sigve
raises his hand and she comes over right away and Sigve says that
he'd like to order two more beers and Gunvor says that'll be fine
and then she takes away the empty glass and empty bottle and
empty coffee cup that The Namesake left and then she walks
away and Sigve says yes, her name is Gunvor, and she married
into the family, and then there's silence and then Asle thinks so
it was The Stranda Hotel that Sigve broke into back in the day
and Sigve says that it was The Stranda Hotel that he and the other crook broke into to get more to drink, but he'd accepted his
punishment and settled things with Gunvor and her husband, he
says and then he says that he assumed Asle wanted another beer
too, yes, at least one and I'm lying on the bench with the grey
blanket wrapped around me, the one Grandmother had on her
when she was lying on the bench in The Old House after she'd
had her stroke and that I took with me when I moved to Aga
to live in a rented room and that's followed me everywhere I've
lived since then, I think and I see that now there's just embers

lit in the stove, and it's a little cold in the room now, so I should put a couple more logs in, I think but I stay lying down because sometimes it takes a real effort just to get to my feet, I think and then I suddenly hear footsteps and I see the door to the hallway open and there, yes, right there in the middle of the hall is Åsleik and he's downright brandishing a cured leg of lamb waving it back and forth over his shoulder like he's about to throw it at me and I think I must have dozed off a bit yes

You're too old to be driving to Bjørgvin constantly, Åsleik says

It tires you out too much, he says

You're wearing yourself out, he says

Your hair's gone greyer in just a few days, I can see it, he says

and Åsleik says was there really any rush to drive those paintings down to Bjørgvin? and anyway why didn't I take them with me on Monday when I drove down to Bjørgvin not once but twice? he says, why did I have to drive them down separately yesterday? what am I doing? Åsleik says and he says now I need to relax a bit, and get some food in me, because even if I am a bit on the heavy side, and you'd have to say I am, I have to admit, at least I'm not a liar, then I've gotten thinner in the last couple of days and the last time he stopped by he saw that there wasn't much meat left on the leg of lamb hanging in the kitchen so he thought he'd bring over a new one, but it's not, it's not without an ulterior motive, as I've probably guessed, because it's about the time I'll be cutting up the rest of the cured lamb bones into parts and cooking them with potato dumplings and once they've been cooking long enough I'll add a little smoked sausage and carrots and turnips to the water, Åsleik says and then I'll fry up some bacon and that'll be dinner, he says, the way I've always done it, I usually ask him to come over a couple of times a year for potato dumplings cooked in stock from what's left of the leg of lamb, Åsleik says, and he can see that it won't be long until the next time, because there's not much meat left on the mutton leg, as city folks call it, that's hanging in the kitchen, Åsleik says, but first they should probably have their Advent dinners at each other's houses, and even though he felt like having the Christmas lamb ribs that he's been soaking since yesterday and today he took The Boat to Vik to shop on both days, the water was calm and beautiful today, and he bought a lot of turnips, potatoes he has from his own garden of course, and he's told me again and again that I could have some of his potatoes but I've always said no thank you and he can't understand why, but I just don't want potatoes, only Christmas lamb ribs and lutefisk and dry-cured mutton and a little salt cod, and it's true that that's the best he has to offer, but he doesn't grow turnips himself so he had to buy them, but what with the price of turnips these days he should just grow the turnips himself next year, Åsleik says and he says that it's cold in my room and I sit up on the bench and I see that the fire's gone out in the stove and Åsleik goes over to the stove and now I can feel how cold it is in the room, but of course I didn't feel it that much when I was lying there sleeping, and I must have been asleep since I didn't hear Åsleik's tractor, I think and Åsleik says he walked on over today because it's important to keep active, and it's not that far anyway, but it is a ways, he says and what was it Åsleik was saying, that we should eat Christmas lamb ribs today? yes well we usually have Christmas lamb and lutefisk at each other's house during Advent, along with always doing that on New Year's Eve we usually have some during Advent and every other year I go to Åsleik's for lamb ribs and he comes over to my house for lutefisk, and in the other years it's reversed, that's how it's been for years, and this year it's Åsleik's turn to make the lamb ribs, but anyway we usually invite each other to these Advent meals well in advance, so this is rather sudden, isn't it, yes, Åsleik just decided that we should have lamb ribs today and so that's that, today already, and it's just because Åsleik felt like having lamb ribs, but I don't feel like lamb ribs, not right when I've just woken up in any case, I think, and the truth is I don't feel like having any food at all, I think, so I think I'll say thank you but no to Åsleik's invitation and he can just have his lamb ribs alone, I think, but that would probably be wrong? and lamb ribs certainly are good, because Åsleik's lamb ribs always taste unbelievably delicious, and I've already eaten up, by myself, one of the two sides of lamb that I get from Åsleik every year, yes, sometimes I make a few potato dumplings to go with it, and two carrots, and then I melt some margarine to put on the dumplings, and that tastes at least as good as lamb ribs with mashed turnips, maybe even better, I think and I then think that Åsleik and I always talk about food, it seems like that anyway, I think, and now is that anything for two older guys to talk about, one of them, Åsleik, almost totally bald with just a little long thin white hair around his bald spot, and then he has a big grey beard, and he trims both of them himself, hair and beard, with scissors, and that's why it's always cut so unevenly, and he can't be trimming his hair and beard too often either, I think, but it's not like I look any better with this long grey hair of mine always tied back with a black hair tie, I think, but it doesn't help much, because my hair is so thin up top that a bald spot shows through, so even if I tie my hair back with a black hair tie the bald spot is still visible through the strands of hair, and I have a grey beard too, at first I trimmed my beard with scissors too, that was when I had a really long beard, but then I got an electric trimmer and I started keeping my beard short, really short, so almost as soon as I wake up I trim my beard, but that doesn't make me look all that much better, no, neither of us looks too good, Åsleik or me, I think and then Åsleik stands there by the stove and he looks at me and he says I need to come over to his house tonight and have dinner, Christmas is getting closer, in spite of everything, and we usually always have dinner at each other's house during Advent, these Advent meals of ours, he says, so if the invitation's a little sudden for me maybe I'll want to come have dinner with him once I collect my thoughts a little, he says and I say yes I guess I will

And it's a good thing you woke me up, otherwise I wouldn't have been able to get to sleep tonight, I say

It's not good to sleep too much during the day, no, Åsleik says and I say no, I can't just sleep the days away, and Åsleik says that the whole time he's known me, and it's getting on many years now, he has never seen me drive back and forth to Bjørgvin on the same day and then drive back to Bjørgvin again that same day and drive home the next day and then drive back to Bjørgvin yet again the day after that, no, he doesn't understand what's going on with me? he says, what's come over me? and I don't need to tell him, of course, yes well the last time was because I had to take in the paintings for the regular Christmas exhibition, which always opens right before Christmas, that makes sense, and a couple of days before that, yes, on Monday, I had shopping to do in Bjørgvin, both for myself and for him, he says, but why did I drive back a second time that same day? and why didn't I bring the paintings with me on one of those two times I drove down? no, he doesn't understand, and it doesn't seem like I'm doing too well, yes, he can't say I'm looking too healthy, Åsleik says, or actually I'm still healthy but it's like something's happened that's worrying me, and to tell the truth that was really why he decided I could use a little hearty food, Åsleik says, yes, he thought a lamb-rib dinner would do me good, and a little juicy mutton, he says and again he holds the mutton leg out to me and I say thank you and I just sit there on the bench and Åsleik says so we'll talk more tonight then? at seven o'clock? he says and I say yes, yes, thank you, it's a little sudden for me but I'm sure it'll be delicious, I say and I just sit there on the bench and Åsleik says that I'm clearly not in the mood to talk much right now and he probably should be getting home anyway, maybe he shouldn't have bothered me, and even woken me up? he says and I say again that no, it was good, if I'd slept any longer I wouldn't have been able to get to sleep tonight and I don't like lying awake in bed, so many thoughts come into my head, I say and then I don't say anything else and Åsleik says he'll go home to check on the lamb ribs in the steam cooker, he's never overcooked the lamb ribs before but still you need to pay attention, he remembers that his mother used to stand there the whole time and check to see that there was still water in the pan, yes, actually she was most likely really doing it to enjoy the good smell of the lamb ribs, that was the main reason, Åsleik says, but anyway he shouldn't stand here chit-chatting, he'll just leave me alone now

We'll talk tonight then, I say

And I'm looking forward to the meal, Åsleik says

Yes, we'll talk later, I say

Around seven o'clock, he says

and then Åsleik says that he'll leave the mutton leg on the kitchen table and I can hang it up myself and he stays standing there and I'm sitting on the bench and I look at the round table with the two chairs, there was one for Ales and one for me, and Ales's chair is still there and I look at her empty chair, and now surely Ales will come soon? I think, yes, I always think that, and then with her chair standing there empty like always, and I couldn't bring myself to get rid of it either, it was like I would be desecrating Ales's memory in a way if I did that, and that was something I didn't want, yes, that's what I would have been doing if I did that, but constantly thinking that Ales had to be back soon now, seeing the empty chair and thinking that Ales was still alive and about to come home, no, being like that was no good either, I think, but the chair is still there, and one day when Åsleik was over and I was sitting in my chair he sat down in the empty chair next to me and I was suddenly shocked and afraid, yes, it was like I was suddenly jealous and I told Åsleik he had to get up

Get up, I said

and he stood up right away and he looked at me taken aback

I didn't know, he said

and I felt ashamed of myself

Sorry, I said

I didn't know, he said again

No of course, I say

But that's Ales's chair, I say

and then it was quiet for a long time and then Åsleik asked if maybe it was a bad idea to have the chair always there, the chair where Ales used to sit, he said and I said no, no, it's not bad, but I didn't want anyone else to sit there, because it was like desecrating Ales's memory, I said and Åsleik said that when Ales was alive he used to sit in that chair all the time and I sat in the other chair and we'd sit there and look out at the water and I said that's how it was but that was when Ales was alive and was either in the room with us or was somewhere else in the house, but now, now that she's gone, yes, now it's only her chair, even I never sit in it, I said and then Åsleik asked didn't I want to get rid of the chair, maybe move it into The Parlour? he said and I said I wanted the empty chair to stay where it is now and Åsleik again said sorry

I didn't know that's how it was, he said

No, how could you, I said

No, he said

and I stand up from the bench and I go and sit down in my chair next to the round table and I look at Åsleik and I say that I often sit and look out at the water, yes, either I'm standing and painting or I'm lying on the bench or I'm sitting in my chair looking out at the water, the sea, out across the Sygne Sea, yes, I say, and I've probably told him that I have a fixed landmark, I say and Åsleik shakes his head and I say that I always look at the same spot in the water, at my landmark, I say and Åsleik says he needs to get home and then he says we'll talk later and then he says that he'll leave the mutton leg on the kitchen table and I see Åsleik go out to the kitchen and shut the kitchen door behind him and I think that the sea is always there to be seen, yes, I can see all the way out to the mouth of the fjord and the open sea, yes, I see the Sygne Sea and the islets and reefs out there, the holms and skerries, and the islands protecting the mouth of the fjord, and then I see the spaces between the islands where it opens out and you can see the ocean itself, yes, even if it's dark or snowing hard or a heavy rain or there's a fog I can see the water, the waves, the ocean, and it's impossible to understand, actually, I think as I sit there in the chair at the round table and I take my bearings and I look at the spot I always look at in the water and I see Asle standing in the hall outside the classroom waiting for The Teacher who teaches English and French and he sees The Teacher come walking up to him and he's wearing his grey trousers and white pullover with blue stripes again today and he's carrying some books and when he gets to Asle he says why aren't you going into class?

But, Asle says

Yes, The Teacher says

I, you know, Asle says

Yes, The Teacher says

Yes I, Asle says

Yes I, I, I'm too scared to read aloud, he says

Scared to read aloud? The Teacher says

and it's like he can't believe what he's hearing

Yes, Asle says

and The Teacher looks at him and Asle can tell that he doesn't believe what he's saying and Asle says he wants to ask him if he could not read out loud in class and The Teacher looks at him and then he says that he often has some student or a row of students recite something, as he's noticed already, so it would be a bit strange if he didn't read too, he says and Asle can tell that The Teacher doesn't believe him and then The Teacher says that he'll try to take this into consideration so Asle won't have to read so much, maybe just one or two sentences, but it is important that he practise his pronunciation, The Teacher says and then he asks if Asle would prefer that he ask him questions? to hear whether or not he's done his homework, his reading? and Asle says that would be great and there's something like mockery in The Teach- er's voice and then Asle says that that was all he wanted to say and The Teacher says they should go in then, today in any case he won't have to read anything out loud, because he'd heard him stumbling and skipping words last time, but his pronunciation is good, yes, his English is good, so he'll be able to learn to speak English well, and they'll see how it goes with French but anyway they need to go into the classroom now, The Teacher says and Asle goes in and he has his brown leather shoulder bag on and he goes over to his desk in the very back of the classroom near the middle and I look at the water, there at my landmark, at the waves, and I get up from the chair and I go out to the kitchen and there on the kitchen table I see a big leg of mutton, yes, Åsleik is generous, I think, he likes to give people things, and plus he's so proud of the food he's prepared, the Christmas lamb ribs, the lutefisk, I think, but it is rather sudden being invited over for a lamb-rib dinner tonight, because strictly speaking I don't feel like eating any food, I have absolutely no appetite for anything, but it'll still taste good anyway, I think and then I take the new leg of lamb and it's heavy in my hand and I put it back down on the kitchen table and then I take the lamb bone off the hook on the wall where it's hanging, and it's almost just bone now, and I put it on the kitchen table and then hang the new leg up and I look at the old leg of lamb on the table and I think that I am hungry, but I'm not in the mood for any food today and I think that later I'll cut it up into pieces and then boil it with potato dumplings, but I won't do that for a while, so I should just stick this leg of lamb in the freezer I have in the hall, I think, and then I'll cut it up into pieces later, I think and I go out into the hall and I see the telephone sitting there and it doesn't ring very often, it sometimes happens that Asle calls, and now I need to call The Hospital and ask how he's doing, and whether I can see him, I think, but that can wait a little, I think, and it sometimes happens every now and then that Beyer calls me, and then there's Åsleik sometimes, usually to ask me if I can buy him something he needs the next time I'm in Bjørgvin, and that's why I keep a notepad and pencil next to the phone on its table there in the hall, that's where I write down what Åsleik's asking me to buy, or when the appointment is if Beyer and I are arranging to see each other, and sometimes every now and then I call Asle too, and then we usually set a time to meet at The Alehouse and then I always call The Country Inn to book my regular room, Room 407, and then Asle and I meet at The Alehouse and have a big dinner, and he has a lot of beer and stronger stuff with it, I used to drink with him before and quite a lot too but that was before Ales and I moved to the brown house, yes, you'd have to say that strictly speaking we moved out of Bjørgvin to the brown house to get away because I was drinking too much, to tell the truth, for a while it was almost nothing but drinking and no painting, and Ales thought I had to stop drinking, and she was completely right, and strangely enough I was able to totally stop drinking, I think, but I don't want to think about that anymore, I think, and first I stopped smoking, because I smoked all the time, lighting each cigarette with the end of the other so to speak, and then one day it felt like I had smoked as much as I was meant to smoke, and I stopped, first smoking, then drinking, and after a while I hardly ever went to restaurants or bars, just to cafés, aside from meeting Asle at The Alehouse every now and then, at The Last Boat, that's how it was, I think and when we met there Asle's always had a little to drink beforehand, and when I see that I start getting a little anxious and I say that it's night for me, I go to bed early, I always turn in at around nine o'clock, I would say and then Asle says he'll stay for a while at The Alehouse, because someone needs to man The Last Boat, he says and he laughs and I say yes we've drunk a lot together over the years you and me and Asle says yes we sure have but that was before I moved out of Bjørgvin and before Ales got me to stop drinking, because it was she who got me to stop, wasn't it? yes, he was sure it was, just as I'd said, because after Ales and I left Bjørgvin it wasn't like we never drank together again, we still met at The Alehouse sometimes, but then I would only drink coffee or water, or else we'd sometimes meet at The Coffeehouse instead, that was usually in the mornings before I went to mass at St Paul's Church, I think, and I think that I need to call The Hospital to hear how Asle is doing, and check if I can come and see him? or if I can bring him something from his apartment anyway, if I can maybe buy him something he might need? I think and no sooner did I think that than Bragi is standing there next to me looking up at me with his dog's eyes and I ask if he wants to go outside and I go and open the front door and Bragi runs out as fast as he can and I leave the door open and I think I need to call The Hospital, because even if I can't see Asle maybe I can bring him something from his apartment? books, maybe? because he was always reading some book or another, and I can give the books or whatever to the woman at the reception desk and then she or someone else can pass them along to Asle, I think, because while I don't read much and am only now thinking seriously about starting to read, Asle has read constantly, yes, it's almost impossible to truly believe how much he's read, or how much he's drunk, for that matter, yes I need to call The Hospital, I think, but not just now, I'm too tired, and anyway I can't drive back to Bjørgvin today so I can call in the morning, because then I can maybe drive back to Bjørgvin to see Asle, that's certainly possible, I think and I feel tired and I step into the cut-off boots I keep by the front door and I go outside and I see snowflakes coming gently down one after another, so now it's already started snowing again, snow one day and rain the next, like always, I think and I see Bragi standing there and doing his business and then running around in circles while the snowflakes come gently down over him and stick to his fur and then I call for Bragi and he comes running over right away and he runs into the hall and I shut the door and I think that I should have painted a little, and right away something like a darkness falls down over and inside me and I think that I don't have the strength to paint anymore, I've done my part, I've done all the painting I'm going to do, I'm done with painting, I don't want to paint anymore, I think, enough is enough, I think and I go into the main room and over there on the easel I see the bad painting with the two lines that cross in the middle, no, I can't look at it, I can't even take the picture down from the easel and put it in the pile with the other paintings I'm not totally done with yet, that I'm not totally satisfied with, I just can't, I think and I look at the easel and I think that when I look at the easel now, isn't it like, the thought comes into my head, isn't it like God is there too, in the easel? like, yes, like God is looking out at me from the easel? I think, and now I just have to not go crazy, I think, because it's like God is looking at me from every single thing, I think and I look around and it's like God is in everything around me, I think, and like he's looking at me from every single thing, I think and I think isn't the round table clearly saying with its silence that God is nearby? and the two chairs? and the one Ales always sat in, especially clearly, God is so clearly looking at me from that chair, I think, and I think that it's when I'm most alone, in my darkness, my loneliness, because it really is lonely, to tell the truth, and when I'm as quiet as I can be, that God is closest, in his distance, and I really have, almost like a monk, I think, and then I start laughing because you can hardly imagine anyone less like a monk than me, I think, or maybe well maybe there is a similarity, because maybe I've withdrawn from life too, a little like a monk, I think, into this wordless painting, yes, into loneliness, I could probably put it that way except it sounds so wrong, I think, but I really have withdrawn into the wordless prayer of painting, maybe it's all right to put it that way, and it does sound wrong, I think, and it's also the peace painting gives, I've also withdrawn into that, I think, but this is the wrong word, it's too big a word, the truth is just that I stood there and painted, day in and day out, all these years, with all the humility I have in me I stood there and painted, and I probably need to keep standing there painting because what else can I do, really? but I don't

want to paint anymore, I think, and if I don't want to paint anymore I don't have to, I think and then I think that God has been
staying hidden this whole time, yes, it's like he shows himself by
concealing himself, in life, in things, in what is, yes, in paintings
too of course, and maybe it's like the more God conceals himself
the more he shows himself, and vice versa, yes, the more he
shows himself, or is shown, you can say it either way, the more
he conceals himself, I think, yes, God reveals himself by hiding,
and it is in the hiddenness of God, God's hiddenness, that I can
forget myself and hide myself, and only there, I think, and this is
not something I can understand, there's nothing comprehensible
about it, but it's when you understand that you can't understand
God that you understand him, and isn't that so obvious that it
doesn't even need to be said? doesn't need to be thought? yes, it's
just as obvious as the fact that God's words are silent, I think,
because they are, but that's completely obvious too, because
God's language speaks silently from everything that exists, and
this silence was first broken when The Word came into the
world, when Christ came down to earth, only then could God's
word be heard, yes, and be thought, too, but do I really believe
this? I think, does it mean anything? I think, no, maybe not, but
maybe a person can be hidden in Christ, in his word, and that's
because there's hope in God's great silence? but do I believe that?
no, maybe not, not literally, but God's nearness isn't something I
need to believe in, because the darker I am the closer God is, I
think, that's a fact, I think and it's something I'll always think
even if I don't get any farther with my thoughts than that, it's
only with painting that I get any farther, but, farther? what do I
mean by that? I think, I've just now thought that I don't want to,
that I can't, paint anymore, I think and I look at the chair where
Ales used to sit and I think that this silent language from the
chair is real, it's true, it's ridiculous but that's what I seriously
think, yes, that God's silent language comes from the chair, yes,
that God is looking at me from Ales's chair and silently speaking

to me, I think, because there's a silence hidden in everything that is, and it's this stillness that is the innermost part of everything real, I think, and it's this stillness that is God's creative silence, as Ales used to say, because God is an uncreated light, she said and I've experienced myself that the black darkness is God's light, this darkness that can be both in me and around me, yes, this darkness I now feel that I am, because in the darkness is a stillness where God's voice sounds in silence, I think and I see the chair where I always sit next to the round table and I go over to the chair and I sit down and I find my bearings and then I look at my landmark, at the waves, and I think that often when I sit like this and look at the water I pray a silent prayer and then Ales is near me too, and my parents, and my sister Alida, and Grandmother, and Sigve, and I get very still inside, and I think that everyone has a deep longing inside them, we always always long for something and we believe that what we long for is this or that, this person or that person, this thing or that thing, but actually we're longing for God, because the human being is a continuous prayer, a person is a prayer through his or her longing, I think and then I look at the chair next to me and I see Ales sitting there and then she starts singing softly, almost inaudibly, she sings Amazing grace How sweet the song That saved a wretch like me I once was lost But now am found Was blind but now I see and then I see Ales stand up and disappear and as she disappears I hear her singing again in an almost inaudible voice Amazing grace How sweet the song That saved a wretch like me I once was lost But now am found Was blind but now I see and I grip the edge of the table tight and then I look at Bragi standing there and looking at me with his dog's eyes and I think that dogs understand so much but they can't say anything about it, or else they can say it with their dog's eyes, and in that way they're like good art, because art can't say anything either, not really, it can only say something else while keeping silent about what it actually wants to say, that's what art is like and faith and dogs' silent understanding too, it's like they're all the same, no now I'm getting in over my head with these thoughts, I think, because I've never been a thinker, and the only language I've so to speak mastered is the language of pictures, I think, and all my thoughts are sort of jumbled together, it's like they don't exist in any order but sort of all at the same time, I think and I look at Bragi and I think maybe he's hungry or thirsty, and it's good to think about that, I think, because I'm trying to comprehend the incomprehensible but it doesn't work, I think and I get up and go out to the kitchen and Bragi follows me and I see that there's no water in his bowl and I fill the bowl with water and he laps and laps at his water and then I cut a slice of bread and break it apart into pieces and put the pieces into the other dish I've set out for Bragi, but he just sniffs at the bread and then he slinks back off into the main room and I think that I really need to find something else for Bragi to eat soon, I think and I think that now I'll go sit in my chair again and then I'll pray for Asle to get better, I think and I go into the main room and I see my black velvet jacket hanging over the back of the chair where I always sit and it's always like that, I always hang my velvet jacket over the back of the chair, I think and I think that I never got rid of Ales's clothes, I put them in boxes nice and neatly and put the boxes up in crates in the attic room, the room where I keep my paintings, so that if Ales one day decides to rise from the dead and come walking into her old house she won't be missing a single article of clothing or anything else of hers, because I've taken care of everything, yes, it really is complete madness, I think, but I couldn't manage to give Ales's clothes or anything else she owned to The Second-Hand Shop, it was too much, and so everything just stayed how it was when she died, it stayed that way for a long time but eventually I gathered her clothes up and put them in boxes and stored them up in the attic and one of these days I need to get hold of myself and come to my senses and drive the boxes of clothes to Bjørgvin and give them to The Second-Hand Shop so someone else can use them, because now they're no good to anyone, I think and I think that in one attic room there's now the portrait I painted of Ales out, leaned against the back of a chair, because that's one of the pictures I didn't want to sell, and that I'll never sell, that is the only picture I will never sell, all the other pictures I'd be happy to sell, as I'm now thinking I'm going to do, but I want to keep the portrait of Ales, and that's so obvious it doesn't even need to be said, I think and when I thought I'd sell all the pictures it was so unthinkable that I'd sell the portrait of Ales that I didn't even think that I wouldn't sell it, I think, and her portrait has been leaning against the back of a chair between the two small windows for such a long time now, I think, several years at least, I think and I stand in the main room and I look at the empty chair where Ales always sat and I think that either I need to get rid of the empty chair or else let Åsleik sit in it, or anyone else who comes over for a visit, but who would that be? I can't remember having anyone else come visit except Åsleik in all these years, just him, no one else, I think, but I just don't want Åsleik to sit in that chair, or anyone else for that matter, so that means the chair is going to just stay there empty, I think, so maybe I should ask Åsleik if he wants to carry the chair into The Parlour? where all of Ales's paintings still are the way they were, where everything is still the way she left it the day she went to The Hospital never to return, I think, and so should I ask Åsleik to put the chair in front of the window there, I think, but no, how can I even think that, of course Ales's chair has to stay where it's always been, how can I even think otherwise, I think and I go and sit down in my chair and I look at the spot out there in the Sygne Sea that I always look at and I look at the waves and I see Asle sitting on the bus from Aga to Stranda and he's thinking that actually it's going pretty well at The Academic High School, because even if he put it off much longer than he should have he did eventually talk to The Teacher who taught Norwegian and History, the homeroom teacher, and to The Teacher who taught German, and they'd

understood right away what reading out loud was like for him
and they'd both said that they wouldn't ask him to read out loud,
but, they'd both said, if he did feel able to read something should
raise his hand or give a sign in some other way that he felt able to
do it and then they could ask him to read, but if he didn't they
wouldn't, they'd said and Asle was so grateful to them for understanding him, and they'd both said that they'd had no problem
understanding it, and then Asle thought that people sure were
different, because these two teachers had understood how he felt
while The Teacher he had in English and French hadn't believed
him, he'd thought Asle was trying to trick him, that Asle wanted
to get out of doing work or something, that he didn't want to do
what he was supposed to, while these two other teachers had
understood at once the fear that was torturing him, so there was
a big difference between people, he'd learned that then and there,
Asle thinks, and then he thinks that every day after he finished at
The Academic High School he went to see Grandmother at The
Hospital, and even if she couldn't talk anymore, even if the only
words she'd been able to say for a long time were gone now, they
were still together in a way, he and Grandmother, and there was
life in her eyes, and she could laugh if he said something funny,
he thinks, but these last few days she'd changed, she'd turned
kind of bluish over her whole face but especially on her lips, her
lips had been a bit blue for a long time but now the blue was
stronger, whiter and stronger, Grandmother had turned so white,
and when he went to see her today her face was almost grey, Asle
thinks, sitting there in the bus going to Stranda because he's out
of white oil paint and he needs some, because he can't paint without white, he thinks, even if painting if you look at it in a certain
way is the art of colour there's no way he can paint without also
using a lot of white, and that's obvious enough, it's pretty straight-
forward, but he also needs to use a lot of black since you often
need black to get a picture into harmony, and everything needs
to be right in a painting, everything needs to go together, there

needs to be a very precise balance in the picture, and to get that balance black can be really useful, Asle thinks and I sit at the round table and now I can feel so clearly that Ales is sitting in the chair next to mine, and she puts her hand over my hand and then we hold each other's hand and stay sitting like that, holding each other's hand, and neither of us says anything and I see Asle sitting on the bus to Stranda and he's thinking that when he gets there he'll go straight to The Paint Shop and buy a big tube of white oil paint and then he'll take the same bus back to Aga that he came on, because the bus goes back to Aga fifteen minutes after it arrives in Stranda, Asle thinks and the bus stops in Stranda and Asle gets out of the bus and then he goes straight to The Paint Shop, because he has hardly any time, since the bus is heading back to Aga in fifteen minutes and he wanted to catch the bus, Asle thinks, because he's in the middle of a picture, and if he wants to do more on it he needs to get hold of some white oil paint, Asle thinks and he goes into The Paint Shop and who should he see standing in front of the tubes of oil paint but The Namesake, his long brown hair, the black velvet jacket, the brown leather shoulder bag, the scarf around his neck, and Asle thinks that of course they're dressed the same today too, and of course he should go up to The Namesake and of course now he'll have to talk to him, and wasn't once enough? Asle thinks, but he needs his white oil paint and he's going to get it so he doesn't leave The Paint Shop, he doesn't have time to leave and come back to The Paint Shop after The Namesake has left, Asle thinks, he needs to just pick up a big tube of white oil paint right now and then go back home to his rented room so that he can keep working on the painting he's in the middle of, Asle thinks and he walks straight to the shelf where the tubes of oil paint are and The Namesake looks at him

No, it's you, he says

Nice to see you again, he says

and he holds out his hand and The Namesake and Asle shake hands

Yes, a lot has happened since we last saw each other, The Namesake says

and Asle thinks he needs to say he doesn't have time and then he sees the tubes of white paint and he picks up two big tubes and The Namesake says yes you can't do anything without white

Yes, a lot's happened, The Namesake says

I, he says

Yes, you need to hear this, he says

I've been accepted at The Art School, The Namesake says

Yeah I took the bus to Bjørgvin and went to The Art School and showed my paintings to the first person I saw, I showed him the best paintings I'd done and he said I had talent, it was a long time since he'd seen pictures that showed such talent, so even if I didn't have an examen artium, yes well what did that really have to do with being able to paint? yes, he was completely sure that The Principal would let me start at The Art School, The Namesake says

and he says that then they went to The Principal and The Principal said that since his paintings showed such clear talent of course he could start at The Art School without an examen artium and The Namesake asked, The Namesake says, if he couldn't maybe start right away and The Principal said that there was always a place for a talent like his, so it would be fine, he said and The Namesake said that he lived in Stranda but that he was going to try to find a place to live either in Bjørgvin or near Bjørgvin as soon as possible so that he could start at The Art School as soon as he could and The Principal asked if he had money, and he'd said hardly any and The Principal said that now that he was a student at The Art School he could apply for an artist's stipend and then he asked for his name and address and birthdate and he asked to see his ID card, because he had to see that if The Namesake was going to start at The Art School and when The Principal saw his birthdate he'd said that his age was also a factor in letting him start right away at The Art School and then The Principal wrote

out a letter stating that he had been accepted to The Art School
because his paintings showed clear talent and he gave Asle a form
and said he had to fill out the form and include it with the letter
and apply for an artist's stipend, yes, the students who went to
The Art School got a higher stipend than other students, which
was reasonable enough, The Principal said and then he shook
hands with The Namesake and it was really great that he got into
The Art School, he says, because Liv, yes, Asle probably remembered he'd told him about her, she was very pregnant now, her
belly had grown so big that it looked like it was about to burst,
and she wanted to give birth in The Hospital and she said that
she wanted to go to Sartor where her parents lived as soon as she
could, because the childbirth was getting close, she might be
giving birth any day now, and he could come along to Sartor and
they could stay for a while at her parents' house until they got a
place of their own to live, preferably in Bjørgvin, she said, and
now, yes, he was actually just standing there looking at the tubes
of oil paint without planning to buy anything because he had to
pack up everything he owned, all of it, and Liv had to pack up
everything she owned, and she found room for everything in her
one suitcase but it was harder for him since he had to bring all
his paintings with him, and of course the easel and brushes and
all the other painting things, but he didn't have many clothes to
pack, so if The Bus Driver wasn't too difficult there'd be enough
room for everything in the baggage compartment, he says

Congratulations on getting into The Art School, Asle says

And you'll be next, The Namesake says

I hope I get in, Asle says

You will, I'm sure of it, The Namesake says

and then Asle says that he doesn't have much time, he just got
off the bus from Aga and he's in the middle of a painting and he
ran out of white paint again so he was planning to take the same
bus back, he says and The Namesake says he won't hold him up
and keep him from catching the bus and he says he's never spo-

ken to Liv's parents, who live in Sartor, and she hasn't asked them either if it's okay that she, or they, come there, or if she, well, they, can live there for a while, she hasn't even told her parents that she's pregnant, she doesn't talk to her parents much, but she did tell her mother over the phone that she'd be taking a trip home soon, she went down to the phone booth in the centre of Stranda and called her mother, and her mother had said of course she was welcome to come, she was so happy she'd be seeing Liv again, it had been so long since the last time, and she was sure that her father felt the same way, of her three sisters who used to live in the house the youngest sister had moved out too in the autumn, she too had gone away, the same way the three other sisters had done before her, so now there was plenty of room in the house, and it would be so nice to see her again, her mother had said and then she'd chattered on about this and that, about the difficult neighbour lady, about Liv's uncle, her father's brother who'd ended up homeless in Bjørgvin and so on and so forth and Liv didn't say a word about being pregnant and that he as the father was going to be with her, he says and Asle has already gone over to the cash register and The Namesake has walked next to him and the man at the register says so you're still painting are you, it's a good thing we have customers like you, he says and Asle says that he doesn't have much time since he needs to catch the bus to Aga and then Asle pays and he leaves and The Namesake leaves with him and The Namesake says that the one thing he's dreading is going home to Liv's parents in Sartor, because what if they don't want him there? maybe Liv's father won't want him to paint because he might get the floor dirty or something? he thinks, he says, and also he was about to be a father, and he was so young, and he didn't own anything, an easel and a few brushes and some pictures and that was it, and he who had thought he would never get married or have children because he'd never be able to, he, yes, he was about to be a father soon, he says and the bus is luckily still there, Asle thinks, so now he can finally get rid of The Namesake, he thinks

The bus is there already, The Namesake says

It's lucky I made it, Asle says

And you were also lucky because they don't always have tubes of white oil paint at The Paint Shop, at least not big ones, The Namesake says

and he says that there've been a few times he's had to wait almost two weeks to get white oil paint, yes, it was unbelievable, it was almost like The Paint Shop was intentionally trying to not carry white oil paint, he says and Asle says that the bus door is open so he better get on right away and The Namesake says yes he should, and so he hopes they meet again at The Art School, he says and Asle says he hopes so too and The Namesake holds out his hand and they shake hands and then The Namesake says that they'll see each other at The Art School in Bjørgvin then, sooner or later, and Asle says that the only question now is whether they'll take him and The Namesake says he's sure they will and Asle thinks now how can The Namesake be so sure that he'll get into The Art School too, he has never even seen one of his paintings, so it's just something he's saying, Asle thinks and he gets on the bus and he tells The Bus Driver that he's going to Aga and The Bus Driver says so he wants to go back home right away and Asle doesn't answer and he pays the fare and he goes to the back of the bus and he sits down in the back seat and then he looks out the window and he sees The Namesake standing there and the bus starts up and pulls away and The Namesake raises his hand and waves at him and Asle waves back and he thinks well now The Namesake has already gotten a spot at The Art School while he's still slogging away at The Academic High School and is afraid to go to school, he's constantly thinking that he might have to read out loud, because The Teacher in English and French who clearly owns only a grey pair of trousers and a white pullover with blue stripes, or else he has several of the same kind of trousers and pullovers, now rarely asks students down a row one after the other to read out loud but he does constantly ask this or that

individual person to read aloud and Asle has noticed that he looks
at him and that he kind of threatens to ask him to read, so now
he'll just have to start skipping school on the days he has English,
because French classes are just words and Asle thinks that the
pronunciation is impossible, he will never be able to make those
sounds, and there's not one of the other students in the class who
can do it either and The Teacher in the grey trousers and white
pullover with blue stripes moans and groans and beats his breast
and says that this is hopeless, it's patently clear that the situation is
hopeless, and he uses those two words all the time, hopeless and
patently, and it'll be a long time before they can read any text out
loud in French so he doesn't have much to worry about there,
but two days a week, Tuesday and Thursday, he has two hours of
English each day and now he'll just have to cut school on those
days, he's thought many times that he should but he's gone to
school anyway, but now he'll miss two days of school every single week, and whatever happens will happen, Asle thinks sitting
there on the bus and he thinks that every Monday and every
Wednesday he's scared all afternoon and all evening, frightened
of the next day, that he might have to read out loud, and so that's
when he usually goes to see Sigve and Sigve answers whenever
he knocks on the door, even if he's not always so glad to see him,
but he always invites him in, and usually Asle has a couple of
beers with him or else they go to The Hotel and buy a glass or
two there, and that helps, but first he goes to see Grandmother at
The Hospital, but she's just getting worse and worse, it's like she's
disappearing into her own world more and more and her face is
getting kind of greyer and greyer and she's asleep more and more
often when he comes by and when she is he leaves right away
and just lets her keep sleeping since if he does wake her up he's
often not sure if she knows he's there, only sometimes does she
look at him clearly and recognize him, and she's entirely stopped
talking, now she just nods or shakes her head, Asle thinks, but he
always holds Grandmother's hand, and her hand is always cold,

he thinks sitting there on the bus and then he thinks that The Namesake got into The Art School without going to The Academic High School, without an examen artium, he could do that too, so one of these days he'll take some of his paintings and get on a bus to Bjørgvin and show the people there the pictures and try to get a spot at The Art School, because exceptions are made for people like them, people who haven't gone to The Academic High School but who get in by reason of talent alone, and if he gets a spot at The Art School he'll stop going to The Academic High School that same day, Asle thinks and he sees that the bus is getting close to The Shoemaker's Workshop where he lives and he pulls the cord and the bus stops and Asle gets out and he goes straight home and he knows exactly where the painting needs a little white paint, there are three places, one place that needs a light thin stroke with movement in it and two others that need a thin overpainting, he thinks and he thinks that tomorrow he has English again so he won't go to school, he's decided that, and before long he'll take the bus to Bjørgvin and then he'll bring the two books that Sigve lent him a long time ago, that he still hasn't read, and he'll read them on the bus, because he hasn't even opened the books, Asle thinks, and then he'll go to The Art School and show them some paintings and try to get a spot even though he doesn't have an examen artium and if he gets a spot he'll stop going to The Academic High School, and this is already a huge relief, he thinks and I sit there and I look at my fixed spot in the water, my bearings, the tops of the pine trees in front of the house need to be in the middle of the middle pane on the right, because the window is divided in two and can be opened from either side and each half of the window is divided into three panes and it's the middle of the right-hand pane that the treetops have to be in, I think and then I look at my landmark and at the waves and I see Asle get out the old suitcase he brought with him from the attic in The Old House when he moved to his rented room and he chooses several pictures and wraps them as well as he can in the grey blanket he got from Grandmother and puts them in the suitcase and he thinks that he should have gone and seen Grandmother at The Hospital but he'd rather go see Sigve and maybe they'll have a beer or two at The Hotel, he thinks and then he puts on his black velvet jacket and brown leather shoulder bag and a scarf and then he'll goes straight to Sigve's, Asle thinks, because now he's finally taken the big decision that he's been thinking about for such a long time, he put it off for too long, he thinks, but now he wants to try to get into The Art School without finishing at The Academic High School, and The Namesake could do it so he should be able to do it too, Asle thinks as he's walking from the old house to Sigve's and he knocks on the door and no one answers so he waits a little bit and he hears someone walking around inside so he knocks again and he hears footsteps coming towards the door and it opens and there's Sigve and he is definitely not so happy to see Asle

No, it's you, Sigve says

and Asle says that he has to tell Sigve something and Sigve invites him in and then Asle says that he's going to try to get into The Art School in Bjørgvin without having graduated from The Academic High School, because if The Namesake could get into The Art School in Bjørgvin without having gone to The Academic High School, just on the strength of his pictures, he should be able to as well, so tomorrow he's going to cut school and take some paintings and go to Bjørgvin and go to The Art School and ask if he can go to The Art School without having finished The Academic High School and taken an examen artium, Asle says and it seems like Sigve isn't entirely following him and Asle sees that the picture he painted of Sigve's house, which had been standing on the floor in front of the bookcase for such a long time now, isn't there anymore, so Sigve must have moved it somewhere else even though it really isn't such a bad painting, Asle thinks and he thinks that it looks like Sigve has been lying down, asleep, and that Asle woke him up, and Sigve says that's very nice and then Sigve says that he was asleep, he was drinking really late last night but he did make it to work, and he got those damn armrests and chair legs attached but it wasn't exactly a great day, no, he says and then Asle says that maybe they could go get a glass or two at The Hotel and Sigve says that after yesterday he really shouldn't, but it sure feels like he could use a glass or two, he says and Asle says that they can go to The Hotel and Sigve says yes, okay, they'll do that and then Sigve says that it was like something snapped in him yesterday a little, no, he doesn't know exactly what came over him but anyway he got angry, and it was mostly himself that he was angry at, because he's never been the type to blame other people, no, he says and then Asle says, saying he doesn't really want to say it, that he wants to apologize for giving Sigve a painting of his house that wasn't the way Sigve wanted it, but actually he'd stopped painting pictures like that, he had painted enough pictures like that, because they weren't real pictures, they were just pointless, really, anyway they weren't art, Asle says and he says that he said he wanted to paint a picture of Sigve's house to be nice, since Sigve had asked him to, and Sigve says that he'd only asked Asle to paint a picture to be nice to him, and then they both laugh a little, and then Sigve says that Asle can just go to The Hotel and have a drink and he'll come a little later, he needs a little time to get ready

In that case I'll go see Grandmother at The Hospital first, Asle says

Yes you go see her every day, Sigve says

She'll miss you if you move to Bjørgvin, he says

I hadn't thought of that, Asle says

and then Asle goes to The Hospital to see Grand- mother and he sees her lying in bed and she's asleep and her face is almost totally grey, with a little blue on her whole face, and he sits down on the edge of the bed and he takes her hand and it's so cold and stiff and then he says something but Grandmother doesn't answer and he hears her breathing but there's a long time between each time she breathes in and breathes out and Asle thinks that since he and Mother never got along too well it was Grandmother he was closest to when he was growing up, always, if it wasn't for her he doesn't know what would have happened to him, Asle thinks and he thinks that he's seen her anyway even if she didn't know it, and he thinks that now it's decided and there's no doubt about it, tomorrow he's going to skip school and take the bus to Bjørgvin, he thinks and now it'll be good to have a couple of glasses of beer, Asle thinks and he goes to The Hotel and he sits down and he orders a glass of beer and then he thinks that Grandmother is going to die tonight, and that's another reason to quit at The Academic High School, so tomorrow he'll skip school and go to Bjørgvin and The Art School and then whatever's going to happen will happen, he thinks and I sit on my chair and look out at the fixed point out on the Sygne Sea, like I'm in the habit of doing, and I notice that Ales is sitting here next to me and she's holding my hand and I think that yes, really, it was the night before I went to Bjørgvin with my pictures to try to get into The Art School that my Grandmother died, I think and then I hear Ales say your Grandmother's in a good place now and I feel that Ales is so close so close, she's sitting in the chair next to me and I can feel her hand in mine so clearly and I look at the chair and of course I don't see anything and I let go of Ales's hand and then I put my arm around her shoulders and I look at the waves and I see Asle and Liv, and she has a big belly, they're sitting on the bus to Bjørgvin and they look so strange sitting there, she with her jacket open because she can't close it since her belly is so big and he with the brown leather shoulder bag on his lap and he thinks that now he's given up the room he was renting in the basement and Liv has given up her job at The Stranda Hotel, so now there's nothing keeping them in Stranda anymore and all their earthly goods, as they say, are packed up and sitting in the bus's baggage compartment now, and The Bus Driver wasn't a problem, he was helpful and put their vanload of stuff into the baggage compartment in the best way, Asle had his things in two empty boxes he'd gotten from The Co-op Store in Stranda and his pictures put away in an old suitcase, and he'd packed his clothes and the other things he had, painting supplies, some books, not much more than that, in two boxes and Liv had her big suitcase and now they're sitting there in the bus and Asle thinks that he's worried about going home to Liv's parents, because what will they say? she hasn't told them she was pregnant, and hasn't told them anything about him, and hasn't told her parents that they'd be arriving today, and what will Liv's father and mother say? Asle thinks and it seems like Liv is thinking the same thing because she says she wishes she'd called her mother and said they were coming and that she's expecting a baby, and that Asle is coming with her, but she was so worried about doing it, she says, and now, now that it is the way it is, her parents can't very well do anything but let them stay in the house, in her childhood home out on Sartor, there's nothing there but some rocky hills and heather and they can see the ocean if they walk just ten or twenty feet up the hill sheltering the house where she grew up, she says and Asle says that he's thinking about the same thing and he says that when they get to Bjørgvin they'll have to get everything they have out of the bus and then hope that the bus to Sartor leaves from the terminal not too long after their bus arrives, and so he'll carry all their stuff over to the terminal, he says and Liv says that she can carry her suitcase herself and Asle says that in that case he'll only need to make two trips, there's the two boxes with the clothes and painting supplies and then the easel and the paintings in the suitcase, and he can't carry all of that in one trip, but he can do it in two, he says and Liv says that if she remembers correctly it's not very far from the gate where the bus from Stranda stops to the gate that the bus to Sartor leaves from, so that'll be fine, but it'll be harder when they get to Sartor, because it's a good long way from the bus stop there up to the house where she grew up, she says, so maybe she should go up first? and she can take her suitcase with her, and then Asle can stay and wait and she'll come back down for him, because then her parents will see the condition she's in, and at the same time she'll tell them that he, Asle, is with her and is standing and waiting down at the bus stop with their things and then maybe her father, since he'll already be home from work, he works at a fishery, will come with her and help carry their things up to the house? she says and Asle says that that sounds good and he says that she needs to tell them at the same time that they're going to be staying there just a short time, until they've found a place to live in Bjørgvin, and that he's about to start at The Art School there, and that they'll probably be able to rent an apartment at The Student Home, he says and Liv says she will tell them that, she says and I sit in the chair here next to the round table and I look and look at the same spot in the water, in the Sygne Sea, and I have my arm around Ales's shoulders and I think that I should have said a prayer for Asle, and then I collect myself and then I pray for God to let Asle get better, and if he can't get better then for God to take him into himself and give him peace, take him into his kingdom, God's kingdom, God's peace, God's light, I pray and I look at the waves and I see Asle sitting there at the table in The Hotel and he's finished his beer and now he's sitting and looking at the woman who's standing behind the reception desk and she's not that much older than him, and it must be the daughter of the owners of the hotel, that's what Sigve has said, so he can order another glass and Sigve'll be here soon too, Asle thinks and I take my arm off Ales's shoulders and I say to Ales now I'm going to drop by Åsleik's and then Ales says that she is always with me, she is always near me, wherever I am, she says and I think now I should probably drive to Åsleik's, shouldn't I, and even if I'm not that hungry it'll be nice to have some good tasty lamb ribs, it's been a long time since I've eaten that, and Åsleik is a good cook, I think and I get up from the chair and Bragi falls down onto the floor and I never seem to remember that he always comes and sits in my lap when I sit in that chair, I think and I put on my black velvet jacket and my shoulder bag and a scarf and I go outside and it's mild, it's stopped snowing, and it's only snowed a little, and I wipe the snow off the windshield with my hand and anyway it's not cold, I think and I get into my car and then I drive slowly over to Åsleik's, it's not very far, but it is a certain distance away and the road is winding and covered in snow and I think it'll still be good to have some of his lamb ribs, even if I don't really feel like eating I can still tell I'm hungry now and that it'll be good to eat something, I think and I drive carefully over to Åsleik's house and I look at the white road and I see Asle standing at The Art School stammering and stuttering and he's taken the paintings wrapped in the grey blanket he got from Grandmother out of the old suitcase and he shows them to the painting teacher he met who's said his name is Eilev Pedersen and he says that in his opinion Asle can get in without having graduated from The Academic High School and taken the examen artium, but it's The Principal who decides, he says, but he can follow him and they'll see The Principal, he says and they go to The Principal and he says to Asle hasn't he just recently come and showed him his pictures already? and Asle says no he hasn't and Eiliv Pedersen says he'd been wondering exactly the same thing too, yes, Asle and someone else who had recently come and asked for a spot looked so much like each other, and their pictures were similar too, Eiliv Pedersen says and The Principal asks Asle if he can see his ID card and he says that if he's old enough and paints that well then yes he can come, that's clear, The Principal says and he congratulates Asle and says that he can now say he is, or is about to be, a student at The Art School in Bjørgvin, but he's so sure that Asle has already come and been given a spot, he says, but it must just be someone who looks like Asle, he says, or maybe he's gotten so old now that his memory is going? yes, well, be that as it may he's certain that Asle paints well enough that it would be a big mistake not to give him a spot at The Art School even without an examen artium, it's precisely to let in people like him that this rule exists, The Principal says and Eiliv Pedersen says that he's in complete agreement and Asle feels so relieved that he could almost faint, because now, now he can stop going to The Academic High School right away, he thinks and he thinks that now that he's about to get an artist's stipend to go to The Art School Father can stop giving him money every month, because Father works and toils and is not paid well for his fruit and even if he does sell the boats he builds, Barmen boats they're called, he used to mostly build traditional pointed rowboats but in recent years he's built them mostly with glass sterns so that it's easy to attach an outboard motor to the boat, because that's the kind of boat people want now, Father says, and he doesn't make all that much money for his boats since most people want to buy plastic boats now, they're easier to maintain, so there's less and less demand for the boats Father builds, on the other hand there are fewer and fewer people who build wooden boats so Father can still sell his boats, and from the money Father makes he then has to give him, Asle, money every month, Asle thinks, but now, now that he's about to start getting an artist's stipend Father can stop needing to part with the little money he makes even though Father works day and night, and Asle will get by with the money Father's already given him until he gets his first artist's stipend, because he has a little money set aside, since he's always been careful with his money, Asle thinks and he thinks that it's hard to believe he can now get away from the grey trousers and the white pullover with blue stripes, now he'll just leave The Academic High School that terrified him so much that he was never entirely free from the anxiety, or whatever you call it, he thinks, now he'll put an ad in *The Bjørgvin Times* looking for an apartment and then as soon as he's found an apartment he'll move from Aga to Bjørgvin, Asle thinks and I drive slowly and I look at the white road and then, all of a sudden, I see a deer leaping across the road and I stop the car, there are constantly deer here, because there are a lot of deer in Dylgja, and especially when it's dark they like to leap out into the road, and right across the road, and right in front of cars too, I think, and it's pure dumb luck that I've never hit a deer, I think and I've stopped the car but the engine's still running and the lights are still on and I look at the white road and I see Asle walking towards the room he's rented at The Shoemaker's Workshop and he's thinking that everything went great, he put an ad in *The Bjørgvin Times* and got a letter and few days later, it was an older woman who wrote to him, she lived alone, she wrote, and she was a teacher, or rather a retired teacher, but she still taught classes every now and then if a teacher was sick or something, she wrote and she had always had renters and a student from Hardanger had lived with her for several years, lived there the whole time he'd been a student, and now she was hoping to get a new renter to live there like the one from Hardanger, someone who was going to study in Bjørgvin, so if he wanted he could come and look at the room she had to rent out, it was on the sixth floor in a townhouse, and she's sure they can work out the rent, the only requirement she had was that he take out the rubbish for her once a week and lend a hand if there was something that needed lifting and she couldn't lift it alone, and change the lightbulbs when one of them went out, she wrote and she gave him her phone number and that same day Asle takes the letter and walks to the phone booth next to The Co-op Store and calls her and they agree that he'll come by the next day, and Asle says that he'll take the bus from Aga to Bjørgvin early in the morning and then go back that afternoon or evening, and the woman, who is from Bjørgvin and speaks like a Bjørgvinner, says that it's best if he comes by around three o'clock, and Asle says that's fine, and then she says that she lives at 7 University Street and it says Herdis Åsen on the door, she says and University Street runs from the city centre up to The University and the apartment is on the sixth floor, with no lift, so there're a lot of stairs to walk up, she says, so it's settled, she says and if Asle can't come then he has her phone number and he can just call her and they'll figure out something else, she says, and then she says that if Asle does live there then he can use her phone as long as he doesn't make too many calls, and as long as other people don't call him too often, she says and I think that I can't just stay sitting like this in my car and I look at the white road and I see Asle sitting on the bus to Bjørgvin, he is sitting in his black velvet jacket and he's put his brown leather shoulder bag down on the seat next to him and he's thinking that he doesn't know his way around Bjørgvin at all, yes, he's probably been there only a few times, he thinks and he remembers nothing or hardly anything about it, he thinks and I sit in my car and I look at the white road and I see Asle standing there and he asks The Bus Driver if he knows where University Street is and he says he doesn't but that it must not be far from The University, as the name says, so he'll just have to go out the door of The Bus Station and turn right and go straight until he gets to a big square, and from there, from The Fishmarket as it's called, take a left and go straight for a while towards a church and The University is behind the church and University Street must be around there somewhere, he says and Asle thanks him and then he walks just the way The Bus Driver told him he should and he gets to the big square and he sees a church up on a hill and then he walks towards the church and then he sees a sign that says University Street and then he walks to a door that says 7 on it and he looks at his watch and it's only twelve, and he wasn't supposed to come look at the room until three, so he has plenty of time, and what should he do now? he thinks, because he can't just stay standing outside the door for three hours, he thinks, and so he goes back the same way he came, because he'd seen that there was a café at The Bus Station itself, he'd seen a sign saying Bus Café over a door, Asle thinks, and then there was a kiosk next to the café selling newspapers so he might as well go to the kiosk and buy a newspaper and then go to The Bus Café and buy a cup of coffee, or maybe a glass of beer, Asle thinks and he walks back the same way, and that goes fine, and at The Kiosk he buys *The Bjørgvin Times* and then he walks through the door with Bus Café over it and he goes over to the counter and he says he'd like a glass of beer and the woman standing behind the counter says there's no way he's old enough to buy beer, if he wants a beer he needs to show an ID, she says and Asle takes out his wallet and takes out the ID card and the woman standing behind the counter looks at it and then she hands it back to him and then she pours a pint from the tap and puts it down in front of Asle and he pays and goes and sits down at a window table, and there's nobody else in The Bus Café, but someone will come in soon, Asle thinks and he looks out the window and people are constantly walking by outside The Bus Station, young and old, and there's a street right in front of The Bus Station and it has two lanes and cars are driving by the whole time, life was going by at breakneck speed out there, Asle feels, and then he opens *The Bjørgvin Times* and starts flipping through the paper and he turns to the pages called Arts and there are a lot of book reviews in there, and a review of an exhibition that the painter Eiliv Pedersen is having now in The Beyer Gallery, and that must be the man Asle talked to when he went to The Art School to show them his pictures, the one who'd recommended that he be given a spot at The Art School, the one who'd taken him and his paintings with him to talk to The Principal, Asle thinks and the woman who wrote the review was named Anne Sofie Grieg and she wrote that this may be the best show Eiliv Pedersen has ever had, it says, and it's been too long since Eiliv Pedersen has shown his work and that must have something to do with the fact that he works as a teacher at The Art School, where he is almost solely responsible for all the courses in the Painting track, which is taking up too much of his time, and really it's too bad that such an eminent painter, with such clear and obvious gifts, because no one with eyes can be in any possible doubt about that, has to spend so much of his time teaching instead of painting, and since it's so rare that Eiliv Ped-

ersen has a show everyone needs to take advantage of this chance
to go see the show at The Beyer Gallery, the critic apparently
named Anne Sofie Grieg writes and Asle looks up and he sees
that a few tables away from where he's sitting there's a girl alone
at a table, and she wasn't sitting there when he came in, when he
sat down, but now she's sitting there facing him, and their eyes
meet, and it's like right away their eyes rested in each other's and
neither her eyes nor his eyes looked away, she has dark eyes and
they're so clear and then she has long dark hair, and he didn't
really know why they were sitting there and looking into each
other's eyes, it kind of felt right that they do that, but eventually
Asle decides that they've sat looking into each other's eyes long
enough and he drinks a little beer and sees her drink a little of her
coffee and he looks down at the newspaper, and he takes another
sip of beer, and it's still cold and good, and he rereads the review
Anne Sofie Grieg wrote about the exhibition of Eiliv Pedersen's
paintings and it says there that The Beyer Gallery is open every
day between ten and seven, on weekends too, and people now
need to take the opportunity to see these paintings by Eiliv Pedersen, one of Norway's foremost artists, even though he's never
been given anything like the recognition he deserves, yes, even
The Bjørgvin Museum of Art owns just one painting by Eiliv
Pedersen, and what a shame that is, and what about The National Museum of Art? isn't it time that they buy one, or better yet,
several of his paintings? she writes, and anyone who has wanted
to buy a single painting ever in their lives has to take the chance
they have now, she writes and the whole time Asle feels the eyes
of the girl sitting across from him looking at him and it's good, it
feels good that she's looking at him, Asle thinks, but he'd still
rather not look up, even if it was good when their eyes met, good
to look her in the eye, he thinks and the exhibition, in The Beyer Gallery it's called, he would like to go see it, he thinks, but
does he even know where The Beyer Gallery is? it says that it's at
1 High Street, but of course he doesn't know where that is, Asle

thinks, so he'll probably never get to see an exhibition of paintings by Eiliv Pedersen, who paints so much in grey and white, and who likes to paint a woman sitting by a window, as it says in the review by Anne Sofie Grieg, and who paints pictures that have such great stillness in them, as Anne Sofie Grieg also writes, Asle thinks and he drinks his beer and he thinks that it's always so good to have a glass of beer, yes, several glasses, it makes him calm, and life begins to feel livable, he thinks and he looks up and again he looks into the dark eyes of the girl sitting a few tables away from him, facing him, the girl with the long dark hair, and he looks down at the newspaper again and then he looks at the watch that he got from Grandmother as a confirmation present and he sees that's it's now one o'clock, so it won't be long now before he can go to 7 University Street to look at the room he might rent, and he doesn't remember the landlady's name, but her apartment was on the sixth floor, and he has the letter from her with him, and her name is in the letter if he can't remember it, but he thinks it was Herdis Åsen, Asle thinks and he takes the letter out of the pocket of his black velvet jacket and yes, yes, it says Herdis Åsen at the bottom of the letter and he sees that it says 7 University Street and he puts the letter back in his pocket and he drinks a little beer and he sees that the glass is about half empty, there's a little more than half the glass left and he sees the girl a few tables away from him get up and Asle looks down at his newspaper and then she stops next to his table

    Nice to meet you, she says

    and she laughs and Asle stands up

    You too, he says

    and they hold out their hands to each other and then they stay standing and holding each other's hand

    My name's Asle, he says

    And my name's Ales, she says

    No, are you joking? he says

    No, no, my name's Ales, she says

We have almost the same name, Asle says

Yes, strange, she says

Yes, Asle says

and she says well isn't that strange and then she asks what Asle is doing here in Bjørgvin and he says that he's going to go look at a room, because he's about to start at The Art School, he says and they're still standing there holding each other's hand and Ales says that she is too, if she gets in, because last year she went to The Academic High School, The Cathedral School, she says, but as Asle can understand she doesn't go every day, sometimes she skips school, yes, she really and truly doesn't want to go there, because she's unhappy whenever she's there, but her mother, yes, her mother Judit, that's her name, thinks that she needs to graduate from The Academic High School, she says and Asle nods and he says that he stopped going, or is about to stop going, to The Academic High School so that he can start at The Art School and then he says that he took his paintings to The Art School and asked if he could start at The Art School even though he didn't have an examen artium, just based on the pictures he's painted, and that a teacher looked at them, he says, and then the teacher took the pictures to The Principal who said there was a spot for him, it's been a long time since he'd seen such a clear talent, The Principal said, Asle says and he feels a little embarrassed and Ales says that the teacher must have been Eiliv Pedersen, because he's the one who teaches oil painting, in the track called Painting, and then there's another track called Drawing, and she thought she would like either track just as well so she's going to apply for both, she says and Asle says that he's moving to Bjørgvin soon, yes, as soon as he finds a room to rent, he says and Ales says she understands exactly how he doesn't want to stay at The Academic High School any longer, she doesn't either, but now she'll be done in the spring, and even if she has bad marks in almost every subject she thinks that maybe her drawings and paintings aren't the worst in the world, or anyway they might be good enough for her to get into The Art School as long as she's finished at The Academic High School and taken her examen artium, she says, but it probably won't be as easy as it was for him, she'll still have to go through the usual admissions process, and maybe she'll get accepted and maybe she won't, she says and Asle asks how the process works and Ales says that first you have to spend two days drawing from a live model, and he probably knows the difference between a nude and a sketch? she asks, and Asle shakes his head and says he hasn't heard of that and Ales says that when you draw a nude you draw a whole body and the model has to sit in the same position for a long time, taking breaks every once in a while, but when you make a sketch the model holds their pose for a very short time, maybe ten or twenty seconds, and you have to make a drawing in that amount of time, yes, that's kind of the most important thing, finishing, Ales says, and you draw with pencil or charcoal, yes, that's the admissions test, but she isn't so good at drawing, she just thinks it'll go better if she draws in charcoal, and erases with a kneaded eraser, because that doesn't just erase the charcoal it kind of spreads it around a little too, and she thinks that that can make a more or less bad drawing at least a little better

Kneaded eraser, Asle says

Yes it's a kind of ball of putty that you erase with when you're drawing in charcoal, she says

You don't know that? she says

No, Asle says

I've always just drawn with a pencil and I've never used a ball of putty, for whatever reason, so I just keep the mistakes and let them be wrong, because it's often the mistakes that eventually lead to something right, he says

and Ales says yes and that the sheets of paper for drawings in the admissions tests are twenty inches wide by sixty inches high and you're supposed to draw a whole person on that, a man or a woman who's sitting there, and you're supposed to draw him or her from head to foot, and that'll be hard for her, well, she isn't so good at drawing, she'd asked her mother to sit for her as a model, but it ended up with the two of them laughing and joking, and then, when she applies for a place at The Art School, she'll have to turn in between three and five of her own pictures, drawings, paintings, watercolours, whatever she wants, yes, but there needs to be at least one painting, and then one of the pictures has to be a still life, she says and she does have two watercolours she's happy with anyway, and then, yes, you have to go off and wait a few days until they decide who's going to get a spot and who isn't, and the names of the people who get into The Art School are written up on a sheet of paper that's hung up on the bulletin board by the entrance, and the worst thing is that you don't know how long it'll take for the admissions to be decided, she thinks it usually takes a week but the decisions can also be made soon- er, so people go and check the bulletin board constantly, yes, of course, that's how it is, Ales says and since she can't get into The Art School like him without going through the normal admis- sions, it's only the exceptions who get in that way, and people who clearly have talent but who haven't taken an examen artium for whatever reason, and age is also a factor, Ales says and Asle thinks so it's because he, or Sigve, faked his ID card that he got into The Art School and not, as he thought, because his pictures were so good, he thinks and they let got of each other's hand and then Ales puts her arm around Asle and pulls him towards her and then lets go of him

You have such nice long hair, she says

You too, Asle says

You have brown hair and I have dark hair, Ales says

and she says she usually has her hair in a ponytail or a braid, and she was wearing it like that when she got to The Bus Café too, but when she saw him she untied her hair and let it fall loose, she says, and Asle says that her hair is dark, and it's almost as long as his hair, and while his eyes are blue hers are dark

Can I sit with you? Ales says

Yes of course, Asle says

and then Ales sits down and Asle says that he's just read a review of an exhibition that a painter named Eiliv Pedersen has up at The Beyer Gallery and he says that he thought it was maybe Eiliv Pedersen that he showed his paintings to and Ales says that it definitely was, and that it's a good exhibition, actually she doesn't know how much she likes Pedersen's paintings but she has to give him one thing, that he always uses such muffled colours, there are a lot of different greys and almost-whites in everything he paints, you almost can't call what's in his paintings colours in the usual sense, and then they all run together, there are no clear and definite edges or transitions in his pictures, everything kind of runs together, Ales says and Asle says that he'd really like to see the exhibition but he doesn't know his way around Bjørgvin at all and he has to go to the house of the woman who might rent him a room at three o'clock and she asks where that is and he says it's on University Street and then she says that in that case it's no problem to go to The Beyer Gallery to see the Eiliv Pedersen exhibition and then she can go with him to University Street after that, she says and Asle says yes, yes, he'd really like that, if she doesn't mind, and she says no of course not, there's no harm in seeing the exhibition a second time, she says, because she already saw the exhibition the day after the opening, with her mother Judit, she says

Because both you and I are going to have Eiliv Pedersen as a painting teacher, she says

Yes well you will anyway, and I will if I get into The Art School, she says

His show got a very good review in *The Bjørgvin Times* anyway, Asle says

and he hands her the newspaper and she reads it and she says that was really a good review, and Anne Sofie Grieg knows what she's talking about, she doesn't have a degree, she used to be a housewife, but she and her husband, a lawyer, travelled a lot to lots of European cities and they visited most of the great art museums, plus she's read a lot, yes, her mother and Anne Sofie Grieg are friends and they see each other now and then, Ales says and she says that it's unbelievable how many art books Anne Sofie Grieg has at home, she's been to her house a few times with her mother Judit, she says and then they stand up and Asle puts his brown leather shoulder bag on and Ales says that it's a nice bag and then she takes his hand

Because now we're a couple, at least sort of, she says

and then they leave The Bus Café and they go straight up the road, the way Asle had already gone, and then Ales takes a right and they walk down a few little alleys and Asle has no idea where they are

Now we're boyfriend and girlfriend, Ales says

Yes, Asle says

Have you ever had a girlfriend before? she asks

No, Asle says

I've never had a boyfriend either, Ales says

But I do now, she says

and I sit in my car, and I'm sure that a deer is about to come leaping across the road or that I'll be able to see one or more deer in the light from my car, I think, but I can't just stay sitting here like this because Åsleik is waiting for me, I think and then I see a deer standing by the side of the road and then the deer stands there and looks at me and I look into the deer's eyes and he looks me in the eye and I just sit in my car and the deer just stands there by the side of the road and we look into each other's eyes and then the deer turns slowly away and vanishes into the darkness and I start driving and I look at the white road and I see Asle sitting in a living room and Liv sitting next to him and Liv's mother comes in with a plate of open-faced sandwiches and puts it down on the coffee table in front of them and she says that Liv's father should sit down too and Asle thinks that they can't stay here at Liv's parents' house, because even if it is all right with Liv's mother it isn't all right with her father, he hasn't said a single word to Asle since they arrived, not even Come in or Welcome, and hasn't greeted him, and now her father is saying he's not hungry and that he thinks he'll go lie down, it's been a long hard day at work and he's tired, he says and then he says good night and Asle thinks they need to leave, but where will they go? yes well there's got to be someplace to live for them too? he thinks, but if he doesn't have money, well, then what do they have? he thinks, so they'll probably have to stay for free at Liv's parents' house for a while, but then, and it won't be long, then he'll get an artist's stipend and maybe they'll also get assigned an apartment at The Student Home, since they'll have a child, that would be good, anyway Asle has applied for a place there but surely there's a waiting list for the places like that, so he doesn't know, but anyway he'll find some other place to live, plus maybe Liv would rather live with her parents until they're ready to get their own place to live, Asle thinks and I sit in my car and I look at the white road and I drive slowly and now I see the turn-off to Åsleik's farm and I drive up the driveway and the light from my car is now shining on Åsleik's house and damned if I don't see Åsleik standing out there in front of his house, next to his tractor, yes, Åsleik is standing there waiting for me, I think, even though it's pretty cold out, and at least those lamb ribs are sure going to taste good, I think, because it was good that I slept for a couple of hours today, yes, that did me a lot of good, so now it feels like I'm back on my feet, I think and I pull up in front of Åsleik's house

Finally you're here, he says

Am I late? I say

Yes well I'm hungry in any case, he says

and Åsleik says that the lamb has been sitting and steaming for hours but that's not a problem, it only makes the lamb better, since it's from a ewe and not a lamb, he says, but it's been hours since the mashed turnips were done, and they're good, and the secret to making good mashed turnips is easy enough, you just cut the turnips up into small pieces and boil them for a long time in their own juice, yes, much longer than you'd actually need for the pieces to get soft, and it's fine to mash them, and then you have to pour out all the cooking water, of course, and then the rest of the water steams from the cut-up turnips and then you add a lot of butter, really a lot, and then of course you mash it and finally add a little salt to taste, and maybe a little pepper, Åsleik says and I say well I know that much, I say and I notice that Åsleik seems a little offended and then he says let's get inside, it's too cold to be standing outside, and I say that I was surprised to see Åsleik standing outside the house and he says he was waiting for me, hunger was gnawing at his stomach, and when the gnawing got worse he had to come outside to see if I was driving up, and finally I did, and the potatoes were done a long time ago too, but they've been covered and with lots of dishtowels on the lid of the pot so he hopes they're still fairly hot, and if they're not totally hot that doesn't really matter, Åsleik says and I say I'm sure it'll all be delicious and Åsleik says that Sister called him today and she said she'd seen me at The Coffeehouse yesterday but she hadn't had the courage to talk to me, even though she wanted to, she'd just gone into Bjørgvin to do some Christmas shopping, and when she was waiting for the ferry to take her back home, first she took the ferry to Instefjord and then the bus to Øygna, yes well I knew how it was, when she was sitting there waiting she saw me come into The Coffeehouse and she'd thought about telling me that her house was full of my paintings but she hadn't dared, she'd said, and then she'd asked him again if maybe I'd think about coming to celebrate Christmas with them

    Yes, maybe, I say

    Seriously, you think you will? Åsleik says

    You're not just fooling around? he says

    You've always said no before, he says

    Yes, I say

and Åsleik says it would be so nice if I came with him on
The Boat and the two of us took it to Øygna, there's a bay there,
and it's a good harbour, he says, and it would be so nice for both
him and Sister if I would honour them with his company, he says

Yes, yes, I think I will come this year, like I said, I say

I hear you saying it but now I'm having a hard time believing
my own ears, Åsleik says

and he says he doesn't know how many times he's asked me
to come, and I never wanted to, and I think that I don't really
understand it myself, yes, why I want to go with Åsleik to celebrate Christmas at Sister's house this year, and so it was her I saw
sitting in The Coffee- house yesterday, all the way at the front,
by the door, the woman with a suitcase and some shopping bags
on the floor next to her and who looked exactly like the Guro
who lived in The Lane, I think and so this year I've said that I
want to go with Åsleik and celebrate Christmas at Sister's house
in Øygna, I think, and I think that I have no desire to paint any
more pictures, I've painted enough, I think, and now I want to
try to sell all the paintings I have and then I'll have done my part,
said what I have to say, I think, and Åsleik asks me to come in and
I take off my shoes in the hall, they're just the cut-off boots, and
then I go into the main room and everything there is the same
as before, I don't think Åsleik has changed anything since his
parents died, the cushions, the pictures, everything, everything
is the way it's always been, I think and I realize that it makes me
feel comfortable that everything's the way it's always been and
Åsleik probably feels that way too, so that must be why he hasn't
changed anything, I think, and Åsleik has set the big table in the
middle of the room nicely, with his nice silverware, and there's
the tablecloth, and there's a pitcher of water on it and a bottle of
beer and a bottle of stronger stuff and in front of where Åsleik
usually sits, facing the hall door, there are two glasses, a beer
glass and a shot glass, and then opposite Åsleik there's just a big
regular glass, and the pitcher of water is next to it and Åsleik says

that I should sit down at the table and then he'll just warm up the mashed turnips a little but it won't take long, he says and Åsleik goes out to the kitchen and he comes back in and he says that it's so nice that I'm thinking about spending Christmas with him and Sister in Øygna, not least because it'll be much nicer taking The Boat to Øygna together, because to tell the truth he's never liked being alone in a boat, and he always is, yes, it's only because he doesn't have anyone to come with him, because it's much nicer, and safer too, if there're two people, Åsleik says and then it was also quite a coincidence that Sister and I ran into each other yesterday, because we've never set eyes on each other before, no, well, not that he knows of, Åsleik says

No I've never met your sister, I say

and I say that I noticed someone sitting at the first table at The Coffeehouse, right by the front door, next to the window, she had medium-length blonde hair and she had a suitcase and some shopping bags on the floor next to her, I say and Åsleik says that must have been Sister, anyway she does have medium-length blonde hair, and her name is Guro, yes, he says, and in those shopping bags, in one of them, was both wine and spirits, because Sister, yes well Guro, she likes the stronger stuff, yes, maybe a little too much even, no, it's not that she drinks all that often, no, she doesn't have the occasion to, seeing how she lives, and then she also doesn't have that much money, he says, but when she does get the chance she likes to toss 'em down, yes, Åsleik says and he goes out to the kitchen and then he comes back with a dish of potatoes in one hand and a dish of mashed turnips in the other and then he goes out again and comes back with a huge plate with a heap of lamb ribs, yes, they're really long ribs and the smell of the smoked Christmas lamb is incredible and Åsleik puts the plate down on the table

And here we go, he says

and he gestures to the plate of lamb ribs with both hands to sort of present it and I take a generous helping right away, three good-sized ribs, and then Åsleik opens the bottle of beer and he pours himself some and then he opens the bottle of spirits, it's only about half-full, and he says he hasn't tasted spirits since the Christmas ribs last year, and he pours himself a little shot and I pick up the pitcher of water and fill my glass

Yes well you're sure missing out, Åsleik says

and he raises his shot glass to me

I've had my share, more than my share, I say

and Åsleik says well then that's the way it is, he says and then he serves himself, he also takes three large ribs and then he passes me the dish of potatoes and I serve myself and I pass it back to him and while Åsleik serves himself some potatoes I serve myself mashed turnips and I pass the plate on to Åsleik and he looks at me and he raises his beer glass

Cheers, Åsleik says

Yes, cheers, I say

and I raise my glass of water and then we toast and drink, he drinks his beer and I drink my water and then he takes a little nip of his stronger stuff and I cut off a bite of the perfectly tender lamb rib and damn if it doesn't taste incredibly good, I think and I say that Åsleik, yes, when it comes to food he's a real genius, I say and Åsleik says that Sister's lamb ribs are even better, he has to admit it, and I'll soon see for myself, Åsleik says and then we eat slowly and in silence and then Åsleik says now isn't that strange, that I've lived in Dylgja for so many years and never once set eyes on Sister before today, and that was only because we both happened to be in The Coffeehouse

No, it's odd, there aren't that many people who live around here, I say

You're right it is, Åsleik says

Yes, and Sister's name is Guro even if I always just call her Sister, he says

Guro, yes, I say

So it's agreed, this year we'll take The Boat together and celebrate Christmas at Sister's house? Åsleik says

Yes, I say

Let's drink to that, he says

and Åsleik raises his shot glass and I raise my water glass and
we toast and then something comes over me suddenly, something
like terror, yes, I'm almost overwhelmed with the same fear, the
same anxiety, that came over me when I had to read out loud at
The Academic High School and I say I need to get back home, I
say and Åsleik looks at me not understanding

Well that was a rush job, he says

Yes, well, I say

and I've stood up and I say thank you for the wonderful meal,
it tasted unbelievably good, I say

But why do you have to leave so soon all of a sudden? Åsleik
says

and I don't know what to say and just say that I remembered
something and I say we'll talk soon and I go out to my car and I
feel that some of my fear has gone away and I start the car and I
think that I need to say an Ave Maria to myself, that usually helps
when the fear comes, which does happen, even if not too often,
and never without some specific reason, and then I say Ave Maria
and that usually helps, I think and sitting there in my car I take my
rosary out from under my pullover and I think now do I really believe in this, no, not really, I think and I hold the cross between my
thumb and finger and I say inside myself Ave Maria Gratia plena
Dominus tecum Benedicta tu in mulieribus et benedictus fructus
ventris tui Iesus Sancta Maria Mater Dei Ora pro nobis peccatori-
bus nunc et in hora mortis nostræ and I move my thumb and finger
up to the first bead and I say inside myself Pater noster Qui es in
cælis Sanctificetur nomen tuum Adveniat regnum tuum Fiat voluntas tua sicut in cælo et in terra Panem nostrum quotidianum da
nobis hodie et dimitte nobis debita nostra sicut et nos dimittimus
debitoribus nostris Et ne nos inducas in tentationem sed libera nos
a malo and I move my thumb and finger down to the cross and
I say Our Father Who art in heaven Hallowed be thy name Thy

kingdom come Thy will be done on earth as it is in heaven Give us this day our daily bread and forgive us our trespasses as we forgive those who trespass against us And lead us not into temptation but deliver us from evil and I hold the brown wooden cross between my thumb and finger and then I say, over and over again inside myself while I breathe in deeply Lord and while I breathe out slowly Jesus and while I breathe in deeply Christ and while I breathe out slowly Have mercy and while I breathe in deeply On me

JON FOSSE was born in 1959 on the west coast of Norway and is the recipient of countless prestigious prizes, both in his native Norway and abroad. Since his 1983 fiction debut, *Raudt, svart* [*Red, Black*], Fosse has written prose, poetry, essays, short stories, children's books, and over forty plays, with more than a thousand productions performed and translations into fifty languages. *I is Another* is the second volume in *Septology*, his latest prose work, to be published in three volumes by Transit Books.

DAMION SEARLS is a translator from German, Norwegian, French, and Dutch and a writer in English. He has translated many classic modern writers, including Proust, Rilke, Nietzsche, Walser, and Ingeborg Bachmann.

Transit Books is a nonprofit publisher of international and American literature, based in Oakland, California. Founded in 2015, Transit Books is committed to the discovery and promotion of enduring works that carry readers across borders and communities. Visit us online to learn more about our forthcoming titles, events, and opportunities to support our mission.

TRANSITBOOKS.ORG